AN ABIDING FIRE

Thomazine & Major Russell Thrillers

Book One

M J Logue

SAPERE
BOOKS

AN ABIDING FIRE

Published by Sapere Books.

11 Bank Chambers, Hornsey, London, N8 7NN,
United Kingdom

saperebooks.com

ISBN: 978-1-912786-81-7

In a very real sense, this book is dedicated to Aphra Behn.
It's also dedicated to — as ever — my boys, the big one and the little
one. Anny, without whom Hollie Babbitt, and by extension Thankful
Russell, would not exist.
Diana and Antoinette, who love the gallant Major about as much as I
do, and without whose encouragement the boy Russell would never have
had a romantic life at all.

Prologue

Four Ashes, Buckinghamshire, England
November 1663

She looked up as he entered the room, her eyes narrowing to see him in the gloom of a few meagre tapers. A paltry display for such a family, and on such a bitter midwinter night. It gave him enough light to see her clearly, though, and he was astonished at the change in her: but then it had been ten years and they had not been kind years for Fly-Fornication Coventry.

She had always been for the King, during the late wars, and it must have gone hard with her to have had a brother who was not only a most notorious rebel and subversive, but who had narrowly escaped being executed for his political beliefs with a pack of fellow Dissenters and horse-thieves calling themselves the Levellers. And he had not had the grace to slide into obscurity after his grudging pardon, but instead had gone on to serve quite conspicuously in the Army of General Monck after the King was restored.

It must have been bitter as wormwood for her to know that he was still out there in the world, that those sins of which she had spoken, at such length, with such contempt, had gone unpunished and that he was still unrepentant.

Bitterness had withered her. Her hair was hidden by the same stiff starched cap, untouched by fashion or flattery, but her eyebrows were as dark and uncompromising as ever. She was not an unattractive woman for a widow in her late fifties. She was as tall and slender as her brother and her shoulders were straight. He found himself quite admiring her, actually.

Not as a woman, but as a fierce thing of beauty, like a falcon or a well-made sword.

"Well," she said. And that was all.

He bowed with as much ostentation as he could because he had been on the peripheries of court these four years and more and he had learned the weapons of vicious courtesy. "I am glad to see you well, Mistress Coventry. After so long absent."

"As a dog returneth to his vomit, so a fool returns to his folly. Should I say I am as glad to see you? Well, I won't." She smiled, which was unexpected. "I do not lie, sir. I am not in the least glad to see you. Prinked out in your degenerate finery — 'For when they speak great swelling words of vanity, they allure through the lusts of the flesh, through much wantonness.' Do you seek to impress me, you nasty, womanish thing?"

"Good lord, no," he said mildly, and she lowered her head and glowered at him.

"Less of your blasphemy. This is a godly house. What do you want?"

She had not invited him to sit or offered him hospitality and he was glad of that. She still made him nervous, for all he had not set eyes on her in ten years, though she had no power over him because for all her malice she was no more than a woman, and a thin, bloodless, bitter one at that.

"I wanted to assure myself of your continued good health," he said and dropped his eyes to hide that particular lie.

"Did you. Well. I wonder why, since you never did before when you were drinking and whoring all over the county, keeping your low company?"

"They say hereabouts that you are grown … odd, mistress. That you grow overly zealous, even more than you were previous, and that none of your servants will stay longer than a few weeks with you, for your harshness. That you can be cruel and whimsical in your ways." He took a deep breath and went on, "That you are often alone in this house at night, for such staff as can bear your intolerance will not stay under the same roof. Is that true?"

Her dark eyes, ringed about with tender blue shadows, lifted to his face. "True? What concern is it of yours?"

He was still on his feet. It was easy to go and stand over her and set his hands on her shoulders. Such slight, narrow shoulders, for all their straightness. Her bodice, close to, was shabby: a little shrunken at the seams, unevenly faded, as if it had been remade from another garment and covered by an old-fashioned linen collar that had a darn at the fold. A fine darn, but a darn, nonetheless. "There is not the money here to pay a servant's hire, is there, mistress?" he said gently. "You have lost all, since the wars. Have you not?"

She almost rose from her seat, an unlovely blush mottling her cheeks and her neck. "How dare you, sir —"

And he put his hands about her slight throat and snapped her neck, as simply as that. Like snapping a coney's when it was snared, and with as little emotion.

She was not expecting it and she did not struggle, after that initial convulsion; she only hung between his two hands with her dark eyes blank and staring at him and her mouth slightly ajar.

He was not as frightened as he thought he would be. She was dead and it had been easy. He did not feel anything, apart from a slight repulsion as a sliver of saliva drooled from her lolling mouth.

Such little bones. So frail. Not like her brother, not at all like her brother, in the end. For Thankful Russell was still alive and Fly was distinctly dead.

She would not be missed until it was too late. Of that he was very sure. He wished her eyes would close, though, and that she might not keep looking at him. Well, he had done what he came to do, and now he knew. It would probably not be so easy again, but he had done it and perhaps — well. Perhaps he must needs try again, to be sure, and with someone who would be more of a challenge, less well-deserved, than this bitter, unmourned woman.

She was very limp and she had soiled herself and he wrinkled his nose at that. Her head flopped on her shoulder when he lifted her and she was unwieldy, her feet dragging on the bare boards as he laid her on the floor in front of the hearth.

He took one of the smouldering logs from the fire and laid it underneath her skirts. He stood back and admired his work. It was a meagre, thin, smoking fire and he had to kick it and poke it till it flared into sullen life, tightening his lips at the smuts it left on his good stockings. Her plain woollen garments smouldered but did not flare and he touched flame to the rest of her. Her loosened hair flared like a banner across the boards where her cap had spilled.

The old-fashioned rushes on the floor caught like tinder and he backed away, scrambling with a loss of dignity as flames began to lick at her skirts, outlining her in a bright halo, and to trickle outwards, starting to crackle, with the first wisps of greasy smoke as her flesh started to scorch. So quick.

And then the first of the wall-hangings that rippled in the old house's draughts caught light and he turned and left the hall. Not running, because why should he run? He felt nothing, except the satisfaction of a job well done — that, and a sense of relief that it was done so quickly and so easily. He could move on.

PART I: TINDER

1

October 1664

Major Thankful Russell sniffed surreptitiously at the stiff, lustrous collar of his court suit. It smelt faintly of stale rosewater and tobacco and sea-coal fumes, with an acrid note of sweat and a slight overlay of wine. Under that was the strange, fugitive scent of silk, of tar, and the sea and the spices of the hold of an East Indiaman — although that was possibly in his imagination, for he had never set foot on a ship bound for anywhere more exotic than the Low Countries.

He'd been told in no uncertain terms that he'd shirked long enough. That an officer of some seniority, even a supply officer of no great military significance or birth — General Monck had been very specific on that last and Russell could still hear his commander's round rural Devonshire accent in his head at the memory of it — it was his duty to present himself at court and pay his respects to His Majesty, on the glorious event of his restoration to the throne after eleven years of misery under the Commonwealth.

And then Monck had glowered and narrowed his little bull's eyes, pouched in sagging red flesh. "You'll do the pretty, Major Russell, for all ye were a damnable Roundhead."

The which Russell could not argue, for with a name like Thankful he could scarcely deny his staunch Puritan upbringing, and having almost had himself executed as a political subversive at Burford with the rest of the Leveller ringleaders he had to admire General Monck's perspicacity.

But, he had thought that after twenty years of keeping his head down, of being a ferociously good supply officer of no great military significance or birth, of waking and sleeping lists and requisitions and logistics — after a life of ruthless and selfless service, he might not, actually, be forced to show his face at court. Monck had said it was a matter of respect. Russell was a god-damned administrator, a jumped-up pen-pusher, who the hell did he think he was to refuse to present his respects to His Majesty in person?

They forgot, you see. They saw this neat, slightly austere, mouse-haired gentleman in his forty-second year, tall and a little stiff in the shoulders as a result of stooping over his requisitions these last twenty years, slightly deaf in one ear and scarred in the face where a Royalist pike had ruined his youthful beauty forever in the early days of the civil wars, and short-haired where preposterously curled wigs were the fashion, and so they called him Old Crophead, for his old Parliament leanings and his present lack of vanity. He was not given to excess of any nature, but a most prim and sober and respectable senior officer, the sight of whose marred face could be relied upon to damp the high spirits of any sociable gathering.

They forgot that twenty years ago he had been a firebrand and a rebel. He looked cold and implacable, but how else might a man look who had taken the thrust of the shattered butt of a pike through his cheek?

And so it had been a matter of duty, and a direct order, that Russell should present himself at court. Well, he had. He remembered little of it. He had, admittedly, fortified himself with perhaps more wine than he ought to have: anything to stop the shaking of his hands, his absolute bone-deep horror of being so conspicuously displayed in a public place, of being stared at. More than that, though, it had just been dull. Nothing happened. Just a lot of people talking a lot of nothing in a big room that smelt of stale bodies and tallow and too much scent. He didn't remember being presented to the King, though he supposed he must have or Monck would have made him go back. He smiled politely at everyone, because he didn't have a clue who was sleeping with whom, male or female, and it did not do to cut the reigning favourite or the court wit. They had called him Bosola, which he did not understand, but which had been kindly explained to him some time later by a friend who had read such old-fashioned tragedies that it referred to a most notorious court malcontent and bird of ill omen in an old play. He had been told, by a gaggle of cackling, bewigged striplings, that if one gilded a turd, it remained, regardless, a turd. In return, he had suggested to their braying whelp of a ringleader, a drawling jackanapes who gave himself out as the Earl of Rochester, that if he passed such remarks in Russell's hearing again, Russell would take Rochester's ungodly pet ape and insert it where the Lord's grace did not shine.

Russell had known poets in his youth. The men he had known would have hesitated to scrawl such lewd doggerel as Rochester wrote on the wall of a troop latrine. He was not impressed by the seventeen-year-old libertine.

Mostly, though, he'd stayed close to the wall, trembling, with the small of his back against the moulded plaster, taking some comfort from that cool strength and holding to his duty, because that was what he did, what he had done since he was seventeen and first a young officer, and he had no idea how to do else. Twenty-five years of duty above all became a sort of habit. He had felt like an impostor, in his charcoal-grey lutestring silk with a jacket that was so short and tight it barely covered his backside and great billowing shirt-sleeves hanging from under the shrunken sleeves, festooned with ribbon, like a damnable maypole, with a cravat that trailed in his supper if he was not cautious how he sat.

He had been a little drunk and a lot nervous, his teeth chattering on the rim of his delicate Venetian glass goblet even before he'd seen a face he knew, however vaguely: the chubby, deceptively amiable countenance of Charles Fairmantle, a distant neighbour from back on his home Buckinghamshire chalk hills. A member of Parliament now, he thought he'd heard. He had gone to school with Russell and done well for himself after the wars, they said. Fairmantle was a lecher and a pathetic ageing hanger-on to the peripheries of Rochester's lewd young cohort. The touch of his chubby hand made a sweat of sheer repulsion break out on Russell's top lip, but Fairmantle was familiar for all that and even his seedy familiarity was a small comfort in this glittering company, like a pair of worn but stinking boots.

They exchanged idle pleasantries — or at the least, Fairmantle made idle pleasantry and Russell stared blankly at him for the most part. And then,

"Accept my condolences, Major. A bad business. A bad business, indeed. You must be devastated."

"Oh. Indeed," Russell said blankly. "Which condolences?"

The pudgy hand on his sleeve was solicitous, leaving a faint, damp print on the glimmering silk.

"But I am so sorry, sir. I had assumed you knew. Your sister, Major. God rest her, she — Four Ashes was burned, not three months ago, and poor Mistress Coventry with it." Fairmantle shook his head. "I am sorry. I had not meant — I had not known — sir, you turn positively pale —"

And Russell, who had hated his sister and not set eyes on her in the better part of ten years, had crushed his glass goblet to pieces in his shock nonetheless.

He thought that had been the moment when he had decided to come back to Buckinghamshire for good, though it had taken him a few months of despair and soul-searching to work out how he might rebuild the house at Four Ashes, and then there were a further few months of despair and soul-searching when he realised that there was only one woman he'd have entertained as mistress there and that she was as utterly, irrevocably not for him as the moon for the moth. Possibly he ought to have mentioned that uncertainty to Thomazine Babbitt, for she was under no such doubts at all, as it turned out. There had only ever been one man for Thomazine, from when she'd been knee-high to him, and the Lord be praised, it turned out it had always been Russell. It seemed she'd considered him her especial property since she was two years old and he twenty-one and her father's lieutenant in the old New Model Army. It might have saved him some considerable distress if she'd thought to tell him, though, he thought wryly.

Well. He smoothed the charcoal silk again. He'd thought to do her honour on their wedding day and wear his finest, but she was marrying a plain gentleman, not a courtier. He'd given all that up, along with his commission, just under a year ago. He was no man's but his own. And hers, of course. Always hers.

He took a deep breath and pulled on the pewter-grey wool waistcoat with the plain silver buttons and the old-fashioned, straight-fitting coat that went with it.

"At least the lass will recognise you," he told himself, smiling wanly at his reflection in the mirror. He ruffled a hand through his hair — grown to his shoulders now and no longer so indeterminately mouse as it had been when he'd worn it close-cropped but streaked fair and dark as a field of wheat when the wind blows through it. She liked it so, worn long and straight.

He was scarred and worn and weary, and his head hurt when the wind was in the north. But Thomazine loved him. And further than that, he did not care.

Russell turned his head to look at Thomazine as she walked in under the dripping arch of leaves and everything Thomazine's mother had been fiercely telling her about comporting herself with dignity — about walking slowly, not loping like a dismounted cavalry trooper (she got that from her father), about behaving with a becoming shyness and grace on her wedding day — she forgot most of it in the sheer joy of seeing her own dear Russell standing at the altar.

Thomazine stood under the weeping trees with her mother's hand under her elbow and felt the chill wind lift her loose hair. Loose, for the last time as a maiden, and she was quite looking forward to not being one. This was the crowning day of her womanhood, her bridal day. Oddly, she wasn't frightened, not at all, not even when every eye in the church was bent on her and she heard the little catch of a collective intake of breath. She hadn't turned out in borrowed plumes, either. In point of fact, both she and her mother had taken one look at the weeping grey skies and decided that a plain but decent birch-green skirt and bodice in a good warm wool were much more sensible than silks.

No, Thomazine wasn't afraid at all. He was though, poor sweet. Even though that kind candlelight gave his pallor a slightly healthier colour than perhaps it merited, he was white to the lips and although he was facing in her direction she had the rather unsettling impression that he was beyond seeing her, or indeed anything at all.

"That lad," her father said grimly down her ear, "that lad of yours is about to keel over, Zee. Go and poke him or summat."

And all those well-meant instructions about dignity and deportment went out of her head and she went laughing to his side so hastily that the last candle in the aisle guttered and went out in a wisp of acrid smoke in the draught of her passing.

"Thankful!" she hissed, and he shook himself and a little life came back into his eyes.

"Thomazine?" — wonderingly, as if he had not truly thought she'd come, the silly man.

"You were expecting someone else?" she said, and he ducked his head and grinned, which was neither pretty nor seemly in this house of God, but which was reassuring.

His hand was cold on hers and his fingers squeezed hers much too tight, but she braced herself and said nothing because she suspected that her betrothed, who had been a soldier and a rebel and a leader of men, was depending on her to get through this day unscathed.

Thankful had managed to get through his entire marriage vows without taking a breath, so far as she could tell, and was now staring at her as if he'd forgotten how to do it.

"I, Thomazine Dorcas Babbitt, do take thee, Thankful —" she couldn't say it, she was going to laugh, and she heard her father, who hadn't known either, choke slightly at her elbow — "Thankful-for-his-Deliverance Russell, to my wedded husband to have and to hold from this day forward, for better for worse, for richer, for poorer, in sickness and in health, to love, cherish, and to obey, till death us do part, according to God's holy ordinance; and thereto I give thee my troth."

And then his hands were shaking so much he dropped the ring and it went rolling away under the feet of most of the great and the good of White Notley. It was so still in the church she heard it tinkle — well, save for Joyeux's exasperated intake of breath at her sister's clumsiness — but by then it was funny and she forgot herself sufficient to stoop to pick it up at the same time as he did and they almost bumped noses, and the ring came to rest quite neatly under Uncle Luce's foot, at the front of the congregation. And that was almost funny, too, until she met his eyes and then neither of them could look away from each other and the rest of the world ceased to exist. His eyes were intent and oddly shy for a man who had been so confident in the commission of his duties but was still so uncertain of himself as a lover.

She wanted to take his other hand and put her head against his chest and have him hold her against his steady beating heart and for them to take comfort from one another, but she could not, of course, not here, not now. She couldn't do it, but the unscarred corner of his mouth lifted in a tiny smile of understanding and he dropped his eyes briefly. He knew.

It was not, perhaps, the most ostentatious of bridal feasts, but then it would have been somewhat of a mockery, in the dark days of a sodden October, with so plain a family and so unromantic a bridegroom, and so it was a quiet affair and no one minded that Thomazine sat with her feet in Russell's lap and he absently rubbed her toes while he was talking because her elegant slippers had let in the damp in the church and her feet were frozen.

Uncle Luce, who had been her father's junior officer in the wars and was now a mildly successful surgeon in his own right had brought his sprawling brood of children and they were careering about the house chasing the striped kitchen-cat (who was used to it and bore no grudges, having met the Pettitts en famille on a regular basis.) His wife was expecting her fifth any day now and so she was saying very little, but looking somewhat white about the mouth and holding very tight to her husband's hand.

Thomazine's father had got changed from his own finery, a deep smoke-blue suit that you only ever saw him wearing on high days and holidays and which made him nervous every hour of the day for fear he might spill something on it. He claimed that he wasn't going to do any work with his horses today, but his eyes kept straying to the window, watching what there was of the light fading and the rain streak the glass, and you could see he was thinking about putting in another hour gentling the new colt.

Joyeux and her equally-fashionable husband had made their excuses and left as soon as it was polite, claiming a long way to travel.

And so it was just the people Thomazine loved on her wedding night, at the last. It had been a day of courteous, smiling busyness, of many kind wishes and many blessings and congratulations, but as the dusk came down there was no air of wild festival about it and that was as it should be. There was only a quiet joy, a settling at peace, like the rose-gold ember at the heart of a flame. There was a rightness about it, because neither she nor Thankful were ostentatious in their loving, but quiet — and faithful, for they had loved one another, all unspoken, for almost six years before this day. Marriage set a crown on their happiness, but it was only a recognition of a thing both of them had known already.

The parlour was not a room that was often used, a room full of Thomazine's mother's precious things, her embroidered seat-cushions and the odd trinket that her father had remembered to bring back from travels about the country in the wars. Old now, but comfortable and sweet, and it had a scent of home and cleanliness about it, and Thomazine closed her eyes and sat smiling with the warmth of the fire on her face while her husband poked her cold toes and made little fond irritable noises reminiscent of a man who thought his wife wanted for common sense. (He'd told her that already. Twice.) Frannie Pettitt leaned with difficulty from her chair by the fireside and lifted a fold of Thomazine's heavy woollen skirts. "There," she said, "I'm that glad you didn't end up wearing that lovely silk today after all, Thomazine. You would have been perished, in that church."

Thomazine gave her new husband a secret, happy glance, sharing the little conspiracy. She had been relieved to see that he'd come to his wedding as his own plain, unpretentious, Sunday-best self: but he had been equally relieved to see her in her good wool gown and her lace collar. She had a suspicion that he might yet have broken and run at the last had he faced a fashionable stranger in silks and satins at the altar.

Frannie smiled and took a pin from her kerchief. "I'd not have liked to put pin-holes in your taffety," she said, pinning a silk ribbon bow to Thomazine's skirt and straightening up with a little huff. "There you go, my dear. I wouldn't have you go without a little frivolity."

"Not altogether without," Thankful said, with that shadow of a smile that was always more in the eyes than the lips, if you knew to look for it. "Zee?" And he put a hand to the breast of his coat and handed her a little package. He'd bought her pearls, a string of them, probably better ones than he could afford and there was a little outcry of admiration from the party as they were passed about. "Every pearl a tear, they say," he said. "Your mother reckons if you have them for your bridal you might never know sadness. You — like them?"

"Tears are for joy, as well as sorrow," she said gently, and then, because they were at home and amongst friends and none might laugh, she touched her fingertips to his wet lashes, because Thankful was the biggest watering-pot she knew, for all his austere demeanour. "Are they not?"

Quite unselfconsciously he took her hand and touched his lips to her fingers. "Happiest day of my life, my tibber. Bless you."

Thomazine had come through the day with absolute serenity and Thankful had taken much of his lead from her, because he would have been lost, else. Surrounded by old comrades gone respectable, he had felt a little awkward, being the last bachelor of their old company, at forty-two. Forty-two and missing in action for the better part of twenty years, in Scotland and in one place and another afterwards. Never quite settling, never quite at ease, never quite finding his own place, and he'd thought he never would, actually. Not till he'd had news of Fly's death and even then, he had assumed if he lived at Four Ashes at all, it would be alone. He'd never dreamed that he might have a hearth of his own one day and a girl of his own to sit at it.

Thomazine Babbitt sitting by the hearth and placidly spinning? Aye, right. Thomazine Babbitt in one of her father's scruffy old coats walking the chalk hills with him and muttering darkly about sheep, more like. She might be his dear love but she was her own self first. That was fine

His new father-in-law and old commander, Hollie Babbitt, was half a head taller than just about anyone else in the room and for once in his conspicuously russet-haired life was wearing something other than grey or black. Judging by the mutinous look on his face, the slate-blue silk was a source of some contention between Babbitt and his wife. And Het — well, Het was what you'd expect, from any lady who had had the misfortune to have been married to that engine of domestic destruction for over twenty years — plump and placid and imperturbable, regardless of what disasters and surprises her beloved husband dumped in her lap. Sturdy and round and freckled as an egg, and since he doubted that Het had ever suffered much in the way of the storms of passion, as comfortably devoted to her Hollie as she had been when they married.

And set against the glowing fire, was Thomazine — Thomazine Russell, now, with her amber hair unbound on her shoulders for the last time as a maiden and her rosemary-grey skirts kilted above her knee. He laughed quietly to himself. He still expected that one of these mornings she'd wake up and look at him and change her mind, but she hadn't so far, and since he'd been Thomazine Babbitt's plaything since she was two years old, he was a fool for her and he always would be. Here she was, twenty-one, beautiful, very slightly drunk — he was not going to meet her father's sardonic gaze across the table, because if Hollie even suspected that his eldest daughter was tipsy, he was more than capable of up-ending her under the stable-yard pump, big as she was.

Actually, take that back, because Hollie was nuzzling his stout, middle-aged lady's ear in a way that Russell suspected might be the result of a comfortable degree of inebriation on his own part and Het was squirming without much conviction. "She'll end up in his lap before long," Zee said happily, following her husband's gaze. "How old is Mama, d'you know?"

"Your mother? Um — fifty-something?"

"Too old for another baby, I suppose. Well. That's a relief."

He probably should be shocked. Instead, it made him laugh. She had a habit of doing that.

"Russell." She settled herself comfortably against him, her bare shoulders warm against his arm even through the layers of linen and sensible wool. "Russell, will we have babies?"

"What?"

"Every time I've seen Mama get — that friendly — with daddy, I end up with a sister."

"Would you mind?" He wouldn't. God help him, he wouldn't.

"What — another sister? Well, no, but —"

"No, Thomazine, our own baby."

"It would be nice."

Thomazine sat on the edge of the bed wearing only her prettiest shift, running a brush through her thick, unbraided hair. She looked up at Russell and smiled, and he smiled back at her, that loving, lopsided smile that lit up his whole dear face. "Oh tibber I do love you," he said softly.

She loosed the ribbon out of his hair and ruffled it onto his shoulders and he shivered. "Cold?" she said, and scooted up the bed and turned the covers back, sitting up against the pillows with her hands round her knees.

He took a deep breath. "Thomazine — wife — I —"

She wasn't daft, and she was the daughter of a man who bred horses. She did know what country matters were. "Out with it," she said firmly, and he almost said it, whatever it was, and then looked quickly into his lap.

"I think I should be grateful for a hug," he said feebly, and she held him so for a moment, and then drew back, looking down quizzically. "Thomazine. I don't want to hurt you," he muttered, scowling fiercely into his lap.

"Hurt me?" Thomazine looked at her husband blankly. "Why would you —"

He lifted a shoulder in an awkward shrug. "Because it does. Apparently. So I am told. By people who know about these things."

"But Russell." She went and sat closer to him and he edged away as if she might burn him. "It's our wedding night and you don't want to be anywhere near me. That causes me distress." She wriggled her fingers under his arm and poked him in the ribs. "Hey. Thankful-for-his-Deliverance." Which got a small smile out of him. "I love you. I don't mind if you hurt me a little bit."

"I do!" He gave a great sigh. "Oh, Zee. What are we to do?" He put his head on her shoulder, very gingerly, and she put her arm round him.

This was ridiculous, she thought. He had known women before, in a very practical and Biblical sense. Quite a lot, actually, if what Daddy said was anything like true —it was remarkably absurd that it should be him that was gone all stiff and shivery, as if he was come innocent to his bridal bed. "There," she said firmly. "Is that better?"

"No," he said, equally firmly. "Thomazine, I have not —"

"Yes you have."

"Not for the better part of ten years," he finished through gritted teeth, and realisation dawned.

"Oh." She didn't know what to say to that, but she felt all hot and uncomfortable about having said it anyway. "You do want to, though?"

"Yes," he said honestly, "yes I do, very much, but —"

She leaned forward and tugged his shirt free of his breeches, and he made no move to stop her. She knew what he felt like in her arms with all his clothes on, of course. They'd done that. But without — he was more solid and smoother and altogether much nicer.

"May I return the compliment, husband?" she said, and he shook himself like a wet dog and grinned down at her and he was himself again. Not frightened. Not worried. Just himself, with nothing between them.

Nothing at all. Not even a layer of thin linen.

And it was much, much nicer even than she'd thought it would be.

Russell was still lying there at gone midnight, flat on his back with his hair fallen in his eyes and a silly grin on his face, watching the moonlight move in squares across the clean scrubbed boards of Thomazine's own chamber.

She snored a little and he liked her snuffling, whistling breathing, and the way she growled in her sleep when he might have taken more of the coverlets than she thought he was entitled to, and the way she was holding him as tight as if he might take it into his head to disappear in the night. He felt — married. The thought of it gave him an odd feeling about his heart again and he put his arm around her shoulders and squeezed her in ardent silence, and she muttered something incomprehensible and buried her face in his armpit.

He was loved. Loved and loving. He had a place. It was currently a grace and favour place in the Babbitt household — his old commander's son-in-law, by God, who'd have ever thought it? — till there was a roof on the house at Four Ashes again and the place wasn't falling to bits about his ears. But that was in the future and for the first time since he'd been a passionate boy in the New Model Army there *was* a future. There would be children at Four Ashes again, and laughter and joy. He would make it so. He would make it a home again, for his bright girl and the bright babies they would fill it with one day. And no child of his would ever know imposed fear, or humiliation, or darkness, not the way he had known it as his sister's hands. She had been a monster and he was not sorry she was dead. A cruel, unloving, vicious, inventive bitch, and the Lord be thanked she had never whelped children of her own, for she would have twisted them worse than she had managed to twist him. She had almost managed to break him of his faith, but he still had a God and he prayed to Him nightly that her black and rotten soul might be brought to look on what she had done to her little brother in the name of godly zeal. He couldn't forgive her, though it was his duty as a good man to do so.

He had not visited her grave and they could make of that what they would at Four Ashes. And nor would he, unless it was with a stake and a rowan-tree to make sure that the bloodless bitch stayed buried.

Thomazine stirred, pushed her knee against his and her hand tightened around his waist in a proprietorial fashion, which was startling but nice.

He wanted to take her home as soon as may be. He closed his eyes, snuffed the clean scent of her hair and thought of Four Ashes. The whole west wing had gone down, and he had stood knee-deep in charred timbers and shattered stone, the dawn gleaming wet and red on shards of broken glass where the windows had burst through in the blaze. It had been an odd thing, to even dare to dream of the future. At first he had considered good plain furnishings for a house that did not yet exist, fitting for a middle-aged retired soldier of quiet tastes and then, given free rein, he had discovered rapidly that his tastes in furnishings were neither subdued nor quiet, but inclined somewhat shockingly towards the magpie. He had stood in warehouses in Wapping, up and down the stinking river docks, stroking silks and holding trinkets up to the light, talking of a young bride who might care for fashionable blue and white china from the Low Countries, or who might prefer porcelain of China, a Turkey carpet, a bolt of green-gold silk the colour of her eyes. Pearls. (She had liked the pearls. She'd pretended not to — she'd called him fond and foolish and said he'd spent far too much money on her — but she had liked them. He would have covered her bed with pearls and precious rubies, if she'd asked it of him.)

He wanted her to see Four Ashes and she would and they would be happy. And Fly-Fornication's joyless spirit would turn in its grave. He would fill their garden with the most fragrant roses his pocket might command, that Thomazine might always have rose petals beneath her feet. A future filled with warmth and joy and sunlight, and a place in the world. And a girl who loved him, and for some unfathomable reason of her own, desired him. What more could a man wish for?

He was almost asleep, and thinking of nothing more useful than the comfort of the soft breathing weight of her in his arms, when he heard the first scream.

2

Russell came bolt upright with a yell of his own and Thomazine came upright with him, though she was barely awake. He could smell smoke.

"Fire," he said, every hair standing up on his neck and the flesh cringing on his bones. "Tibber!" He took her by the shoulders and shook her till her head lolled on her shoulders and her eyelashes fluttered but she would not wake. He could hear the crackle of flames and the warm orange glow of firelight under the door, could hear raised voices and running feet on the stairs, the roar of the flames and the first splintering crash as the windows —

"Wha'?" she said drowsily, and he was half out of bed and pulling her with him, dragging her by the arm across the crumpled sheets.

"Fire!"

The wench was heavier than she looked, deadweight, and she pulled her arm free and blinked at him sleepily, "What?"

"Smoke!"

"There's no smoke," she said, perfectly calmly. "Russell, you're dreaming."

"I heard —"

"It's all right," she said, and he half-believed her, and she shook his arm until he looked at her. "Thankful. It is all right. It's —" Another yowl of bloodcurdling ferocity split the air and Thomazine's eyebrows rose. She opened the door a crack as a further set of footsteps went thumping down the landing. "Mama? What's amiss?"

The sight of Het Babbitt on the shadowy landing, as plump and four-square as a little hedgehog in her stout flannel nightgown, was oddly comforting. "Nothing, dear," she said blithely. "There have been babies a-plenty born under this roof before, and I imagine there will be plenty more to come. Everything proceeds as it should. And really, Thankful, to be so squalmish — I recall you standing in that very doorway when Joyeux was born, dear, you are no stranger to childbirth." She gave a fond, reproving shake of the head. "Now, young lady, I am needed elsewhere, for I very much suspect you will be an auntie again by dawn. Go back to bed, the both of you. Your father is gone for the midwife, Zee, so I am sure there will be much commotion shortly." She pottered down the landing towards the stairs. Thomazine closed the door again, firmly.

"There, now, you see? We are not besieged, the house is not falling —"

She was laughing, and he was not. In his head, he knew that he was in a place of safety with the woman he loved and that all was well. In his heart — a woman screaming, the sound of hoofbeats crashing on the stone flags of the yard, the leap and flare of firelight —

"Russell?"

He shook his head.

"Come back to bed," she said gently, "you are shaking with cold, lamb."

Not cold, but fear, and he hated it, all the more for knowing it was not real, that he was afraid of a phantom in his own head. His mouth was very dry and his marred cheek stiff as wood, but he choked down the bile in his throat and said, "My. Sis. Ter." And his voice was slurred, odd, and she glanced at him with a look of understanding. She crossed the room again, barefoot and tall and slight and radiant as a white candle, to squat on her haunches in front of the dying fire and shake the jug of spiced ale that had been left there. She poured the last of it and offered it to him wordlessly.

He didn't taste it, but the warmth of it eased the shivering cold in his bones and he swallowed it gratefully.

Thomazine set the jug back in the ashes and perched herself on the bed, cross-legged.

He was awake now. He could not see Thomazine with her skirts blazing around her, or her loose hair burning like the tail of a comet. He could not smell roasting meat, or imagine the shattering roar as the roof fell in to obliterate her dear body under a ruin of charred wood and broken glass. "Four Ashes burned," he said softly, his voice under control again. "That much you know. Well. My sister burned with it. She was in the house. I dream of it, sometimes." He thought, but did not say, that sometimes it was not Fly he saw in his dreams, but other people, the people he loved. Burning. Always burning and begging to be saved, and he was always standing outside. Standing in the thin rain of a Buckinghamshire winter night, with the heat on his face and the whirling sparks like scarlet snow and the roar and whoosh of collapsing timbers.

Thomazine touched his hand and he snatched at her fingers and held them, hard, and in his head he was pulling her free from the falling timbers. Too hard, he thought, for her level brows drew together in a tiny wince. He was sorry for it.

"Yes," she said. "I imagine you would." And then, after a little pause, she freed her hand and linked her fingers through his, that he might not squeeze them quite so hard anymore. "I'm sorry, Russell. I don't think I have said that before. I am truly sorry."

He was tired and his head was beginning to ache with lack of sleep, so he was honest and he said, "I'm not, tibber."

He thought she might be shocked. She took a little sharp breath, but then she glanced up and looked both sad and angry at once. "I am sorry for you, love. Not her."

"No one deserves to die so," he said softly, and it was the first time he had said as much aloud, and the closest he had yet come to forgiveness. "No matter how vile a sinner they may be. No one deserves that death. I am sorry she died so hard. I am not sorry she died, and I cannot find it in my heart to mourn her."

Thomazine's gilded russet lashes dipped and she said nothing. The house was still again, so still that you could hear the murmur of voices in the room at the end of the landing and the creak of floorboards where Frannie Pettitt was walking to and fro to ease the pain of bringing a new life into the world. So still that the disconcerting, all too audible grunting snarl from the far chamber made Russell jump and blink, imagining the worst, and made Thomazine smile at his discomfiture, for being a woman she had more knowledge of these matters than he did. He stared at her, wide-eyed, and she leaned forward till her forehead touched his. "What was it you always used to say to me," she said gently, "all will be well, and all manner of things shall be well?" He nodded, slowly, reassured. "All proceeds as it should, Russell," she said, and disentangled his hand from hers and pushed his loose, fear-sweaty hair out of his eyes. "Come back to bed and be comforted."

Frances Pettitt was the lighter of a daughter by dawn and the house was buzzing like an upturned ant's nest.

Het was crumpled and teary-eyed, reminded of her own babies, all grown up now, and Uncle Luce said he had half a mind to have the child christened Rosamund, the Rose of the World. Thomazine's father, who looked a little misty-eyed himself, muttered darkly that he'd only ever thought Luce had had half a mind at the best of times and to give the poor little mite a sensible name in all charity.

"Like Thomazine, you mean?" Luce said tartly, bouncing the little bundle of spotless drapery in his arms. The infant gave a tiny mew, like a sleepy kitten, and nestled against her father.

Thomazine caught her father's eye and he smiled and scratched at his cinnamon stubble. "I'm happy with Thomazine," he said softly. "Now, lass, I'd never have suspected that man of yours of idleness. Is he likely to appear before breakfast to admire this child prodigy?"

She had left Russell sleeping. She did not know what he might make of a new baby, whether he would turn sentimental, or be timid, or distant, did not, in all truth, know if he liked children or not. There was a deal she did not know about Thankful Russell. She had not known his given name was Thankful-for-His-Deliverance until yesterday, for one thing, and the memory of that rather ludicrously godly and well-concealed Christian name lightened her mood suddenly. She returned to him.

"A what?" he said muzzily, without opening his eyes.

"A baby. Uncle Luce's baby. She —"

Russell sat up then and slithered out of bed and ended by bounding downstairs barefoot, a solitary stocking trailing from his pocket. "She? He has a daughter? Oh, bravely done, Frances! About time!"

He liked children, then, she thought, following in his wake. The baby, being a matter of hours old and not objecting at so tender an age to being passed from pillar to post like a little parcel, had not been frightened by his marred cheek, but had simply lay cuddled in the crook of his arm and looked up at him with unfocussed blue eyes.

Russell had looked at Thomazine and Thomazine had looked at Russell and an unspoken understanding had passed between them. She had not cared who might see the look of dazed joy on his face, or the tenderness on hers. It was a fragile understanding at best, though, and not the sort of thing that could be shared in a room full of people, with a nursing mother upstairs and all the talk of the new one's beauty — how she might have Luce's height, such long legs for a tiny wee one, and wasn't she a sweet poppet, and did you see, so young, and she smiled, truly she did, and did you think she would be dark like her mammy or fair like her father.

Russell handed the child back to Luce with an air of one having successfully carried off a frightening duty and absented himself to his wife's side. "So small!" he murmured and there was an edge of marvel to his voice that made her look at him sharply. She found him still with his hand cupped as if he were still cradling the child's head. She moved her foot against his and gave him a shove.

"Russell, people will think you are a mooncalf. Have you never held a child before?"

"Only you, tibber," he said, "I didn't dare any others, after that. You were sufficient wriggly to frighten the life out of me." He gave a happy sigh. "We'd not be missed, lass. If you'd care to see our home. Travel light, we'd be there in — a week? Maybe?"

Afterwards, Thomazine looked back on that week as their honeymoon, for all it was spent trailing hock-deep along deep-rutted muddy lanes in the rain. She learned a number of things: that it was possible to ride holding hands with a man if your respective mounts were amicable enough and if you were able to slip the disapproving eye of your maid and his groom for more than an hour at a time. That amongst his many admirable abilities Russell's ability to command a hot meal and a warm bed in short order in even the busiest inns was amongst his finest. That he could be remarkably intimidating if you put his back to the wall; that he was fierce in his defence of his own and would brook no insolence from his subordinates. She wondered if he had always been so, as a fiery young officer, or if that trick of arrogant command was a thing he'd learned later.

"Boots," he said firmly and that was something else she had learned about her new husband. She sat and put her muddy booted foot into his lap obediently with a sigh.

"Russell, do we really have to —"

"Dry boots, clean stockings." He rolled her stocking down over her foot, rubbed her frog-cold toes between his hands and looked up at her. "You ask my bailiff, my tibber. He was with me in Scotland and I have never seen men as miserable as those without good boots. Can't be warm when your feet are damp, Zee, no matter how many clothes you have on."

"I'm not a soldier, Russell," she said patiently, and he'd planted a kiss on his palm and placed it on her instep.

"Surely. But you're my wife and I have a duty to look after you."

"Oh? Indeed? So dragging me halfway across the country in midwinter is looking after me?"

"Character-forming," he said sweetly. "Anyway, you're enjoying it."

And actually, she was. She had never been so far outside Essex before. The people sounded different, the sky looked different, the trees looked different. Everything was a little wider and paler and colder than it was in Essex. When they had reached Buckinghamshire it had seemed that they would be obliged to call at every little manor in the county, at Radnage and Walters Ash and Wooburn, that Major Russell might introduce his draggled bride in company. She fell to wondering if perhaps she might not take to her new home after all, for Russell at his stiffest and coldest was as nothing to the stiffness and the coolness of the people he claimed as friends and neighbours, moving politely around each other, offering cakes and wine with a brittle social gloss.

"My new bride," he said and his voice had the same pride to it as it had had the first time he'd said it.

Mistress Eleanor Lane of Everhall Manor inclined her head graciously and looked at Thomazine with some curiosity.

The house was big, venerable and — Thomazine sniffed, surreptitiously — not very well kept, for despite its grandeur it smelt of mice and damp. Not as clean as White Notley. She restrained herself from craning her neck to observe the creamy cobwebs in the corners of the ceiling that her domestic soul itched to take a broom to.

"Indeed, Mistress — ah — Russell?"

"Indeed," Thomazine replied, returning her stare for stare, for Mistress Lane evidently fancied she resembled a blush-rose in her stiff pink silks. In point of fact, with a roll of creamy fat over the stiffly-boned shoulders of her fashionable gown she resembled nothing so much as an undercooked sausage. Thomazine was a little crumpled, for they had spent the better part of a week on horseback and the greater part of her baggage was as yet at White Notley, but her plain steel-blue wool gown was good, for her mother had a taste for line and colour that was unsurpassed throughout Essex. Thomazine drew herself up to her full height and looked down her not-inconsiderable nose at Mistress Lane as though she was the Queen of England herself. "We are new-married. A week, no more."

"How charming. Such pretty hair." With a smile that said, such a shame about the lamentably prominent nose, dear, and the unfashionable length of your bones. "You have such a lot of it, Mistress Russell. I always find long hair so difficult to keep tidy, don't you? Such a relief that the prevailing fashion is for *en déshabillé*, I think. It must make things so much easier."

"Indeed," Thomazine said again, unsure whether or not she ought to give the sausage-lady tit for tat, or whether perhaps she had misunderstood that last. For, after all, it wasn't Thomazine who was crouched on a spindly stool like a toad on a mushroom with her sagging bubbies thrust up as a kind of ghastly support for her jowls, simpering at polite company. Perhaps Mistress Lane had only meant that the prevailing fashion was not to finish putting on a bodice before receiving guests. She glanced up at Russell, hoping to take her lead from him — was it meant, perhaps, as a joke that he might understand?

"Well, madam, I must not keep you from your journey," the sausage-lady said and the rude baggage actually twitched her head aside, tinkling a little bell with one podgy hand to summon a servant.

"No," Russell said, equally curtly, and he had that slightly wide-eyed, rigid look about him, as if by holding himself very stiff he might also hold his temper in. (It was not a look she had often seen at White Notley and she put her hand out and touched his wrist. He smiled down at her, but he stayed rigid.) "No, we have a way to travel before we reach home."

She was not surprised that Russell was as slight as he was, if the only refreshment anyone ever offered guests in these parts was thin, sugary wine, well-watered and stale cake, and even that grudgingly. At White Notley any guest who arrived at the supper hour would have had a place made for them at table and be expected to do service to Williams's good food. "Perhaps you would do the honour of calling on us when we are settled at Four Ashes, Mistress Lane," Russell said icily.

"Perhaps. Although it will be a while before the house is fit to live in, so I believe. I understand the house to be gutted, sir. Wholly gutted."

"It was," he said. "My bailiff has had men working on it this six months and more."

"No expense spared, indeed."

"None."

She inclined her head again, dismissively. "How very fortunate that Mistress Coventry's untimely death should leave you so well provided for, Major Russell. My congratulations on your — most unexpected — marriage, sir. And my husband's, also, were he here to offer them. I bid you a good day."

"Well. That went well." Russell had sniffed and hunched his shoulders, and looked so remarkably uncomforted that she nudged the black mare up close to his big grey horse and took his hand.

"I imagine we are going to get any number of odd looks for a while. It is a little unexpected of you to turn up with a new wife, when you've been the county's most eligible bachelor for so long. She's probably been secretly in love with you for years herself."

That startled a laugh out of him. "Thank you, Thomazine, for that piece of shameless flattery. A patent untruth, but thank you. They've not set eyes on me for the better part of twenty years, tibber. I could have had six wives, for all they know."

"All at once?" she said delicately. "That would have kept you busy."

"If they were all like you, mistress, I should be even greyer than I already am." The corner of his mouth lifted in a reluctant smile. "Unexpected. Aye. You might say so. I had thought — well, I was a regular guest at their table before the wars. Am I so changed? No, don't answer that, Thomazine. A regicide, a most notorious Roundhead, and now I'm turned up out of nowhere with a beautiful young woman to wife. They probably think I've spent the last twenty years selling arms to the Dutch or something." Thomazine's mare heaved a blubbery sigh and shifted her weight onto one back foot. "I'll not have them be rude to you, Zee," he said, and she looked up expecting her watery husband to be blinking back tears. Instead he looked rather frighteningly purposeful. "I'll tell you one thing straight off, mistress. They rent a farm at Walter's Ash off my estate and that lease is terminated as of now. I will be instructing my bailiff to write and put an end to that agreement and they can have till the end of the quarter to find new grazing for their benighted stock. She wants to play silly buggers and I intend to play silly buggers right back. I bet Henry Lane won't thank her for that when they're put to the trouble of finding new pasture."

"There's no need for —"

"She was discourteous to you, Thomazine. And I will not tolerate insolence from an aged parasite in — in borrowed finery!"

"Borrowed?"

He raised an eyebrow at her. "Well, unless Lane's been spending the rent money on those god-awful gowns of hers I'm fairly sure they're not paid for, tibber, since I've not had a penny off 'em since the turn of the year."

Thomazine looked down at her gloved hands on the mare's reins. Neatly gloved, as well they might be, since they'd been made by Luce's father and he'd been a member of the Guild of Glovers. Well-made and well-kept, in plain russet leather, but a little worn and neatly mended in places. She looked at the lace on her husband's cuff, which was narrow and hellish expensive. "Dear," she said, carefully, "I had always assumed you were, well, you were. Ah. I don't really know how to say this. I had assumed you were like us." He was looking amused now, that long, slow cat's blink that was the closest he ever got to a smug grin. "Would I be right in guessing that you are ... significantly better placed than I had assumed?"

"Tibber, you behold the last of the noble Russell household." He gave her a sly sidelong glance. "I don't take much feeding. I am, I would argue, cheap to keep."

She took another deep breath. "Your land. Lands. Which bits are yours? I mean, did the King — did His Majesty — does he not mind, with you being a, you know…?"

"If you are asking do I own half of Buckinghamshire, mistress, I may assure you, I do not. And does the King mind that I do happen to own a proportion of it, well, as I have no objection to his mistresses being my next-door neighbour, then I trust he has no objection to a notorious regicide living next door to Radnage Manor. Why, Thomazine, I do believe you are shocked!"

"You live next door to one of His Majesty's mistresses?"

"There is a respectable distance between us, madam, I guarantee. I have yet to see the lady in question, but I am assured she is in no way remarkable and nor does she live as to excite comment in the neighbourhood. Although my bailiff assures me that she is frequently visited by a plain country gentleman who goes by the name of Rowley. That being why he gave her the wretched place in the first place." He turned his head and looked at her solemnly. "That's the King, dear. Though I've only met him the once in a — civilian — capacity."

"Goodness," she said faintly.

"Goodness had very little to do with it, tibber. Although I'm told His Majesty is a very nice man and very kind to his friends. And madam," he looked down at her and there was a smile lurking in his eyes, "I have been involved in regicide once already and if Master Rowley thinks he's going to make frolic with my wife, I may be moved to become so again."

"Why, Russell. I do believe you're jealous!"

"How very perceptive, madam." He pulled his hand away from hers, gently. "I reckon it's coming on to rain, Zee, and I'd like to make shelter before dark. Twenty years ago there'd have been half a dozen houses where we'd have found a welcome and a bed for the night within an hour's ride of here, but I wouldn't stake my life to it after Mistress Lane's welcome. Welcome to bloody Buckinghamshire, wife. It's raining and nobody wants to talk to me."

"Oh, well, dear." She put her heels to the mare and trotted on a few strides. "I'm not so tired of your company yet that I can't manage a little further conversation with you."

Thank God the turf beneath the mare's feet was solid and firm and the path flat, because as that sweet little mare trotted out willingly her wicked husband set his own horse chasing after her, bounding from a standing start into a gallop and they arrived at the coppice that gave Four Ashes its name in the gathering dusk, laughing and breathless. But as they walked the blowing horses side by side out of the dripping black trees, her first sight of the house where she was to spend her married life broke her laughter off short, for it was a ruin, looming up stark through the gusting rain at the end of an overgrown track.

One wing and the centre of the house were as new as a fresh-minted gold piece, but then the house tailed off, fire-scarred and black, into a jumble of broken glass and charred timber and broken stone, and there was something heart-breaking about that. Beside her the grey horse threw his head up and backed as if Russell had jerked on the reins and then he dismounted with a thump and walked towards the ruin, his hands outstretched like a blind man.

The grey horse, cavalry-trained, dropped his nose to the grass and Thomazine cocked her leg over the side-saddle and went to dismount, to go to Russell, for he looked as if he had been stabbed to the heart. He turned and gave her a brittle, unconvincing smile and brushed the heel of his hand to his eyes. "Well," he said, "there is more work still needs to be done than I had imagined, my tibber. Welcome —" his voice broke a little, "welcome to our new home, wife."

She had wanted to say something bright and clever to console him, but looking at that bleak, black ruin, she could not. It was horrible and pitiful, all at once. The new-built wing and the front door and the centre were lovely, gracefully proportioned and mellow and welcoming, and then the west end of the house was —

It was as if a pretty girl had opened her mouth to reveal rotting, splintered black teeth.

There were no lights in the windows, no smoke from the chimneys, no signs of life. Not so much as a slinking cat crossed the overgrown lawns, no birds sang from the shaggy bushes. It was not only half in ruins, it was uncared-for and eerie and Thomazine was cold and wet and hungry, and she would have given much for a hot supper and her bed. Thankful was looking at her as if he wanted her to say it didn't matter, but she could not, because it did. It mattered very much. She slithered down the mare's flank, missed her footing in the wet grass and twisted her ankle. There was no great damage, but the sharp little pain added to her other woes and for the first time since she had been a baby Thomazine could not get back on her feet smiling, but instead sat in the cold grass in the dark and wept.

She had her head buried in the folds of her skirt that still smelt of her mother's linen-chest and home and a place that had a roof on it and so she didn't see him, but she felt the touch on the back of her neck and batted her hand at it with a most unmaidenly, "Leave me alone!"

Russell laughed weakly and sounded almost as forlorn as she felt. "That's not me, tibber. That's Marlowe. He worries about people."

A horse's muzzle investigated the scant few inches of bare flesh at the nape of her neck between her hair and her collar and blew moistly and she had to laugh even though she didn't want to. Then Russell came and sat in the wet grass beside her and put his arms round her and pulled her into his lap and held her head against his chest and rocked her a little, as if she had been a child again. "Oh, Thomazine," he said, "oh, lass, it will not be so bad come the morning. It looks worse than what it is, I'm sure. And, you know, we can always live somewhere close, and —"

"I want to go home!" she sobbed, and felt him nod.

"So did I, my tibber, so did I. Wanted this to be home and it's not. It looks like the morning after they lifted the siege at

Colchester." He rocked her again and lifted a hand to stroke her hair, as much for his own comfort as her own, she thought. "It'll come good, love."

She wanted to be her brave little mother right that minute, because Het Babbitt would have shaken out her skirts in a martial fashion and rolled up her sleeves and called for soap and hot water and started in on making the place all right and tight. But Thomazine was too stiff and miserable and just about the only thing of any warmth in that whole bleak November world was the patch of her husband's shoulder where she clung, and even that was bony. The grey horse nuzzled at the back of her head again and she frowned into Russell's damp coat. "What kind of stupid name for a horse is Marlowe?"

"Blame your Uncle Luce," he said dryly. "He introduced me to the man's poetry."

The tears still ran down her cheeks, but that was of their own volition and they no longer hurt her eyes and her temples, they just ran, overflowing, like rain. Her nose was running, too, and the breast of his coat would be a horrible sticky mess when she straightened up and so she burrowed her face tighter against him, scenting wet wool and fresh air. He put his hand on the back of her head again and then cursed softly to himself. "Oh, a pox on those hairpins, tibber. There goes another one. D'you want a handkerchief?"

It would be full dark soon and moonless and chill. She wanted to go in to a warm hearth and to her mother sitting beside it with her mending and the smell of cooking and baking bread and scoured cleanliness. She sat up and pushed her hair out of her eyes and wiped her nose on her cuff, though it was so dark he'd probably not see the unfeminine gesture. She took a deep breath and straightened her shoulders.

"No," she said, "no, I shall be fine. A momentary silliness, that was all. A little bit tired. It's been a long day, I think. Do we," it was a forlorn hope, but she had to ask, "do you think there would be anything to eat, within?"

He kissed the top of her head. "Oh, my girl, you are your mother's daughter. Well, I can promise nothing. All I can say is that if I know the gentlemen that have been working on the west wing, and if they have been here as recently as I pay them to be, then yes. There may be a few leftovers. And if not, why, we won't starve before tomorrow morning."

"The horses?" Because if there were stables there might be oats and then there might be gruel. Of a sort.

"Leave them loose," he said firmly and pulled her to her feet.

3

Thomazine opened her eyes blearily to a faint pearly dawn. In the first grey light the kitchens looked like a family crypt, which thought made her shudder: long, rough-planed wood boxes were stacked along the walls like coffins. She hadn't seen those in the dark.

She'd not expected to sleep, but she had been so tired that she had. They had been wrapped in each other's arms, rolled in two wet cloaks in front of a black-empty hearth with a saddle for a pillow. She looked down at her new husband. He looked different in sleep, lying flat on his back with his hair in his eyes and the collar of the cloak pulled right up to his chin. She leaned forwards and pulled the cloak up over his bare shoulder, more for the excuse of touching his bare skin than anything else.

"Thomazine," he said sleepily, and she sat upright with a squeak. "That tickles, what're you doing?" She felt him laugh, rather than heard it. "D'you want some breakfast, then, my tibber? Can't promise you any more than bread and bacon, mind you, and I wouldn't swear to it that my cooking is any better than the common run, but where there are labouring-men in these parts, there is most often a piece of bacon —"

It made her laugh, because he still sounded marvellously prim and dignified, even whilst he was wriggling into his breeches and hauling his shirt over his head, his hair in an abandoned tangle down his back. "Won't take a minute to get the fire lit," he said smugly, and then, a while later, pink and slightly flustered, "It'll catch shortly, I'm sure. No, truly, it will—"

She took the flint and steel out of his hand, and he smiled up at her. "A helpmeet, lady?"

"A friend loves at all times, and a wife is born for adversity," she misquoted softly.

The corner of his mouth twitched. "No doubt. Um, we will have staff to do this kind of thing, usually, tibber. I'm not wholly uncivilised. It's just — I wasn't expecting us to stay overnight."

She caught a spark and blew on it, onto the little pile of wood shavings in the big hearth. "Well, we are here. For as long as may be."

He glanced up at her. "Perhaps we ought to see about employing some servants with all dispatch?"

"And not go —"

"Not go back to White Notley," he finished, with an air of finality. "This is our home, Zee." He must have caught her look of disappointment, because he blinked at her solemnly. "It's not finished yet," he said. "I've not showed you upstairs."

"I am only relieved that there is an upstairs. You told me half the roof had fallen in."

"Ah, well, the lads have been working on that." He held out his hands to her to display a somewhat ungentlemanly black thumbnail and a scar the length of one finger — "Chisel," he said proudly. "I might have been known to lend a hand myself. What kind of man should I be that wouldn't see a whole roof over his wife's head?"

"The sort of man who stands there prattling and lets the fire go out?" she suggested, and he closed his mouth with a snap and looked briefly affronted. He had never been good at being teased and it took him a heartbeat to realise that it was happening. And then he laughed. "Well, there's probably bread. Somewhere. We are not yet so crammed with furniture that there are many places to conceal it."

She had a prowl around the shadowy kitchen, not realising until now how big and dusty an unfurnished, untenanted kitchen could be. She caught sight of a lumpy linen bag and gave a little moan of shameless greed as the stale bread rolled out of its covering.

"I have not forgotten quite everything I knew on campaign," Russell said smugly, turning around at the sound of loaves as hard as rocks bouncing on rough boards. "See? I told you they'd leave something. And half a side of bacon in the chimney here, and — hm." He sat back on his heels, scowling at the flaring lump of charcoal on the point of his knife. "You any good at toasting bread, tibber? I can't seem to get the trick of this at all."

"Perhaps we could eat it as is?" she suggested, and he raised a very sardonic eyebrow.

"Only if they also left a hammer and chisel."

But she did her best, with great ragged lopsided doorsteps of rock-hard bread. "Hunger is the best salt," he said hopefully, and she looked at the curling grey slabs of meat laid on the smouldering crusts.

"You reckon?"

"Well. Perhaps a little more salt then."

They had just about managed to achieve something that was almost edible, with much laughter and restrained cursing, when they heard hoofbeats on the cobbles and the sound of boots running. The barton door slammed open and a stocky, black-haired man with a brace of pistols about his person stood before them. Thomazine whisked behind a wooden chest and pulled Russell's cloak tight round her.

"What the hell d'you mean by this, ye shameless vagabond? Get out and show yourself like a man, or I swear I'll — Major Russell!"

Facing down the barrel of a cocked pistol Russell put the knife and the smoking bread down and gingerly moved the bacon from its perilous placement at the edge of the flames. "Eadulf, sir, I am delighted to see you taking such an interest in the house, but really." He turned full round, pushing his hair out of his eyes with his un-greasy hand. "It is my house, you know."

"You never told me!" the irate gentleman said. "I might have shot you, you great —"

"Scotsmen," Russell said over his shoulder to Thomazine, as if it explained everything. "Eadulf is my bailiff, tibber. He's been seeing to the estate in my absence."

"Aye, since —" The man's eyes moved very slowly to the shadows, as if he was afraid of what he might see. "Who're you talking to, Major?"

"My wife. Who did you think I was talking to? My sister's shadow?"

The expression on the man called Eadulf's face was a joy to behold. He looked as if someone had punched him in the belly. "Your wife?"

"Someone had to be daft enough to marry me eventually," Russell said smugly, and Thomazine stood up, surreptitiously holding the edges of the crumpled cloak together over her body-linen. "I am delighted to make your acquaintance, sir," she said sweetly and curtseyed so that the folds of cloak covered her bare feet.

"Mistress Russell — Eadulf Gillespie. My bailiff. He lives about a mile up the valley."

"You brought your wife," Gillespie said again, "to this unchancy ruin? Major Russell, that was no' well done! Ye should have sent word, sir! I'd have — well, I'd at least have seen you decently provisioned! When did all this happen?"

"We came over yesterday, at dusk. We didn't intend to stay overnight, but it was raining and near dark."

"God a'mighty, Russell, ye're not twenty-one anymore, have ye not the sense ye were born with? I saw the smoke from out o' the chimney and I knew verra well there'd be none come to here after dark for any good purpose, so I come straight down here to see what was afoot, and — well, here ye are, safe and sound and intact, thank God, but why did ye not tell me ye were coming home? Ye didn't even tell me ye had a — a lass promised, never mind a wife! And this is no welcome for a gently-born maid, coming to this benighted pile of rubble!" Gillespie glowered, running his free hand through his short, ruffled hair. "Well. I've said my piece and I'll say no more. I bid ye welcome to Four Ashes, mistress. What's left of it."

"Oh," Thomazine said faintly. "Thank you."

"I should like to reassure you that I am not customarily addressed in like fashion by my staff," Russell said, sounding very stiff and shocked, and then the unmarked corner of his mouth lifted in that dear lopsided grin. "I don't hardly count Eadulf as staff, tibber. More in the way of a friend."

"You might call it friendship. More in the way of a keeper, I'd argue."

"He pulled me out from under my horse at Dunbar," Russell explained and his hand went to his shoulder, by which she guessed that he had taken some hurt there as well as losing his horse.

"Aye, and you pulled me out of the cathedral at Durham a month after," Gillespie grumbled. "So I call us quits."

"Want a slice of bacon? I reckon it's just about cooked."

"Give that here," the Scotsman said. "I've had the benefit o' your cooking before, Major, and ye're not known for the thoroughness of it. If you don't mind breakfasting on raw meat, mistress, you go right ahead and eat it." He made a disgusted noise, brushing crumbs from the top of the box that was presently serving as a table top. "As if the place wasn't sufficient of a mess already, with those daubers dragging their splatters all over the house. I'll sit and visit with you, mistress, in common civility, and then I mun start looking out some likely staff for this place, or the pair of you will starve."

Thomazine wondered if all Scotsmen growled like dogs and were as fierce as mastiffs, because she had little knowledge of any man north of Lancashire. Even her Lancastrian father had lived in Essex for so long that his North Country burr was only distinctive in some words.

Gillespie was looking around the kitchen as if he did not often step inside. "It's a well-appointed house, mistress. The labourers have worked hard. When," he looked, sharply, at Russell, "we can get them. D'ye want to have a look round? Me and your good man have dull matters to discuss."

"That you need not trouble your pretty head with," Russell said, in a very odd, slightly strangled voice. She glared at him and he bit his lip and looked innocently out of the rain-streaked window.

Gillespie nodded. "Aye, mistress, that you'd not want to be troubled with, unless you've a mind to discuss sheep-scab and the application of Stockholm tar. Though if you're inclined to look over the accounts and see what that shameless rogue at Wycombe has been charging for wormy timber, I'll not say you nay."

Thomazine was increasingly aware, as the chill of stone and plaster struck at her tender parts, that under that all-enveloping cloak she was wearing nothing but a shift, and that as soon as she stood up her naked feet were going to become all too apparent. She shot her husband a quick glance and glanced as quickly down at herself, and his eyes widened briefly as he realised exactly what she meant.

"Perhaps you could show me how the work progresses?" Russell said to Gillespie. "I can see you're hot to be investigating those boxes, my tibber. Well, I've done my best, poor instrument that I am —" he handed her the blackened, greasy knife, point first, and Gillespie stiffened, as if he thought no decent woman should be handling such a utilitarian implement.

"Aye," Gillespie said, with a deep growl of disapproval, "And I'd speak to you privately about that, too, Major Russell! Porcelain, mistress, from the Indies—"

"China," he murmured, and she thought his bailiff might explode.

"China, then! Brought in special, at the Lord knows how much expense, with not so much a stick of decent furniture in the house! So you might have dishes the like of the King's, but you've got nothing to sit down to like a civilized man!"

"Are you suggesting that my husband is profligate, sir?" Thomazine said, bridling.

Russell snorted. "My sister must be turning into her grave then."

"Not exactly profligate," Gillespie said grimly, "but Russell! What were you thinking?"

Gillespie and Russell moved out to the bare room off the hall. The office was little more than a cupboard, windowless and airless, and containing only one large, worn and very utilitarian Army pay chest, big enough to sit on. The lock of the thing had defeated the most determined looters of both the King and Parliament's Armies over a course of almost twenty year's campaigning.

There was a great sword-slash across the iron-bound lid, which caught on Russell's breeches as he shifted uncomfortably. It had been put there by Colonel James Wardlaw and his band of bloody brigands when they sacked the baggage-train after the battle of Edgehill and it had made that pay chest one of the most distinctive in the Army.

Gillespie propped his elbows on his knees and gave another disapproving grunt. The question about what Russell had been thinking was not, clearly, a rhetorical one.

"Can we afford it?" Russell said, though he knew what the answer was. He was sitting on it.

"Aye, we can stand it, as ye well know!" Gillespie said irritably. "But Russell! Look at this place — it's half a house in the middle of God-knows-where, can ye no' wait at least 'til the woman's cold in her grave afore ye start thinking of setting up housekeeping and stuffing the house wi' trinkets and gauds for the lassie?"

"You know the answer to that," Russell said mildly, though he considered himself reproved.

"Aye. I do. But does she?"

"Have you ever known me lie?"

Gillespie snorted. "No. I've known ye evade any number of questions, mind. Well, I'll not have ye perjure yourself, Major, so you'll pardon me if I'm as straightforward as you are yourself. She's a young woman and a pretty one — if ye don't mind that I've noticed?" He didn't wait for an answer, which was as well, because Russell wasn't going to give him one. "I'd not have the two of ye marked for a happy match, Russell, so I'll ask again. As a friend. Does she know ye for what you are?"

"She knows what I was."

"Aye, that's the sort of daft answer I thought ye'd give. Russell, I don't know who that lassie is, or where you found her and I'll not ask. She seems like a nice enough maid and I wish ye both happiness. I will ask, though, for they talk of it. How d'ye come by the money?"

"Army pay," Russell said innocently. "I am a senior officer."

"Oh, bollocks are ye! A retired half-pay one, sir, and well I know it — d'ye take me for a fool together! There was no money in this estate when she — when the mistress died here and well ye know that, too. She couldn't keep a servant in the house for more than a week, given that the old besom was living on bread and scrat. Ye know verra well she failed to thrive under your masters in Parliament, Russell, wi' no man to stand her corner under Cromwell. I'd not say you put them up to it, but I know what ye are on your mettle and I don't say ye'd have lifted a finger to help her. This estate was on its knees and suddenly the mistress of it dies and ye turn up from nowhere throwing gold about like there's no tomorrow? Well, truly, what d'ye think they're saying?"

"The wages of sin is death?" Russell suggested and felt, but did not see, the bailiff's exasperated glare. Even from the grave, Fly's malign influence tried to extend over him. She'd been a nasty bitch in life; had taken a shy, sensitive, lonely little boy, after their mother's death and tried to force him into as frigid a pattern-card Puritan as she'd been herself. She'd failed, of course. Their mother had been a good woman, a decent and godly widow, but she had also been a loving one and a joyful one. Her God was a God of warmth and loving and comfort, and her skirts had smelt of sunlight and roses, so far as he could remember. He had been three, four, perhaps, when she had died and he could barely recall how she had looked now, just the kindness of her voice and the soft folds of her scented skirts. After that had been darkness and Fly-Fornication's cruel dominion. He had been shy before, but under her rule he had grown fearful and timid; unloved and not knowing why, and tormented by it. She had held that unloving over his head like a man baiting a dog — promising that if he was a good boy, if he conformed, if he thought and behaved as she said the Bible told him to, she might love him. God might love him.

It had taken him a long time to learn that love was not a thing of conditions and bargaining. By then there was Thomazine and she had been a small, bright baby, and then a bright girl, who did not care that he was scarred and uncertain of temper, but only that he was her own. He'd never thought that brave, sturdy young woman with her steady green-gold eyes might ever see him as more than an object of pity, but she had.

Thomazine's porcelain was beautiful and fragile, and it had been worth every penny of the money he hadn't paid for it, as had been the bolt of gold-green silk, the colour of her eyes, that he'd bought the same day.

Russell had outworn all his usefulness as a fighting soldier at forty, with little influence and a tertian fever that laid him flat two weeks out of every eight, but he could not bear that he might not be useful somewhere still. So he had become one of the King's intelligencers. Most of the work was dull, painstaking, line-by-line accounting, of the sort that only a clerk could appreciate. Requisition lists that did not add up, or added up to more than they should. Deliveries to occasional places where deliveries should not go, or too many names on a muster roll, or the same names in different places. Men who should not have been where they were, or who should not have known each other, mentioned in dispatches.

But then Thomas Killigrew had taken him to one side, one drizzling wet afternoon in Whitehall, to offer his congratulations on Russell's most unexpected betrothal — which, really, ought to have made him alert to having become a person of some note, that the King's spymaster was congratulating him on his upcoming nuptials. Then Killigrew had confided what was in the wind, the threat of the Dutch and the need for English men to spy in that land, and suddenly gathering intelligence was a thing of importance. Russell had lived through one war already and it had nearly killed him; he would not see his bright girl live amid that chaos, not while there was breath left in his body. What you will, Killigrew had said, so long as you are not caught, for if you are taken up you are nothing to do with us. And he had winked, rather horribly, and said — get your girl a trinket or two, eh?

So Russell had, but Killigrew had called him out on the little black cabinet. It was not often that you heard that most urbane of royal courtiers squawk in outrage — apart from anything else, Master Killigrew's own tastes ran more than a little to the expensive and what he spent on his mistresses alone would have kept Four Ashes for a twelvemonth — but he'd looked at the bill of lading from that gilded lacquer box and his hand had been trembling a little. "How much, Russell?"

"It was needful," Russell said coolly, which was true. It had been needful. It had had a beautiful house and trees on the doors, and a man and a woman standing on either side of it, painted in gold with a brush that must have been finer than an eyelash.

"Do not. Ever. Pull a stunt like that again, sir."

And he wouldn't. Probably. For now he was retired. He had handed in his note of resignation as an intelligencer along with his commission. He had done his duty for the last time and had not met a single one amongst the Dutch men and women he had come across in his times in Amsterdam that he should not have been proud to call a friend; no matter what the common gossip was about their vile and bestial habits.

"When ye're done thinking on that lass in her underlinen," Gillespie said with resignation, "I'll tell ye, Russell. It's no easy task, finding labourers for this house. There's some reckon it's haunted and that's a daft thing to think, but if ye're a gullible fool ye'd believe it, and they do. What bothers me is the ones that don't think it's haunted, aye? I caught three lads from Wycombe a week since, bent on mischief. And they weren't the first. They're saying ye murdered her in her bed, for the sake o' the house and the lands, to have her out of your way so ye could come home. Or that ye had me do it for ye."

Thomazine wasn't precisely eavesdropping. She had a little rabbit in her hand, a tiny thing the size of her thumb, made in a shiny, smooth creamy stone. It was sitting on its haunches with its paws tucked underneath it and it was the smallest, most perfect thing she had ever seen. It had been tucked in the corner of that great wooden crate as casually as if it had been forgotten. It had no purpose that she could see, other than to make her smile.

The fragile blue and white dishes were beautiful and frightened her a little, because they were so delicate, like eggshells, and the silk was lovely to touch and perhaps, one day, she would have a gown made up in it, but it was not practical, not a thing for everyday, for a plain countrywoman and a good wife. But that little rabbit — that solid, earthy little rabbit, who grew warm in her hand from the heat of her skin — was a real, living thing. She did not mind that Eadulf Gillespie thought she was a child, or a silly little girl to be sent away while the men talked of business, because this rabbit was a statement of Russell's loving as public as if he had written it up to be pinned on the church door and she wanted to be with him, so that he knew she understood.

Instead, she was standing outside the door whilst Gillespie accused him of murder, which was the stupidest thing she had ever heard. She pushed the door open, with her indignation a great bubble of speechlessness in her throat. The pair of them had sat blinking at her like two owlets in a hollow tree, dazzled by the watery sunlight. The Scotsman had started to gabble something in his uncouth voice and Russell had simply said, very coolly, that he would hear no more of it.

"This is my house," he said. "And I do not mean to be frightened out of it. Take heed."

"Wi' no food and no furniture in it, save yon spindly bawbees? Aye, and I wish ye well of it, Major! Mistress, will ye no' talk some sense into the man — this is no' a safe place for ye, either of ye, 'til the talk dies down." The grim, badger-haired Scot lurched from his perch and grabbed both Thomazine's hands in his, causing her to jump back with a little yelp, because his hands were hard, callused and warm, and that she had not expected. "In all charity, Mistress Russell — I beg of ye, please. Don't stay in this unchancy place."

"Don't be absurd, Master Gillespie!" she cried.

"Well, at least stay under my roof then, if you will stay here. The house is no' so far from here that ye can't keep an eye on the proceedings, and — acht, Major, at least there is a roof on the place, ye can't expect a gently born girl to sleep out on campaign wi' ye!"

"Master Gillespie, I am the daughter of a most well-respected Parliamentarian commander and wife to another!" Thomazine snapped, finally nettled beyond endurance. "I am not made of glass, nor spun sugar. I will not melt for a little hardship. Now have done!"

They agreed in the end on a compromise. They would eat with Gillespie and share his hospitality and he would bring them blankets, in order that they might spend a night in something that resembled comfort.

"And some breakfast," Thomazine said firmly and her husband had given her a wry look.

Gillespie would see to it himself that a message went to their servants, lodging in the inn at Everhall and awaiting word, that all was well.

With that, the bailiff must rest content.

4

Thomazine had thought she would be tired, after the rest of the day riding around her featureless new estate. Up. Down. Up. Down. One rolling chalk hill dotted with dirty sheep looking much the same as another. She had almost fallen asleep in Gillespie's comfortable flint cottage, over a supper of homely mutton stew and bread and cheese, and rosy autumn apples and warmed ale. She'd have slept where she sat, if it hadn't been for sheer wilful pride that she might not go back on her word before a man who thought of her as a silly child.

Now, back at Four Ashes, she was wide awake. She put her cheek against the cool skin of Russell's back and he murmured something that she didn't catch and wriggled himself closer to her. He was a funny, stiff, loving thing, she thought, with an ache of tenderness. And he hadn't done it. He wouldn't have done it, and he couldn't have done it. Just thinking of it made her overtired head ache and her eyes burn behind their gritty closed lids.

No matter how much he had loathed his sister, no matter what injustice she had done him, he would not have killed a defenceless elderly widow in cold blood. Not for money and not for vengeance. It was not how he was made. She would have staked her life on it.

Four Ashes was a cold house, with the coldness of new plaster and raw wood; the coldness of emptiness, she thought, and that not only from the construction work. Thomazine was not much given to fancies, but she thought she could feel this house's resentment in the dark hours when the new timbers settled and groaned, and the wind hissed through the gaps in the west wing. You could imagine that this had never been a happy house, either.

She lay flat again and looked at her darling, asleep with his hair in his eyes. This was his home. He had been a little boy here, had taken his first faltering steps in the hall downstairs. But it was no consolation, none at all. She lay awake, thinking she smelled burning, wondering whether her sister-in-law had been dead before the roof fell in on the west wing, looking for the blackened patches on the bricks and the shadows on the new plaster where the charring might show through.

Was it here she lay? Or here? And did she know, as the flames came for her? Did she cry for help? Or was she already dead — had she fallen, alone in the dark, or died of an apoplexy, or had she been done to death, as they said, and —

She shook herself. She could lie here all night, watching the squares of moonlight creeping slowly across the floor and breeding foolish, fearful fancies, or she could get up and do something useful with herself, like getting the kitchen fire lit, or starting some bread.

She got dressed, quietly, though she left off her stays because the idea of lacing herself twice in the dark was more than she could bear. She pulled on stockings and sensible boots — oh, a most murderous man, her husband, with his insistence on clean stockings and stout footwear.

Out on the lawn, big grey Marlowe had his head down and his solid dappled backside turned into the gusting rain, grazing peaceably with little black Minna sheltered in his lee. Two less concerned beasts she had not seen. So much for ghosts and boggarts.

Marlowe was pleased to see her. She pushed his enquiring muzzle away from her face when his investigations became too pressing. He heaved a great sigh and pretended to be the most desolate horse in the world while she fussed Minna. It was hard to imagine ghosts when you had a good hundredweight of horse trying to push his head under your arm, while another blew hot, grassy horse-breath into your face.

"Behave," she said firmly, "you daft pair."

Her voice sounded like the loudest thing in the world and yet she was barely whispering. All the hairs rippled on the back of her neck and she was being silly, she knew she was being silly, there was nothing here —

Then a light showed suddenly amongst the ruins, bobbing and wavering. Marlowe suddenly sprang away, as stiff-legged as a child's toy, his head up and his ears flickering, and Minna wheeled with him, the two horses in a plunging panic as far as their hobbles would allow them. Thomazine screamed as a black figure reared out of the ashes.

"What the hell are you doing wandering round in the middle of the night, lass?"

"Gillespie!" she snapped, her voice shaky with relief. "I might ask the same of you!"

He put his hand out to the big grey horse and Marlowe snuffed him warily. "Aye, it's me, you witless beast. Be still." He set down his lantern and the blackened apocalypse of timber suddenly took on a strangely homely glow. "Don't you dare, Marlowe. This thing's yet primed. Mistress Russell, I'd have ye step away from the house, if ye please. Come. And you, ye daft nag. 'Tis not safe."

He took the grey's halter and offered his free hand out to Thomazine. "Broken glass in the ashes, mistress. I'd bring your mare away, too. This part of the house is mostly shored up wi' timbers and they warp in the damp. Ye'll have heard it shifting?"

"I am not a baby, Gillespie," she said coldly, ignoring his hand. She was impressed at how calm and unafraid her voice sounded. "There is no need to frighten me with ghost stories."

"Aye? Well, from things that go bump in the night, may the good Lord deliver us indeed, Mistress Russell, for it's like to be the gable end, and it'll go a sight more than bump."

"I don't —" She was about to say she didn't believe a word of it, but even as she spoke there was a faint, hollow groan, long and low and eerie, from the ruins. He stooped and picked up the lantern and tugged the grey horse away. "Mistress —"

She was still standing like a mooncalf when there was a slithering, hissing sound from somewhere in the skies above her and something came whistling past her head. Gillespie hurled himself at her, his shoulder taking her in the breastbone, and the pair of them hit the rubble at the same time as a razor-edged slab of tile hit the ground a yard from them both and burst into lethal shards.

Thomazine turned her bleeding face into the inimical ash and wept tears of shock and pain.

The lantern was shattered, but Gillespie had brought flint and tinder and he sat and patiently re-lit it in the seeping mizzle. He did not say that he had told her so, but simply went and caught up the two frightened horses and soothed them and petted them, and Marlowe buried his face in the Scotsman's coat with a trust that spoke of long intimacy.

"Now then," he said, when she had cleaned herself up. "I've a job to do, mistress. Can ye bide a minute, or d'ye need my undivided attention?"

He grinned at her, his dark face devilish in the lantern-light, and did not wait for an answer. Still holding her gaze, he drew a pistol from his belt, the lantern-light glinting along its barrel, raised it above his head and fired. "Didn't fancy trying to worm it out in the cat's-light."

The echoes of the shot were still ringing when he drew his second pistol and fired that into the heavens.

He moved aside, unexpectedly lithe for all his muscular bulk, as Thomazine fell to her knees, retching up bile. As taken by surprise herself as he was, she huddled on all fours amongst the rubble with her eyes and nose burning and her whole body shaking, drooling bitter spittle. After a long moment he heaved a great sigh and knelt beside her, rubbing her back awkwardly. "Acht, mistress, I've told him ye shouldn't be staying here, but you know how he is, once that man o' yours has an idea in his head there's not much will shift it save a musket-butt between the eyes. Well, maybe now he'll listen. This is no place for a lass."

"Why?" She was sick, but she wasn't stupid. "What is there here that you must prowl the house through the dark hours with a brace of primed pistols? What are you hiding?"

He snorted. "Hiding? I wish. Well. Ye've seen what state the roof's in." He puffed his cheeks out and blew his hair out of his eyes, looking uncomfortable and suddenly considerably younger. "We get a fair few visitors, mistress, with one thing and another and not all of 'em mean well. Hunting for gold that don't exist is a game, aye, I'd not mind that. Stones through the windows and pulling away the timbers that's shoring up the west wing, that's no game. That's wanton damage, mistress, and I'll not have it."

"Why should they do such a thing?"

She did not see Gillespie spit, but she heard it land with a wet splat. "Don't pretend to be dafter than you are, Mistress Russell, it doesn't become ye. You know verra well. And so does he, though he'll carry on pretending he doesn't 'til hell freezes over, wanting to protect ye. I asked him to take you hence and maybe this time ye'll heed me, for sooner or later it'll end in tears, lass. Someone will get hurt. Or worse."

"I will not be driven from —"

"No one's talking of retreat, mistress. For myself, I'm talking of a tactical withdrawal, aye? Withdraw and recover your ground. And if your man queries me, tell him to remember Dunbar." He snorted again. "Though he'll not, given that he was under a dead horse for the better part of the battle and off his head with fever for nigh on a fortnight afterwards. Aye, though enough in his right mind to tell his master he knew me — me, a bloody Covenanter, an enemy soldier, who'd taken up arms against him. Oh, he knew me, all right. I'd hauled him out from under the horse in the first place. I'd not have left a dog to die so. Well, he lied to Cromwell himself, Mistress Russell. He looked him in the eye, all bloody and stinking wi' the dirt of battle as he still was — looked him full in the face and he swore on the Bible I was his own troop lieutenant and had got confused amongst the Scots prisoners in the battle, since I was in no state to speak for myself by then. Your man had me took out of the prisoners, for what I'd done for him, and but for him I'd have perished wi' the rest of my men, in the cathedral at Durham where that black-souled bastard Cromwell put us, the sick and the hurt together, to die like dogs."

Oh, Thankful. "Why are you telling me this?"

"Because he didn't murder anyone, lass. Any man that can save the life of a worthless — worthless by their count, not by mine! — prisoner of war, at the risk of his own neck, is no' a man who goes sneaking about the countryside murdering old ladies in their beds. So. If you care to you can betray both myself and your good man and have me transported and the major hanged. If ye feel ye cannot trust my word as an officer and as a gentlemen." He laughed again, with a weary bitterness. "A Scot can yet be both, despite what Master Cromwell might have ye believe. Both our lives in your hand, mistress, as parole. Have him take ye hence, out of harm's way, and then —" He patted her shoulder again, awkwardly. "In all charity, lass, give him his good name back."

Thomazine was shaking with cold and weariness and sickness, but she sat on the edge of their rough bed of sheepskins and pulled her shoes and stockings off, unhooked her skirt and tugged the laces of her bodice free and left them where they fell, puddled colourless on the bare boards in the first rosy light of dawn. Then she crawled under the blankets and held her husband very tight. *Gillespie does not think him capable of it, either. Go away, Mistress Coventry. Take your vengeful ghost elsewhere.*

Russell turned over in her arms, murmuring sleepily, and buried his face in her hair. "Wassmatter, tibber?"

Her head lay just under his chin, her cheek against the beating hollow in his throat. He was warm and solid and reassuring, and just being held began to still the tremors that ran through her.

"'Bout time we slept in a proper bed again, Zee," he mumbled into her hair. "Still got lodgings in London. If you wish it?"

PART II: SPARK

5

It was a bare sixty miles from White Notley to London. It should have been a couple of days' ride and it had taken them a week. It had also taken almost two months of painstaking correspondence before that, of drafting carefully-worded letters and awaiting replies, of appointments with mantua-makers, shoemakers and tailors before they were anything like ready to travel anywhere. It had driven Thomazine stark mad. By a mutual and unspoken agreement they had returned to her parents and said nothing of that peculiar defamation that had seen them driven from Four Ashes. It would blow over when the next scandal-broth came their way.

Russell had changed, though, since that night. He'd not taken as much care over their marriage as he had with those letters to and from London or with his choosing of the cut and style of her new wardrobe. She carried her tiny rabbit with her in her little hanging pocket, under her skirts against her thigh, though. It was a reminder that her husband was exactly the same man as she had known for twenty years and not quite so fixated on presentation and propriety as he seemed to have lately become.

For Thomazine, London itself was a seeping wet disappointment. It was not full of exotic sights and smells, unless you happened to count the stink of far too many unwashed bodies in too small a space exotic. They put men's heads on spikes and that was just barbaric. Thankful had refused to take her where they said Cromwell's head was exhibited as a warning and a terrible vengeance by the King on his enemies, on a spike above Westminster Hall. He had known Ireton and Cromwell as living men. He did not care to see their decaying skulls impaled for the crows to pick at.

You could buy anything you chose in London. Anything from a ribbon to a life, with dreadful, thin, scrabbling figures scratching in the drowning mud at the side of the river to see what they might scavenge and sell. Thomazine wanted to give them money, she wanted to empty her purse and see them all fed and clothed decently.

"Wouldn't help, tibber," Russell had said, without looking at her, keeping his eyes resolutely fixed on the road in front of them. "Too many."

At least their lodgings were clean and decent, though slightly shabby. The landlady, Mistress Bartholomew, was a timid little mouse who hardly dared look Thomazine in the eye, but scuttled from room to room with her baby clinging to her skirts like a fat white spider.

Russell had come in from another of his interminable affairs of business and laid on the bed without troubling to take his muddy boots off. That was another thing Thomazine did not care for about London. It bred fevers and agues worse than a dog bred fleas. If they had been at home in Essex with fresh air and decent feeding he would not look as if he had aged ten years and lost as many pounds in weight in a little under a week. She passed her hand gently over his forehead and he stirred under her touch, murmuring as if he were grateful for it.

"Are you unwell?" she said, tucking a little of his loose hair out of his eyes and behind his ear.

"Just tired."

"I can ask Mistress Bartholomew to make you up a posset."

"No, tibber, she has enough to tease her without —"

"Without my teasing her further?" Her lips tightened. "I can make it myself, you know. I need not trouble your good lady at all."

"Thomazine, I am fine. I am just tired. Will you not leave me be?"

"Surely," she said crossly, and slid off the bed and stomped to the window, making as much noise as possible with her wooden heels on the bare wooden boards, which was childish but satisfying.

The Bartholomew-baby yelled suddenly downstairs and there was a slam as of a heavy door and then a thumping of footsteps. Few riders came down this far into Aldgate. It was a shabby part of the city, but dignified-shabby, not desperate, not poor. This was where working men and women lived; the silk workers, the seamen, the carpenters.

"Major Russell, sir?" Jane Bartholomew's mousy little voice peeped on the landing. "Major Russell, I have a letter for you, sir. A messenger just brought it. Could you, please?"

Thomazine leaned on the windowsill and said nothing, in a very pointed fashion. But neither did Thankful and so she looked round. He'd turned his head a little on the pillow and one hand — ink-stained, which reassured her somewhat that his business affairs were at least just that — lay limp on his breast, the other trailing on the boards. He looked like a marble effigy of a knight on a church memorial and he was about as likely to wake up as one.

She pulled the door open and glared at the little widow. "My husband is sleeping, madam. He is not to be disturbed."

"I'm glad," their landlady said. A nervous little smile came and went about her lips. "He does work ever so hard. I hope you will take care of him, mistress. I am fond of the major. Could you take the letter, please? It's just that if I keep it

Daniel is likely to gnaw on it." She thrust it into Thomazine's hands — a thin packet, sealed with a blob of expensive blood-red wax and a signet seal. Her mouth twitched again. "He's teething, mistress. I daren't leave him with anything."

Thomazine woke up in bed with the rain pelting on the windows and her husband perched on the end of the bed, humming like an atonal bee, half-dressed with his letter in his hand.

"Good news?" she hazarded sleepily.

He wrinkled his nose. "Not really, my tibber, but better than no news. It seems the Earl of Birstall is willing to condescend to receiving our humble company at an informal little supper this evening."

She stared at him. "Who?"

"Birstall. Not ideal, but better than nothing."

"Thankful —" she was beginning to wonder if she was actually still dreaming, "Thankful, what on earth are you talking about?"

He grinned and tossed her the letter. It still made as little sense to her, but it seemed to be genuine, although it was signed by someone called Fairmantle, not Birstall.

"His name is Charles Fairmantle and he is the Earl of Birstall," Russell explained. "And he is a sort-of neighbour at Four Ashes, though not a man I should care to call an intimate. He is not really a fit person for you to know, Thomazine, but he is a beginning, and hopefully he will act as an introduction to slightly more appropriate society."

"Husband, might I enquire why you think you have the authority to dictate who I may and may not be acquainted with? You brought me here —"

"You wanted to come!"

"*I* wanted to come and live in a garret upstairs from one of your cast-off mistresses and eat stale pies for breakfast?"

"Madam, your temper —"

"You drag me from my family to stay in some mouse-haunted attic in a slum and you accuse *me* of being out of temper —"

"It is a perfectly respectable house, madam!" he snapped back at her. "And you have done nothing but complain since you arrived —"

"Well, you hardly keep your mistresses in comfort, sir, do you? That whore downstairs —"

"Thomazine." He looked as if he might shake her and she sat back hard against the wall, drawing the bolster into her lap for protection. "Is that truly what you think?"

"That Mistress Bartholomew is your light o'love? Well, do you deny it? She seems very fond of you —"

"Your father would be ashamed of you," he said and stood up, smoothing his hair back with both hands to tie it neatly at the nape of his neck.

"For —?"

"Jealousy, madam, unwarranted, unreasoning jealousy — sheer vicious spite! And I should never have suspected you of it! How could you even think it, Thomazine?"

"I hardly know what to think of you, Thankful! I married you thinking you were a retired soldier with no money and all of a sudden it turns out your family owns half of Buckinghamshire! And you might have killed your sister, and your landlady might have whelped your bastard, and on the other hand you might just be as hapless as daddy always called you —"

He stared at her for a second, then he inclined his head with an icy courtesy, snatched his coat up off the floor and stalked past her.

"Then I have no more to say to you, madam. I bid you a good day."

He was walking down the stairs and every line of him said that he wasn't coming back. Thomazine was torn between an urge to launch the chamber pot at the back of his head and a sudden, childish, frightened need not to let him go, because she did not mean those things, any of them, and more than that she did not want to be alone in this place.

"Apple!"

It was her old childhood name for him, from when Hapless had been his old troop nickname and she could not pronounce it. She had not meant it to be a leash, but he whirled on the stairs and came thumping back up two steps at a time. She put her hands to her mouth and looked up at him. She wanted to say that she was sorry, and she wanted to demand an explanation, and she wanted to call him any number of rude names. Instead, she looked up at him and saw that he was furious, indignant and utterly wretched all at once. Her eyes prickled. "Oh, Thankful," she said, her voice wobbling. "I love you."

"Do you?"

She nodded. "That's about the one thing I am sure of."

He heaved a deep sigh. "Tibber, it is about the only thing I am sure of too."

He carefully put his hands on her waist and she equally carefully put her arms around him. "I promise you," he said, "I swear to you, Thomazine, on my hope of heaven, I had nothing to do with my sister's death. And you may trust my word or not trust my word, as you choose."

She moved a step closer, so that her head fitted under his chin and rested her cheek against his beating heart.

"And the widow?" she said.

This time he laughed. "You are persistent, mistress. I am flattered that you think women have been falling at my feet for years, but — no, tibber, it was always you and only ever you. And with that you must rest content. Mistress Bartholomew is the widow of a good man, and a man I knew — moderately well, not an intimate, but he was a decent man. He was a sea-captain and he died when a Dutch man o' war sank his ship a year ago for bearing an English flag in their waters."

"They did — what?" Thomazine said faintly. "Over a flag?"

"Well, the Dutch were supposed to salute it," Russell said. "That was what was agreed in the Treaty of Westminster, when the first war ended. And, ah, well, obviously, they didn't. And Captain Bartholomew took what you might describe as a degree of national pride in his flag. So he decided that if they wouldn't salute his, he wouldn't salute theirs. Matters grew a little heated and the Commonwealth was rendered unseaworthy. Permanently."

"What a remarkably stupid thing to do. I imagine Mistress Bartholomew was somewhat vexed by that, especially when she was put to the trouble of burying him."

"She wasn't, Zee. He was fifteen miles off the coast of West Africa at the time. There wasn't a lot to bring home."

"Are you telling me that we are currently resident in the house of a pirate's widow?"

"No precisely, tibber. Say, rather, a state-licensed privateer."

"And do you often associate with — state-licensed privateers?"

"Matthew Bartholomew was a good Parliament man," Russell said primly, sounding so suddenly and absolutely like

Thomazine's father's zealous young lieutenant that she had to stuff her fist into her mouth not to burst out giggling at the unlikeliness of it. "He was with Cromwell's navy in the first war against the Dutch and —"

That stopped her laughing. "Thankful, you keep saying the *first* war, as if there is more than one?"

"Thomazine," her husband said firmly, "you won't have tried coffee, dearest. Would you care to?"

Fleet Street was a bustling, noisy place, filled with bowing gallants who looked for all the world like an avenue of pigeons, their iridescent breasts pouting as they strutted and cooed at each other. Mr Farr, of the formerly-respectable coffee-house known as the Rainbow, looked up at Russell and Thomazine, as they entered his door. "We don't have women in coffee-shops, sir, it'd make the other customers feel uncomfortable."

"Would it," Russell said dryly. "So far as I can tell the wench in the window is making that gentleman very comfortable indeed. So you are happy to admit the meaner sort of female, but not an intelligent, respectable woman accompanied by her lawful husband?"

"Since you put it like that, sir —"

"Since we are assured of our creation in the image of God," Thomazine said sweetly, "and of an interest in Christ equal unto men, as also of a proportionable share in the freedoms of this commonwealth, we cannot but wonder and grieve that we should appear so despicable in your eyes as to be thought unworthy to —"

"Her father was a Leveller," Russell added by way of explanation, and then, "an Agitant, sir. As I was myself in the late wars. You may be assured, Mr Farr, that the ladies of my wife's household have as an equal interest with the men of this nation as those well-affected women who presented their petition to Parliament, those many years ago."

"A man of principle," Farr said.

Russell smiled grimly. "With a history of taking up arms in defence of those principles. My wife would like to try your coffee, Mr Farr. Make it so."

Farr bowed. "You will, I have no doubt, be as passionate in your enthusiasm for my coffee-house as for your principles, sir? Being, as I perceive, a man of some — influence in the world?"

It might have been the new suit, which had been bloody expensive, despite the plainness of its cut. It might have been that, amongst the brightly-coloured, embroidered, beribboned gallants and the workmanlike tradesmen, Russell looked like a falcon amongst starlings. That, or it might have been the unreadable expression that was so customary on his scarred face, but whatever it was, Farr had him pegged as dangerously unpredictable, clearly.

"Are you trying to bribe my husband, sir?" Thomazine said haughtily.

Farr raised an eyebrow at her, as if she might be a talking dog.

She smiled at him — as balefully, she hoped, as her husband, though she had not the advantage of his marred cheek. "If you are, Mr Farr, I would suggest that admittance alone to your coffee-house may not be adequate. I might even go so far to say that of the females who gain admittance, one or two armed with a mop and bucket might be of greater service. If it eases your conscience I may kilt up my skirts and scrub your floors because your premises stand in need of some attention. Now. Coffee, Mr Farr. And though your floors do not pass muster —"

"His bakery does," Russell said, with a happy sigh. "Coffee, Mr Farr, for two. And a dish of spiced wigs, if you would be so kind. And — we will sit as far from the windows as may be. We are here to observe, not to be observed."

Farr found them the darkest, pokiest, smokiest table, as far from the great bow window that faced onto the street as he could manage and Thomazine was able to sit with her back against the grubby plaster by the chimney breast and observe the fascinating inner workings of a print shop and coffee shop combined.

The first thing she noticed was the smell. Coffee or ink, it managed to be both bitter and oily at once and it caught at the back of her throat and made her gag slightly. And the people and the noise! Such a combination of prentices, gentlemen and tradesmen; all kinds of men together, wigs and polled heads and balding heads and greasy heads all bent together over gossip, news and cups of that bubbling black brew. She could see why such democracy might appeal to an old Leveller like her husband but the roar of ardent conversation combined with the thump of the printing press upstairs and the clatter of the kitchens behind them was fit to give a decent woman the headache of her life.

"You are a hard woman to bargain with, Mistress Russell," her husband said contentedly, through a mouthful of breakfast.

"That is from Mama's side of the family."

Her husband smiled his funny, lopsided smile. "People talk such nonsense in here, maid. If you listen a minute you'll hear all sorts of conjecture. Who's in favour with whom and who's fallen from grace this week. If you listen very hard you'll hear the same names, too." He leaned across the table and snagged a slab of the warm sliced bread from her plate, licking his fingers neatly of crumbs. "Smyrna. De Ruyter."

She shook her head, not understanding.

"Our fleet attacked the Dutch fleet at Smyrna in December," he said, still dabbing intently at her plate. "Admiral De Ruyter's men have taken to returning the favour this last week past." He raised his eyes to her face. "That part is common currency. Everyone knows it."

A slow, shivery feeling spread down her spine, as if cold water was trickling down her shift. "Thankful, when you said the first war, you did actually mean —"

He blinked, just once. "Any time now, my tibber."

"Husband," she said coolly, "if you are hoping to impress me with this — gossip…?"

"Hm? Oh no, love." He leaned across the table and quite absently took the last wedge of her breakfast from under her very nose, buttering it neatly. Looking up from his work, he saw the look on her face, cut the spiced bread in half and set it back on her plate. "I find the fresh air gives me something of an appetite," he said, which was as close as she was likely to get to an apology from that quarter.

"I'm glad," she said and meant it, for he looked — if not joyous then considerably brighter than he had looked last night. "But Thankful, what has a further war with the butterboxes got to do with you?"

"Presently, not a lot." He grinned at her, his lopsided dog-chasing-a-flea grin that showed all his teeth on one side and not on the other. "Not inconceivable that it will become my business, though."

"For why, husband?"

It was not often that her man looked smug. He propped his chin in his hands and his eyes sparkled with mischief. "I'm good at what I do, my tibber."

His looking smug — and remarkably handsome and as bright-eyed as a boy — did not mollify Thomazine. "I see," she said and her lips tightened. "The Navy cannot find itself decent supply officers that it must needs recruit those newly-married ones recently retired from the Army?"

"Ah, now, Thomazine, I've got a new wife to think of and a household —"

"Thankful," she hissed furiously, "if you think getting that bloody ruin of a house fixed up is worth getting your head shot off for I am here to assure you, sir, you are very sadly misguided! We can perfectly well live in Essex — and if you are so desperate to live in a fever-ridden swamp and breed sheep, we can always move to the Dengey peninsula and be done with it! I have a dowry — it is not, I admit, a vast one, but surely to goodness, husband, if we stand in so much want that you must —" She picked up her pewter plate and slammed it back down on the table to relieve her feelings somewhat and heads turned. "There, now see what you have done," she said and her chin wobbled in spite of everything she could do to stop it.

"Oh dear," her husband said. "Oh, tibber, have I —"

"Yes!" Whatever it was, he had done it and she scowled at the crumbs on the table top and would not look at him.

"Would you mind so much?"

"If this is an excuse to have me flatter your vanity, you shameless — you miserable wretch — if you are asking would I mind if you were to go off and be a soldier again, after we have scarcely been married a month — yes, Thankful, yes I would mind, very bloody much I would mind! If you didn't want to be married you should have just said so at the time, and not — not —"

She pushed the table back with a screech of wood and did not care who looked her way. She struggled to her feet — these bloody hampering, trailing fashionable skirts, why could she not just wear the sensible ankle-length homespun of a plain country girl and be done, why must she be draped and festooned and looped like a pagan maypole? — pushed rudely past a gaggle of slack-jawed apprentices and stormed out.

"That maid's breeding, see if she ain't," Farr said sagely and Russell favoured him with what he hoped was a quelling look.

"See why 'ee don't have wenches in the shop, then," someone else added. "Peck o' trouble, they be."

"Disruptive. That's what they are, disruptive. Especially when they're breeding."

"Well, you just going to sit there and let her walk out on yer? Make a fool of you?"

She'd left her furs and her cloak and it was beginning to sleet. Thomazine was hot-tempered, but she wasn't stupid. She'd not go far. Russell got to his feet slowly, aware of every eye in the shop on him. It was an odd feeling, to be stared at for being an irresponsible young reprobate who had broken his girl's heart in the middle of a public meeting-place. He didn't want to go after her, he felt a bloody fool, though he wasn't angry with her, but he could wish she hadn't the sort of fiery temperament that would leave him in the middle of a coffee-shop exposed to every censure while she went flouncing off in a tantrum. And that was nothing to do with a marriage of April and December and everything to do with a marriage of fire and ice. Well, fire could melt ice and ice could temper fire. Fire might, on the other hand, get itself knocked on the head and robbed, if not worse, if ice didn't shape itself and stop sulking.

"No," he said mildly, "I'm going to go after her."

There was a chorus of disapproval from the apprentices, who thought that such a froward wench deserved all she got.

"Married?"

"Month past." He tucked his hair behind his ears and settled his hat firmly on his head.

"Ahhh...."

"Told you."

"Breeding."

"Intending to remain married," he clarified. "If you will excuse me?"

This was not Essex, Thomazine reminded herself. It was a little too late to discover common sense when you were a good quarter-mile away from where you'd started out and pushing your way through crowds that seemed to be thicker by the step, a confused mass of heads and ringlets and hats and feathers.

How dare he. *How dare he.* He behaved like a — a single man with no responsibilities, like the same shatter-brained young officer who had turned up three parts dead on her mother's doorstep on more than one occasion when Thomazine had been growing up, expecting to be pieced back together. Well, he wasn't young anymore and he wasn't an officer, he was a husband with — with —

She stopped in the middle of the pavement, stock-still, and someone thumped into the back of her with a heavy basket of shopping, cursing.

She wasn't — was she? She couldn't be. They had been married not much more than a month. Well, he was as much to blame if she was. How dare he bring her to a public place where she couldn't speak her mind to him and then tell her that he was meaning to go for a fighting officer again, after twenty years and who knows how many narrow escapes, how many scars. How many times could a man put himself in the way of serious hurt and come away with no more than broken bones, or flesh wounds — as if you could call that livid thing on his cheek a "flesh wound", as if it was only his poor cheek that was marred, as if he wasn't shy and stiff and awkward with his disfigurement —

It was someone else's turn. He had earned his peace.

She clenched her fists at her sides and looked up at the sky, digging her nails into her palms because she must look like the worst kind of madwoman, standing bareheaded in the wintry rain with her eyes full of tears and stars.

"How would I live without you, you bloody fool?" she said aloud and a respectable goodwife stiffened as she passed, sidestepping as if profane insanity might be catching.

"Mistress Russell?"

She did not recognise him, though he looked respectable enough. A tall man, though neither so elegant nor so finely put-together as Thankful — tall and running a little to fat, with a very clean, pink face, earnest hazel eyes and possibly the most ludicrous wig she had ever seen: a great confection that tumbled in lustrous curls over his shoulders and rose to two little spiralling peaks at his temples.

"Mistress Russell, my dear, wherever is that neglectful spouse of yours? Surely he has not tired of such a ravishing beauty so soon!"

"Do I know you, sir?" she said. She was almost tall enough to look him in the eye and had she been wearing heeled slippers she would have been. As it was she was stoutly-shod enough to kick him in his silk-clad shins and do some serious damage if he were to endeavour to lay hands on her.

He seemed to be well aware of that fact. His mouth twitched. "No, mistress, although I was on my way to remedy that lack. Charles Birstall — the Earl of Fairmantle — your adoring cavalier, ma'am." And right there, in the middle of the street, with everyone passing by and staring and giggling, he took off his hat and made her the most ludicrously flamboyant bow. "Your next-door neighbour," he said, peeking up from under the tumbling curls with a roguish twinkle in his eye. "And Member of Parliament for Everhall."

"We don't hold much with cavaliers in our house," she said disapprovingly.

He grinned at her and straightened up. "So I understand, madam. I trust I — being smitten by your beauty — may be exempt from the just punishment of other cavaliers? The merest hint of your displeasure renders me prostrate with grief..."

"Sir Charles," she began.

He gave her another cheery wink. "Chas, dear. Honestly. We are neighbours and I hope we will be friends. Calling me Sir Charles makes you sound like my bank manager and he makes me quake. Now. I know where you last had him, because since I received no reply to my little invitation last night I thought I'd pop round in person and see what your plans were for this evening. I am sure you're very much in demand, madam. For the novelty value, dear, I imagine, of thawing Old Crophead's frosty heart. Anyway. I saw that dear little country-mouse you keep as a housekeeper — so novel! — and she said you meant to have coffee — and how fortunate, because here you are, but here he is not. Well, then, young lady, whatever have you done with him?"

It was difficult not to giggle at him, because he was silly like a fond uncle in a sort of harmlessly flirtatious manner and especially with that absurd confection perched on his head. "I left him in the coffee shop," she said with a defiant tilt of her chin.

"Oh dear," Fairmantle said, looking sympathetic. "How very rebellious, dear. Not permanently, one hopes?"

"Um. No."

"It does appear to be — well — raining, rather, madam. Now I appreciate that our gallant puritanical Major probably approves of a little light mortification of the flesh after breakfast, but I am not made of such stern stuff. May I offer you my arm and we shall seek shelter? I fear I am considerably more old-fashioned than your husband, or I should return you to the coffee-house —"

"There is no need," Russell said grimly, from about a yard's distance. "Wife, if you ever pull a trick like that again —" He looked furious. He also looked incredibly relieved. "I thank God that you were mistaken for a fanatic or a hoyden," he went on, completely ignoring Fairmantle, "bare-headed, in the rain, you were distinctive enough that men marked you —"

"And a good morning to you too, Major Russell," Fairmantle said innocently, "I see I find you in good health, sir, and may I offer you my felicitations on —"

"Thomazine, you might have been robbed or worse! You are not in Essex now, mistress, you are in the City of London and these streets swarm with cutpurses and —" Russell's cheek twitched, "I was worried to bloody death, tibber!"

"Dear me, I've not heard anyone called 'tibber' in years," Fairmantle said, rubbing his jaw reminiscently. "My old nurse used to call me that. How sweet."

Russell's eyes flicked over Thomazine's shoulder and she turned round to see what he was looking at. It was a tavern and a rather elegantly dressed, slightly portly gentleman with a face like an amiable pig leaning in the doorway, watching them.

"Master Pepys," he said curtly. "May I be of assistance?"

"On the contrary, Major Russell. I was not aware that you had returned to town." Master Pepys gave Thomazine a polite bow and did not ask, though his eyes were all but popping out of his head with intrigue. "I imagine the Admiralty will be delighted with the information."

"I imagine the Admiralty can wait a day or so, Samuel, before you tell them. My wife. Mistress Thomazine Russell of White Notley, in Essex — Master Samuel Pepys, Clerk to the Board of the Admiralty. Don't you dare, sir."

Pepys' round, cheerful eyes were alight with mischief. "Give you up, Major? Well, if you plan to stand in the middle of Fleet Street making yourself the talk of the City with a pretty girl young enough to be your daughter, I won't hardly need to, will I?"

"Is this turning into a commercial gathering?" Fairmantle said. His gaze rested for a second on Pepys, coolly. "Because I find the smell of ink makes me sick. Smells of the shop, dear."

Pepys' rosy face flushed a darker pink and he turned away, back into the tavern.

"I mean it, Master Pepys," Russell called after him. "If I receive word from the Admiralty on the morrow I am going to come looking for you, sir. And Sir John will have your chambers, because you will not be requiring them further. I am married less than a six-month, sir. Have some kindness."

"I imagine he has some outstanding tailor's bill that you could offer to meet, Major," Fairmantle added cheerfully. "Master Pepys is customarily financially embarrassed, I believe."

Thomazine could tell that Fairmantle did not like Master Pepys and it was also clear that Master Pepys was well aware of that fact and immensely amused by it. She wondered if Russell had noticed Pepys' fascination with the shadowy place where her collar tucked into her bodice, or if he was likely to simply drop him off the bridge into the Thames at a convenient point when no one was looking.

Having escaped the society of both, though, Russell and Thomazine finally compromised on a bakehouse, which was warm and dark, and where she could sit and watch some of the more absurd teetering wigs and pattens that London had to offer go wobbling through the grey sleet past the open windows.

"Perhaps," Thomazine said, "you might like to enlighten me, finally, as to what one retired supply officer has to do with a war with the butterboxes? Dear?"

Her husband laughed his almost-soundless laugh. "Been trying to do that all morning, tibber, but you will keep getting side-tracked. General Monck, is what. My old commander, who is now commander of the Navy —"

"Oh, indeed? And what, pray, are his qualifications as a sailor? And more to the point, what are yours that you should be dragged into this — this — enterprise?"

"Mine? Well, I've been to the Low Countries more than a few times, lass. I flatter myself I am more than conversant with the language. Very glad of it, too, for I imagine that silk gown we had made up will be much admired later."

"You are engaged in trade with the enemy?" she squeaked.

"Me personally? Oh God yes! It's been driving Gillespie stark mad for months. He reckons I've filled the house with gauds and bawbees —" it wasn't a great Scots accent, coming from a man with a faint Buckinghamshire burr to his voice and an even fainter slur to it when he was weary, but it was recognisably Gillespie's dog-bark — "and no' a decent chair to sit on in the place."

"So because General Monck has not the wit to run fast enough when they asked him you must needs pick up his dirty linen?"

"Not quite, my tibber, no. Thomazine, we are at war."

"We weren't first thing this morning," she said tartly.

He sighed. "Indeed. And by now we probably are. According to Master Pepys, who has a nose for such tattle. And no, the Navy does not want for perfectly adequate supply officers of its own, who are doubtless competent in their way. It does, however, want for competent supply officers who can discourse like reasoned human beings in Dutch and who have some reputation for, uh, a want of compromise in their personal dealings. Try how they might, lass, they will be hard put to it to attach any scurrilous gossip to my name, for there is none. I told you I was a dull dog. No, regrettably, I am sufficiently boring in my intimate relations that I have one wife, one household to maintain, moderate personal beliefs, and absolutely no leverage for blackmail."

"Russell, are you telling me that you're an intelligencer?" she said faintly. After only a few months of marriage it was becoming fatally clear to Thomazine that when her man dipped his lashes in that particularly sweet, innocent, doe-eyed manner he was as guilty as sin. "You are, aren't you?"

"Not in so many words. I am not a spy." He cocked his head on one side assessingly. "I am simply a further weapon in the Navy Board's armoury. Well, truly, darling, you've met Master Pepys, you've met Fairmantle, and they're a fair representation of what we have to offer — Samuel negotiates most of his contracts in taverns and puts more of his wages on his back than in his purse and Charles runs with a very dubious set indeed. Though there's no real harm in him, my tibber, I'd not have you think he is a bad man. He's just a vain, silly, empty-headed one. Honestly, Thomazine, can you imagine, were you a respectable, sober gentleman from the Low Countries, expecting to treat with a like Englishman, and Charles Fairmantle turns up in that preposterous wig, reeking of perfume and —" he stopped abruptly, remembering to whom he was talking.

"Girls," she finished for him.

He gave her a reproachful look. "Indeed. Girls. Some of the most notably pious and respectable gentlemen of my acquaintance have been Dutch. They are a good Protestant people. I — well, I hardly dare say, tibber, but — some of the people I know — in an official capacity — some of the Court — dear God, if some of that lot showed up to negotiate, it'd be taken as an affront."

"So —?" He wasn't getting away with changing the subject. Thomazine could see why he might make a good intelligencer, though. He was very good at not answering the questions he didn't want to answer.

"So, I am not likely to be summoned hence to my destruction, Thomazine," he said with resignation. And then when she did not soften, added, "So that — silliness — in the Rainbow was for nothing. Am I attached in a military capacity to the Navy Board? Yes. Hence my acquaintance with Master Pepys. God help me. I have previously had to account for my receipting to Master Pepys in his capacity as clerk to the Board — and having Sam Pepys accuse one of profligacy is, as your esteemed father would say, the kettle calling the pot brunt-arse. My fighting days are done. Other than wrangling with the Navy Board in matters of overdue expense claims."

"Do you promise?"

"Very much so." He raised his eyes to her face and for a minute he was her young rebel angel again, armed with nothing but ideals and a fiery sword. "I love you more than my hope of heaven, but not even for you would I perjure myself. I do not make idle promises, Thomazine. I swear to you, I would swear to you with my hand on a stack of Bibles as high as this house, I am no more than an administrator. I am one of the few people at His Majesty's court with a wholly unblemished name, my tibber, and were I to lose that integrity I should be of no further service to my country."

Gillespie had said almost the same thing to her, that Russell would do the thing that was right, no matter what it cost him, no matter how unpopular or inconvenient, because he could not do else and remain who he was. His uncompromising honesty might set him out of favour in a court that they said favoured strategy and polite pragmatism above all else, but if he said a thing, it could be depended on. Always.

Take away his good name, Gillespie had said, and you stripped him of everything.

6

"You scrub up very nicely, husband," Thomazine said wickedly, as they arrived at the supper arranged in their honour, and slid a surreptitious hand down his back.

That scarred and inscrutable war hero jerked as if he'd been shot as she squeezed his backside in a very familiar fashion and then turned just before the great doors swung slowly open, ducked his head and kissed her with a brief, fierce enthusiasm.

Thomazine — thoroughly kissed — gasped at her first sight of society.

Thankful had warned her, of course. He'd said it was all shadow and glitter, the women with tiny, perfect breasts like pomegranates all but spilling from their stiff bodices, jewelled and scented and ringletted. And the men almost as primped in their extravagant curled wigs and ribbons.

"It is not at all what a gently-reared young lady will be accustomed to," he had said primly and then the unscarred corner of his mouth had turned up in that slow, sweet smile that only she ever saw. "Joyeux would scratch your eyes out, tibber."

The thought of her little sister's envy had seemed unlikely — Joyeux was beautiful and sociable, and she had been the reigning belle of Essex before she married Jack Harrington, and now she was the reigning belle of Hertfordshire. And Thomazine — well, Thomazine was tall, unfashionably slight and unfashionably cinnamon-coloured, and before Thankful she'd never been so much as looked at by a boy.

She had asked Deb to lay out her good yaffingale-green silk gown and her decent shift with the ruffled sleeves and

Thankful had shaken his head. "The bronze," he had said, firmly, and she had been minded to argue for he grew too fond of his own will of late, that one, and the one piece of advice her mother had been firm on was to allow a husband his head in small things, but keep a firm hand on the bridle. Besides, that bronze silk gown was a shocking vanity, almost indecently cut. A pretty enough thing to wear in the privacy of your own rooms, to flirt decently with your husband, but not —

"And the pearls," he had said, and then she had protested because those pearls had been her wedding gift and they were too precious to be worn at any casual supper — "In your hair."

In the end she had acquiesced to his ordering her dress, too stunned to do else. He had directed Deb in a most peremptory fashion and it had taken hours, including the bathing and the curling and the brushing: the sun was set and he had called for candles before they were through, and mousy little Jane Bartholomew had come scampering up and down the stairs with tapers.

The little widow's eyes had almost started from her head by the end and Russell had given her a conspiratorial smile and set his finger to his lips. When Thomazine had turned to the mirror she had not recognised the slender glowing flame reflected there, with her russet hair wound about with a rope of moonlit pearls and curled down her shoulder in a thick ringlet, and a pair of wide-set green-amber eyes looking back at her with far more worldliness than she had ever possessed before.

"That's not me," she said cautiously.

Russell put his hand on her shoulder and squeezed it. "It is, too," he said, meeting her eyes in the mirror. "You see why I should have you wear that dress tonight, my tibber?"

She looked at her white throat, at her shoulders, at her — yes. Well. "For a certain ease in removing it, I imagine," she said shakily, "for if I laugh or sneeze I am almost certain to outrage public decency."

"Not to mention catching your death of cold," he added, smiling at her. "There is a reason for all this vanity, Thomazine. Trust me."

She'd thought it was just his old puritanical streak and she stood on the threshold of that high-ceilinged, glittering room, where the women were plastered and painted as thickly as the walls and she gawked like the veriest country bumpkin. She recognised Charles Fairmantle at least, sitting at his ease at the head of the table in a great carved chair with his wig all askew and his cheerful face glistening with sweat and good feeding.

"Major Russell!" he bawled, "d'ye plan to stand there on the threshold all night, sir, or will you not come in and sit down to supper like a Christian?"

"Only if you'll play Messiah, Chas, and make more loaves, for I swear Sedley's eaten the bloody lot!" another voice yelled from the shifting candlelight.

Fairmantle staggered to his feet. He was not precisely drunk, but it was close. "Now, now, gentlemen. You arrive late, Major Russell. It's unfashionable to be late, d'you hear me?"

"For he who comes on stroke of nine, Must take his chance, and forfeit wine," a sepulchral voice intoned. "Strephon, damn your eyes, can I take you nowhere?"

"Oh indeed — Once to go, and once to apologise!"

"Gentlemen!" Fairmantle roared. "And Wilmot — leash that damnable ape and be seated!"

It *was* an ape. What Thomazine had first thought to be a lap-dog was a monkey and it grinned amiably up at her from where it was presently engaged in picking the sky-blue paint from the wall with fingers that were all too human. A tall, dark-haired young man rose from his seat on the far side of the room and lifted the monkey as if it were a naughty child, talking sternly to it the while. "My apologies, madam," he said gloomily, and she deduced he had been the impromptu poet. "We keep him — a reminder of our own baser natures, my lady. I can only offer my humblest apologies for the beast's animal rudeness. A brute — what can I say, except to beg that he has not caused offence?"

With the creature's head nestled against his throat like some sort of hairy baby, she could only stammer that no, of course not, no offence had been taken.

"For if he had caused you offence, Penthesilea," the young man breathed over her hand, "I should tell his wife of his antics."

By the hilarity that followed she deduced that had been a rather unkind joke and not aimed at the monkey at all. "The Earl of Rochester," Fairmantle said, "who thinks he is a wit and is not. You're not funny, Wilmot, and you're drunk. Sit down, sir. Mistress Russell — Major Russell —" he spread his hands — "you see what I have to put up with? I am surrounded by puppies at play —"

"Woof," someone else said, very quietly, and she giggled.

They were late. The company had been at the theatre — "Hence," Wilmot said, "our pitiable state, for news is new come of a second war against the Dutch and we must drown our cares ere the Dutch Navy drown us."

"Def'ntely drunk," the cheerful, slightly balding cherub Fairmantle had called Sedley said firmly. "Being silly now, Wilmot. Don' say that to the lady. Frightening the women. Bad form. You going to hold her hand, Crophead?"

"They are always like this," Russell said grimly, carefully picking his way around the monkey's discarded fruit. "I imagine he dismisses his household staff —" looking up at the stony-faced manservant who held chairs out for them — "should they betray any expression."

"He's not a Crophead any more, Sid," one of the ladies said firmly and Thomazine stared at her in amazement, for she was dressed in silk and jewels and yet she spoke like a good plain countrywoman. "Let it grow a bit, haven't you, lovey? Since you were last here?"

Sedley put his arm round the woman's shoulders and squeezed her familiarly, and Thomazine was unsure whether to laugh or to cry, for these women were whores: gaudy, cheap, noisy whores. Her first supper in London was in the company of blowsy tarts and drunken fat cherubs. She had dressed in her fine array for *this*.

Under the table something touched her hand and she pulled her fingers away, fully expecting it to be the monkey — or worse. It touched her again and this time she looked down and realised that it was her husband's hand. He squeezed her fingers, gently.

"I am holding her hand, Sir Charles," he said, eyeing Sedley balefully. "So the whole poxed crew of you may stop behaving like Wilmot's ape in an attempt to impress my wife. We now comprehend fully that you are carefree gentlemen who know no limitations. Assume that my wife and I are appropriately impressed. May we now proceed to behaving like men of reason?"

It seemed that the doleful young man, John Wilmot, Earl of Rochester was in disgrace with His Majesty for some stupid prank that had earned the King's disfavour and that this riotous affair had begun in sobriety and decency, as a modest supper for friends.

Thomazine looked at the candlelight glittering on plate and crystal, at the great engraved silver bowl half-filled with fruit that the ape was presently selecting the choicest titbits from. Very modest. She was suddenly glad that Russell had insisted on the bronze gown, for in her yaffingale-green she would have felt dowdy and out of place.

"May I help you to some chicken, madam?" Wilmot said gravely.

Thomazine glanced under her lashes at her husband, who was presently engaged in some intense and earnest discourse with Master Sedley.

"I am very sure she did not," she heard him say.

Sedley cackled. "I am very sure she did, too, Major. In the silver-cupboard. With the head footman. Now that, sir, is what you might call a rattling."

The which Thomazine thought might be a dirty joke and she was not sure if she ought to have heard it, so she applied herself to her plate with downcast eyes and tried not to giggle.

"Shocked, my lady Penthesilea?" Wilmot's dry voice was at her elbow.

"Amused, rather," she said truthfully. "Though I suspect I ought not to know what it means."

"Ah. The Puritan does not rattle his lady?"

That stung and she raised her eyes and looked at him — at the solemn-faced boy who was younger than she was, who was stroking his monkey as if he hoped the sight of it might offend her, who had a mocking smile on his lovely mouth that had no humour in it at all. She wondered why a young man who was handsome and witty and learned ought to be so downright mean-spirited, and then decided it was none of her business.

"The Puritan, sir, rattles like a hired carriage," she said sweetly and had the pleasure of watching his eyes widen slightly in shock. *So you see, Master Wilmot, two of us can play at childish games.*

"Good God, Strephon," he said faintly to the monkey. "The age of miracles is not yet past. A wench of wit. Well, Penthesilea, are you determined to set the town about its ears with so devastating a combination of beauty and daring?" He rubbed the monkey's head again and she thought he might be smiling, though his eyes were as modestly downcast as hers. "Or are you so innocent that you still see the world as a place of high romance? *Amor vincit omnia*," he said wryly, "God help you."

"I may be," she said and squeezed her husband's hand where it was comfortably, wickedly settled on her knee under the table. "It may be."

"Good God, my Amazon, next you will be telling me that our gallant Crophead pursues a second career as a highwayman, or some such lawlessness!"

He laughed. Thankful turned round and did not. "My lord, if it amuses you to fill my wife's head with foolishness, I may assure you, sir, I am not amused." He bit into a strawberry and placed the uneaten half back on his plate with malevolent precision. "I will not have her made game of, sir."

"Jealous?" Wilmot said and his lips twitched.

"Very," Russell said levelly. "And violent-tempered to boot. You may do well to remember that."

"You would have done better not to lay — temptation — in my way, then, Major. To bring such a pearl beyond price within my lewd compass —" he said it in such a perfect imitation of Thankful's chilly society tones that Thomazine was hard put to it not to laugh, because could the dear man not see that he was being deliberately baited?

"The pearl has a fairly sturdy oyster," she said firmly and looked over her shoulder at him in case he hadn't quite got it.

"I trust he pays sufficient attentions to the pearl," Wilmot said, and the lady at his side snorted with unladylike giggles.

She'd said something she ought not to have, then.

"If you did not choose to have her admired, sir, you should not have brought her."

"Should she not have the liberty to see some society unmolested?"

"She has a tongue in her head," Thomazine said mildly, and Russell forgot himself and smiled at her, not his careful company-smile but the real one, the slightly lopsided one.

He pushed his plate to her and she picked up his half-eaten strawberry and, very deliberately, set her teeth in the exact same place where his had been. "On the contrary, my lord," she said demurely. "I am entitled to enjoy my husband's company, and he mine. We neither of us can be responsible for your temptation, sir."

Russell looked quickly away, with what might have been a giggle of his own.

Thomazine grew confident after that. She understood little of what Wilmot and Sedley said, it being mostly in Latin, or in tortuous Classical analogy, but she did understand that they thought she was amusing and pretty. She even fed the little monkey on grapes from her plate and it grew sufficiently accustomed to her to allow her to stroke its head. But mostly she watched her husband, which was a thing she liked to do, and sipped wine from the delicate glass that Master Wilmot kept refilling for her, and said nothing. She wasn't sure if she liked the wine or not, but everyone else seemed to be swilling the stuff like ale and even her darling Apple grew a little flushed, which made her prop her chin in her hands and watch him, more animated than was customary, bright-eyed and almost lovely from this side.

Wisps of hair had worked loose to frame his face and she forgot for a moment that they were in civilised company and reached up to tuck it behind his ear, and he glanced at her sideways under his lashes. When he was amongst decent people — when he was at her parents' table — he was different. Here, he was disapproving and cool, but he was not out of place. His wit was less rapier-thrust than plain cavalry backsword, but it was every bit as sharp and true. She left her hand on his shoulder, daringly, because this was not a thing that a gently-born young woman should do in company at supper, even at a table full of whores and ruffians.

Thankful put his hand over hers — his warm, competent, slightly rough hand, that was so out of keeping with his elegant dark grey silk waistcoat and the embroidered ribbon that caught his hair into a tail —

"Oh, Apple," she breathed, and the corner of his mouth lifted very faintly. "Oh, you dear, sentimental — silly!"

For the ribbon in his hair was one of her bridal favours, a length of golden-green silk that she had embroidered herself with a trailing sprig of rosemary. She stroked it with a fingertip and smiled up at him.

Without missing a word of his conversation with Sedley he rubbed his jaw against the inside of her wrist and carried on talking — of taxes, she thought, or the price of barrels of salt fish.

"I see," Wilmot said at her other side and there was that in his voice that was not mocking anymore. "I see."

She thought he probably did not but she had shocked him and that was funny, because around this table these men did nothing but try and shock each other with their casual talk of women and debauchery and Thomazine Russell had shocked him by loving her husband. It was funny and it was sad all at once. "I hope you do," she said, and meant it. "One day."

"Is that an offer, Penthesilea?"

She shook her head, smiling, and Russell turned his head and looked at her questioningly.

"No, Master Wilmot," she said. "I am well content."

7

Russell had thought, the next morning, that his headache was the result of an unaccustomed lack of sleep, but now he was sure it was not. He blinked hard and discreetly rubbed his eyes, but the elegant back-slanting scrawl remained as wavering.

The room he was in was too warm and it smelt of exotic spice. He rather suspected that everything about Clarence di Cavalese was expensive and subtly fragranced with the breath of the Indies. The only sign of his country of birth was a very small, dark portrait of a young woman wearing little but an unfastened fur-lined jacket, putting on her stockings on the edge of an unmade bed.

Russell had very recently left a young woman with very similar breasts, sitting on the edge of their own unmade bed. Dear God, but he found that painting erotic, even when he felt like death. He wondered if Cavalese would consider parting with it, but then he felt guilty for even wondering such a thing for it was not inconceivable that in Amsterdam that pretty girl was sitting on the edge of her bed alone and waiting for her man to come home from his trading in a hostile foreign land.

Across the well-polished inlaid table, Mijnheer di Cavalese's profile remained as impassive as ever, as white and unreadable as a Roman emperor on an old coin. Russell wondered if Cavalese ever got sick, although looking at that impeccable figure in its dark wool suit, he doubted it. He couldn't imagine Cavalese with a hair out of place.

"Major Russell, sir, I await your answer?" Cavalese said crisply.

Russell couldn't do it. His head was stuffed with wool, fit only for spinning fancies around this man's inscrutable domestic arrangements. He simply could not gather his thoughts together sufficient, not only to work through that bloody stupid code of spice and silk and monopoly and export, but that impenetrable code of circuitous courtesies, of what might offend the Dutch, or might not, and what formalities must be observed in one's personal dealings.

"I cannot," he said simply.

Cavalese blinked at him. "Cannot? But sir, we expect to reach some kind of settlement this morning?"

Russell wondered how many other men there were across London this morning engaged in this polite fiction of trade, like spiders, all spinning their own little webs, with the great fat white spider of that erstwhile regicide George Downing in the middle of it, manipulating all those sticky little strings.

Downing had known Russell in Scotland ten years ago: had trusted him with autonomy in this tiny matter of negotiating some trade leeway with the Dutch merchants. George Downing would sell the souls of his unborn children for profit, so long as he retained his mercantile links with the Low Countries and the gold continued to flow unchecked into his pockets, which was possibly what His Majesty wanted in an ambassador, a man whose nose for self-interested profit was legendary. That matter of a day, two days' delay in cementing those tiny fragile links of commerce — it was of no great significance. A few guineas lost, to men on both sides of the North Sea. No more.

"I cannot," Russell said again, more firmly.

"Perhaps you should spend a little less time in debauchery, sir, and a little more time at your work?" Cavalese snapped, and that was so unlikely as to make Russell laugh out loud.

101

"Possibly, mijnheer." And then, because all the bones in his head were hurting and his skin ached, he said with more asperity than was professionally discreet, "And perhaps you should spend a little less time listening to slanderous rumour and a little more time in gathering intelligence, or you would know that I have suffered from a recurrent fever for the better part of ten years."

"A most convenient fever," Cavalese said. "Will you to business, or no?"

Russell owed it to his country — he owed it to his wife's safety, and his family's. He had a duty.

"My apologies, Mijnheer di Cavalese," he said with as much dignity as he could muster. "I will attend you tomorrow. By your leave, sir?"

Outside, the fresh air made him feel a little better. He closed his eyes and put his hand on the nearest wall, grateful for the warm, rough feel of the plaster under his fingers. It was solid and real. It made him feel less as if he might fall on his face. He could smell the river, the salt mud and the tide and the debris that washed up there with every turn of the moon and the damp wood and water of the big ships moored up.

The gulls were laughing, high up over his head in a rain-washed sky and he could hear the slow, faint slap of the water against the hulls of the moored ships. It was chill, but the cold salt felt good against his sweaty skin.

He thought he might have slept for a while, sitting on a coil of rotting rope with his back up against the harbourmaster's wall. The sun had moved between the ragged clouds and the water shimmered, although he thought that was perhaps just in his head. He felt steadier. Hungry — well, perhaps that was what ailed him, a lack of food and no more. They were still unloading the big ship, now down to the last bales, bringing them up out of the darkness in their oiled silk wrappers.

He stood up, swaying a little.

"Y'all right, Major?"

They knew him here. He was here often enough that he went unmolested, though he rather suspected they spun yarns about how he had come by his scarred face that were considerably less romantic than the reality. "Persephone due in by the end o' the week, I reckon. Provided the bloody butterboxes didn't put a hole in her."

Russell had something of a soft spot for the Perse. He would not have chosen her for his enterprises else, she being a good forty years old and as comfortably unfashionable and wide in the beam as a little country goodwife. He'd been fond of the Perse since the first time he'd set foot on her rackety splintered deck. The first time he'd gone to the Low Countries it had been in her comfortable, wallowing embrace, and he had come home safe. "I trust so," he said, turning his face up to the sun. "Though on the wings of the storm, I fear."

Thomazine had just drawn a horse on the hearthstone for the amusement of the Bartholomew-baby. The child's mother had not been as impressed and had huffed at Thomazine's dirtying her clean hearth with such daubery, but the baby was delighted.

"Man shall not live by bread alone," Thomazine said tartly, "but some roses, also."

"You are clever," the widow said grudgingly. "With your hands. It is a good drawing."

"Well, it doesn't look like a dog, at least." Thomazine looked out of the window, out into a street that was touched by sun for the first time since she had been in London and it lifted her heart. "May I do any errands for you, mistress?"

"I have no errands for you to run. And even if I had, Mistress Russell, I am quite sure the major would not think it fitting for his wife to be running his errands like a maid."

"But —" Thomazine was bored, she came from a house where there was always work to be done, where the labourer was worthy of his hire and a man was not judged on what work he did but the quality of it. They had not been in London long enough for any of his linen to require her attention and his stockings were all but intact. He had been mending his own for so long that they were as lumpy as walnuts.

"Major Russell has his position to think of, madam," the widow said.

The street door opened on a gust of lovely cool fresh air and Major Russell's considered position was immediately declared to be hard by the fire.

It was not so cool that he ought to be shivering and Thomazine looked up at him sharply.

"I'm all. Right, tibber," he said, but there was that little break in his speech that she only ever heard when his ruined cheek had locked stiff on him. He did not like her to speak of it — to be pitied — and so she did not, but she put her hand on his scars in passing, because sometimes warmth would ease the stiffness and the widow would think it no more than a foolish display of affection.

His skin was hot, though, and slightly damp to the touch.

The Bartholomew-baby made a happy noise and shuffled on his bottom to snuggle into Thomazine's skirts whilst his mother busied herself warming ale and fetching food that Russell did not want.

"Mistress, my husband wishes to be left in peace," she said. "He needs his bed. Can you not see as much?"

"Sound like your mother," he murmured, and that made her laugh, even though she was worried about him.

He was sufficiently biddable as to frighten her. He lay down — he did not try and incite her to lie down with him — and she pulled the blankets over his shoulders. He tried to smile at her though his teeth were chattering. "Be all right, Zee," he said. "Been so before. Come about."

She sat on the boards at the side of the bed, loosed the tie from his hair and then, for the sake of comfort, kissed his poor forehead. "Poor Apple," she said, and she meant it, for he looked weary and cold. "Let me —"

"Don't." He gave a shiver and twisted to bury his face in her shoulder, "Don't let me go, tibber. Don't ever let me go."

She ran her hand up and down the back of his neck, under his hair where it was already hot and wet with sweat. "Long enough to bring you something hot, perhaps? For you must be hungry, after so long at your work. And you need to eat something, husband."

She thought he meant to shake his head but then he sighed and rubbed his face against her arm, and she could feel him shivering. "I love you," he said, and he sounded desperate about it. "Thomazine, I love you. Always."

The widow looked up from her never-ending mending, as Thomazine pushed open the kitchen door. "My husband is sick," she said.

The older woman nodded. "I thought he might be so. It recurs."

"He has often been so?"

"And did not tell you?" The woman laughed, without much humour. "Why should he? He is a man like any other —" She folded her sewing and stood up. "He is not wholly your fool,

Mistress Thomazine, for all you might think he is at the crook of your little finger. He has his pride. Sometimes it is all he has. Well, then. I have sat up a-nights for the Major before and I see I must again. Will you see to the child?"

"I — no. Will you tell me what to do, madam?"

The widow looked at her thoughtfully and nodded. "Jane. My name is Jane. God grant him a quick return to health, this time, for the Lord knows he is much needed."

"Upright wi' breeches on," Thomazine quoted one of her father's precepts.

Jane Bartholomew's lips quivered. "I have never seen him else, mistress. On my honour, I have not."

"Frumenty," Thomazine said firmly. "And I will see to it my own self. For of all things he likes frumenty the way I do it."

"Eggs," Jane Bartholomew said, equally firmly. "Buttered, mistress. He needs rest and care and nourishing."

"I am more than capable of caring for my own husband, madam!"

To which the widow said nothing, but her eyebrows moved in a manner that was both sceptical and unflattering. "Indeed," she said.

"Now either you or I must go to market and get the makings of frumenty — for tomorrow — and today it seems that the major must make do with his buttered eggs, and be, ah." It was a clumsy joke, but Thomazine had heard him make it often enough. "He must be, um, thankful."

It was not a truce precisely, but more in the way of an armed neutrality and the widow lent Thomazine an apron and between the two of them they managed as pretty a dish of buttered eggs as Robert May and his accomplished cookery could have done.

106

The three of them sat to table, there in the kitchen, Thomazine and the widow and the Bartholomew-baby, and they ate a good half of that pretty dish between them, taking it in turns to spoon the creamy eggs into the child's peeping mouth.

They talked of medicines and of the nature of Russell's illness and how he might best be mended — of what good nourishing things they might give him to eat until he was well and where Thomazine might find some good plain whole-cloth stockings at a sensible price. It was simple housewifely conversation and she had missed it, for much though Thomazine enjoyed listening to the high-flown poetry and politics around Charles Fairmantle's supper table, she had not known how much she missed real talk, of things that mattered.

This was the world she knew: feeding buttered eggs into a little boy's mouth and talking of whether sage oil was a better plaster for a man with phlegm in his lungs than mustard. Of being competent and a woman in your own right, a person of significance and not merely of value for a daring turn of wit or beauty.

"You are smiling, madam?" Jane Bartholomew said, leaning forward to turn the bread on the fork where it toasted fragrantly.

"I was thinking on the nature of power," Thomazine said mildly and dropped her eyes, because she did not think the widow would approve of what she was truly thinking. But it crossed Thomazine's mind that the diplomacy with which she and the widow Bartholomew were setting out their rules of engagement and beginning their peace negotiations was every bit as sensitive and fraught as those her husband was engaged in.

A little commonwealth, indeed.

Russell had not played the obedient husband and he was not in bed. Through the attic window the sun had moved almost all the way round the street and the room was lit with a soft amber light. Thomazine's husband was still half-dressed, shaking hard enough to rattle plaster-dust from the walls and determined that he must go out and finish his business.

"Apple, you're ill, and you should be abed," she said, giving him a stern look.

"I know! You come bearing medicine —"

"I come bearing buttered eggs, sweeting." He was neither that daft nor that feverish and he grinned at her, and she acknowledged defeat. "Well. A little medicine, then. Jane tells me you take these fits, when you are —" *Strained. Worried. Tired.*

"Did she tell you it was a tertian ague? Had it since Scotland. Three days out of commission and I haven't got three days. I —"

"Am going to finish undressing, put on the flannel nightshirt that your loving but impatient wife has so conscientiously put against the chimney breast to warm, take my medicine, and sleep."

"You don't understand," he said, sounding so marvellously like an outraged small boy that had she not been afraid of what Jane had told her the next three days would bring, she might have laughed.

"Dear, nothing is more important than you getting well."

"I —"

"Am sick, and weary, and in need of rest and good feeding. Now hush."

He sat down limply on the bed and let her help him out of the rest of his clothes. He said he was cold and she wrapped the blankets tight about him and got her cloak and her furs from the press and piled them over him, agreeing that it was cold and insisting that he finish his tea.

She slid under the blankets and put her arms about him, and he put his head on her breast with a little sigh of relief.

"I am here," she said, and he felt for her hand under the covers and held it hard enough to hurt.

"I know," he said. His teeth chattered together just once before he set his jaw. "But tibber — may God have mercy on me, lass, I am afraid."

"No need," she said, kissing the top of his head, her eyes squeezed shut. "No need at all, my darling. Rest. I will see to all in the morning."

"You promise?"

"As God is my witness, Apple. Sleep now."

She felt all the tension leave him on one long shaky sigh.

The next day Russell was fractious, restless, ungrateful — distressed and irritable by turns, and Thomazine could not comfort him, which annoyed the hell out of her. She knew of course that it shouldn't and that if she were at home in Essex her mother would have made him comfortable in no time at all. Even the widow Bartholomew would have eased him better than Thomazine, for the unhappy bottom line of it was that Russell was not a particularly placid invalid and she not a particularly competent nurse. When he was lucid enough to know that he was ill he hated it and when he wasn't he scared her witless, although Jane Bartholomew assured her that this bout of his illness was not a particularly severe one. About the only consolation was that he was not contagious.

It was the uselessness that riled Thomazine the most: and that wasn't fair, because it wasn't his fault that nothing she did could make him comfortable. So when he asked for her help she was glad to be of service.

"I am tired, but — mending," Russell told her, though he did not look well. His hair was plastered dark with sweat across his forehead, clinging in limp rags to his back, and his nightshirt was soaked right through. "A night's sleep should do it. But — tibber — could you do a thing for me? I should have been at the table with Mijnheer di Cavalese today already and God knows my credit is uncertain enough as it is with him at present. I would not ask, Zee, but I must get a message to him before the end of the day."

"In a professional capacity?" she said dryly.

He smiled. "In a professional capacity. Indeed."

"And to Mine — who?"

"Cavalese. He is, believe it or not, a Dutchman. He is a merchant — oh, lass, may I trouble you with the details another time, for my head is ringing like a blacksmith's anvil." He sat up stiffly, reaching for pen and paper. It was not like his usual sure, spare script. His hands shook and she had to dip the pen in the ink for him, for he could not keep it still enough to find the ink-bottle. But in the end it was done, a matter of a few apologetic lines that he had not transacted business with Master di Cavalese that day due to the recurrence of a tertian ague and might he be excused without causing offence.

"Can you take it to Master Pepys? You mind his direction — we were there, was it only last week?" He was beginning to shiver again, but she suspected it was the healthy shivering of a man in a wet shirt sitting in a draught and she tucked her tippet about his shoulders feeling, for the first time, competent.

"I should rather stay with you," she said honestly, kissing his forehead.

"I should rather you did, too, tibber. But take your maid and go. Please."

Her maid Debby thought she was mad and the widow thought she had some kind of furtive illicit liaison arranged, and the more they thought she was up to no good the more she was determined to carry out this daring plan and prove the lot of them wrong. Jane wanted to send a boy with the note and that seemed sensible, save that the widow did not personally know a sensible, reliable boy to send for and Thomazine was hanged if she was going to trust a letter that her darling had risen from his sickbed to write into the hands of some dirty little urchin they didn't know from Adam, who might throw it in the river and run to the nearest pothouse on the proceeds.

After she had wrapped herself in her own plain, sensible cloak and slipped on her stout pattens and her thick woollen hood, and when there was little more than the gleam of her eyes visible between the layers of plain dark wool then Thomazine was ready to brave the darkness. She took one of Russell's pistols from the clothes press, primed it and slipped it into her muff. Money she would not take, for what she did not have could not be stolen, but she slipped that letter on which all his hopes rested in with the pistol and crept downstairs.

London after dark was a different, frightening place. This was the respectable end of the poor quarter and all the swathed and muffled bodies that jostled her were no more than workmen and plain women returning home from a day's labour, or from marketing for the last of the day's bargains, or from prayers at St Gabriel's. Tired, hungry, aching people, longing for their beds and their boards — not menacing predators, no matter how much they pushed.

And then she and Debby were out of Aldgate and all changed again, for she barely recognised the bustling streets she saw by daylight in these shifting torchlit shadows. Doors were swinging open on noise and blasts of heat and there was the stench of too many bodies in too small a space. Beggars lay in alleyways and a brawl almost spilled over her feet. She could smell the river, that rich tidal silt of salt mud and decay.

"Mistress," Debby said close to her ear, "Mistress Zee, are we anywhere close to yet?"

That poor lady was near to weeping with fear and yet they were barely a mile from home and not even across the bridge yet.

Thomazine's feet were numb and cold, her hands ached, her nose was running and she was entirely lost. Well, not lost. But she did not know where Master Pepys' office was, for she had only seen him at the Fighting Cocks tavern at Leadenhall, which was no use at all to a woman and a maid, and so all this subterfuge had come to naught, and she could have sat down and wept in the street for the waste of it.

"Mistress?" Debby said woefully.

Thomazine straightened her back. "A little further, Debs. We are to go to Birstall House in Kensington. Sir Charles will see our note of hand delivered."

It was — what? Four miles? It was the longest journey of nightmare she had ever known, dappled with creatures of darkness who loomed in her path and the smell of burning and disease everywhere about her.

She was not sure what was worse: the stinking, bustling streets of the City, or the shadowy, deceptive marble of Kensington, elegantly silent and menacing, where every dark house was haunted. A cat who darted across her path might be the Witch of Endor and reduced Deb to frightened tears.

It came on for midnight, she was sure of it. She could not even hear the chimes of a church to tell her so, or the cry of a watchman, but she knew it, and he would be missing her soon, would be worried, would send someone to look for her —

So, better make haste, then, madam.

She pulled her quivering maidservant up the great moonlight-pale marble steps of Birstall House, with Deb protesting every step of the way — their hair, their shoes, the state of their skirts —

"My lord Fairmantle, if you please," Thomazine said sweetly and then out of the side of her mouth, "It's all right, Deb, they always look like that. They are hired for a certain rigidity of expression. Heaven only knows what goes on in this house."

Deb gave a horrified whoop and the butler gave her a stern look. "The Earl of Birstall is not at home, madam."

"Indeed," Thomazine said. She was of an unwomanly height and she had a prominent nose. That was from her father's side of the family. He'd made a career of using both to intimidate and she'd learned at his knee. She straightened her back and looked down at the butler. "Indeed, sir. Then perhaps you would be good enough to interrupt the Earl whilst he is not at home in the drawing-room and tell him that Mistress Russell would beg a few moments of his time on a matter of some delicacy."

"The Earl is not at home," he repeated.

"Surely. I can hear him not being at home with, I believe, Sir Charles Sedley, amongst others. I count the Earl as a personal friend. I have dined in this house with my husband."

"I am aware of that, madam. I mind the occasion well. The Earl is still not at home to callers."

"Then I imagine I must leave him a note, must I not?"

"He will not be at home for some time, madam, and I —"

"Martin, the hell's going on out there? Send the bitch away!"

Thomazine bridled at the coarse voice from behind the drawing-room door — not Sir Charles, not her friend, surely? — and said, very loudly, "I beg your pardon, sir!"

"It's not mine, you slut, I won't own it, and I won't pay for it — Oh! Mistress Russell!"

Thomazine very slowly withdrew her muff from under the enveloping layers of wool. "If this is what you are referring to, I assure you it is already accounted for, Sir Charles," she said stiffly. "I fear you may be under some illusion, sir. I am not here to importune."

"Dear God, woman, I thought you had — what on earth were you thinking, madam? Have your wits gone wandering altogether? I thought you were a — what d'you mean by it, eh? Wandering about in the dark, like a — has he not got any sense at all, that addle-pated chap of yours? Gad, I should shake the sense into you! If you were my daughter, madam, I can assure you I'd not — well? What d'ye say, then?"

"What I say, sir, is that if you are so discourteous to all your callers as you are to me, I see we have nothing further to say to each other!" She tossed her head and she would have gone — aye, and she would have wept, too, for he was her last hope and she was disappointed in him — had he not put his hand on her arm.

"Oh, don't be so missish, Mistress Russell! I apologise, madam, but —!"

"Whosit, Chas? She going t'come in and entertain us?" Sedley drawled from the dimly-lit darkness.

"You see why I am not at home to lady callers, dear? Now. What errand brings you out on such urgency — and in God's name, be brief!"

She handed him the letter. He expressed blurred sympathy for Russell's indisposition, but no more than that: no surprise. He squinted at the inscription. "Handwriting's terrible, dear. Bad again this time, is he?"

"He will recover. With care."

"Well, he normally manages to come about, so — yes, I'm sure he'll mend nicely. Very wifely, dear."

She took a deep breath. "Will you deliver it for me? To Master Pepys's office?"

"I?" He looked briefly appalled. "Well, but — but madam, you heard — and I wish you had not — I have no wish to taint myself with the shop, no offence to Master Pepys you understand, but — I mean —"

"They will call you names if you are seen to be involved with decent working men such as Master Pepys?" she said with gentle malice.

He raised his eyebrows at her and scratched under his wig. "Madam, if you consider that smellsmock to be a decent anything you have yet to have any acquaintance with his wife. She has a number of stories to tell and none of them reflect very well on her husband."

"But you'll do it?"

"The very first thing tomorrow morning, Mistress Russell, I shall send a discreet footman to slip a note under Master Pepys' office door. Now in God's name, dear, begone, before Little Sid comes staggering out thinking I'm sampling your wares! Let me call my carriage."

"I thought we had agreed on discretion, sir?"

"We had. Only you and I will know that I am soiling my hands with trade, dear. Will I allow you to walk home through the streets at the peril of your life? — I will not. If any harm befalls you, well, I rather fear the major would make my life nasty, brutish and short, as that clever Master Hobbes would put it."

"Why —"

"Don't be ridiculous, dear. Just humour me. There have been a sufficiency of rather grisly murders of late —"

"Oh, will you stop trying to frighten me, sir, I am not a child!"

"No, well, and were you aware of the poor woman who was strangled, Mistress Russell not a mile from here? A most respectable lady coming late from church less than a month ago — no doubt she wasn't a child either, but she was still throttled — aye, and a thing done to her that you and I will not speak of, you being a lady — if you take my meaning, madam. If you were a little more in the world you would know all about that for 'tis the talk of the town this many a day: there is a fiend abroad. So yes, you will take my carriage home and you may instruct the driver to deliver you to so far as you please and walk the rest of the way, if you still have a mind to deceive your husband —"

"Whassmatter, Chas, paying in kind?" Sedley yelled. "She paying you, or are you paying her? Hey?"

Fairmantle's lips tightened and he looked angry for the first time. "Carriage, Mistress Russell. You may not be frightened, but I am. A woman was done to death last night not a mile from this house. We have no idea with what we are dealing, madam, and I would be grateful if you would take all precautions, for there are murderers abroad — rogues and murderers, dear, who would come on us all in our beds. It may even be the beginning of the invasion by the Dutch and we all know how vile they are, especially where good English men and women are concerned!" He clapped his hands together, looking purposeful. "Now. For once, mistress, be obedient and do as you are bid and behave like a conventional woman of town. You are not amongst your friends in Buckinghamshire now. This is London and things are done differently here, and you must abide by town rule, not country ones. Dear God, that I should live so long to be nursemaiding a wench still wet behind the ears!"

Thomazine found herself smiling at him. "I believe you are an old sweetheart, sir."

"Less of the old, you minx. I'll have you know I am six months younger than your husband."

"Sir Charles — did you, did your coachman, um, did anyone find a ribbon in that carriage? It was an embroidered one — I — um — it was a wedding favour, and we — I embroidered it," she could feel a flush rising from her collar, "I think Thankful lost it from his hair, when we journeyed home the other evening."

He blinked at her and shook his head thoughtfully. "No, dear, not that I know. But I imagine it's quite distinctive, if anyone were to find it."

8

Thomazine did not know at first what woke her. She sat up, flipping her braid over her shoulder, knuckling the sleep out of her eyes. Thankful was breathing beside her, a little shaky, a little too fast, but steady. She slipped out of bed and padded across the dark boards to use the pot, wincing as her sleep-warm skin met night-cold air.

"Thomazine."

She stood up abruptly, shaking her shift down. "Er — Thankful? Are you awake?"

A long sigh and then he sat up. "Thomazine, take your shift off."

"I — what?"

"Take it off. I want to see you."

"You want to what?" Outside in the street she heard the rumble of the night soil cart and entirely by reflex she clapped a hand to hide herself from its driver, though unless he could see into shuttered attics her modesty was safe. "Thankful it's freezing, you can't mean it!"

"Then come back to bed. And let me warm you."

"You're ill! You can't —"

"Sick of love," he said, and he sounded so much like his old, dry self that she smiled and shook her head and slid back under the covers. He rolled over, as quick as a hunting falcon and pinned her to the mattress with the whole burning weight of him, kissing her throat and her jaw with barely-leashed ferocity.

118

She should tell him to stop. His hand closed on her hip. Caught a handful of linen. Pushed the crumpled linen up to her waist. She made a noise of protest.

He pushed the folds of her shift up further, up over her tingling breasts and he dipped his head and kissed the salt-cellar of her throat. "Darkness is no friend to lovers," he said conversationally. "I want to see you, tibber. All of you."

She wanted to argue, but then his teeth closed, very gently, on her nipple and she found herself saying something else altogether without having the faintest idea what it was. But she had his shirt over his head and she felt him laugh as the collar gave under her tugging, and then it was his hot skin against her coolness, warming her, melting her…

Afterwards she lay, trembling and panting with her heart thumping so hard she thought it must burst her chest, feeling as if all her bones had turned to warm honey. She thought he slept, afterwards. She surely did, drugged by loving and weariness, rolled safe in his arms with a lullaby of boots and curfews and watchmen in the cold, starry night outside.

Only once, she woke, at the sound of his voice. Quite clear, as lucid as if he were talking to her, or to another in the room with them.

"I know loving, you filthy-souled bitch," he said. "I know what it is, now. You could not steal it from me wholly, and I pray God you burn for your trying."

But when she sat up, they were alone, and he was asleep.

She remembered it, afterwards, as the last bright day before the storm. She awoke to a faint pale sun the colour of primroses shining in slats across the attic floor and Thankful up and half-dressed in his plain wool breeches and his plainest shirt, a little shaky but recognisably himself.

He stopped mid-stocking, leaned across the bed and kissed her with an enthusiasm that still took her aback.

"Feeling better, then," she said wryly, and he tossed his loose hair out of his eyes and grinned sideways at her.

"I'm alive, tibber," he said, as if it explained everything, and she nodded blankly.

"Surely."

"Every time I come through that ague and I don't die of it — ah, sweet Christ, I am grateful! I have not thanked you for either your care of me, or your service. I am at your disposal, so long as we might sit down often. What would you?"

She didn't want much, actually. To walk with him, without fear of interruption or duty. To take him to Leadenhall market and stare at the great wheels of cheese and the piles of herbs and the mounds of fruit. To buy him a pair of stout woollen stockings with her own money and for him to kiss her right there in front of everyone as if they truly were an apprentice and his lass, and not a truanting married couple.

"May I show you the Perse?" he said. "My ship. Well. Not wholly mine. I can walk so far as Wapping, I think, after a rest."

It was busier than it often was with an air of suppressed excitement that was almost feverish.

"He saith among the trumpets, ha ha, and he smelleth the battle afar off," Russell said to Thomazine and squeezed her fingers in his own. She had not a clue what he was talking about but she gave him that sparkling, indulgent look that she often gave him these days, as if they were two adventurers together setting out on a quest to far-off lands.

"There she is," he said and he was grinning for though he had never had the sailing of her — no, nor would he, for he liked the solid ground beneath his feet too well — the Persephone was all things magical to Russell: she was mystery, and hope, and magic, and had she come back with a phoenix for her figurehead and a merman for a captain he would not have blinked an eye.

Thomazine followed his pointing finger and then all the breath came out of her on a long sigh, too, and she looked on that fat old nautical goodwife with her eyes like stars. "Where has she been?"

"East India," he said softly. Then shook his head. "Well, no, truly, the Perse has been no further than Amsterdam. She trades with the East Indiamen, you see." He gave a sigh of his own. "Sandalwood, and cubebs, and silks —"

"My silks?" she said.

He nodded. "Chose them myself," he said, feeling rather shy. "Well. I was engaged in other work, too, but — yes. From India to Amsterdam, and from my heart to yours."

Her eyes were shining. "You are a sentimental old fraud, Thankful Russell."

"I never claimed to be other than sentimental, my tibber. Other people may think as they choose."

They would probably have stood there all day admiring the Persephone, rocking gently at her anchor, if a rather large gentleman in a very conspicuous waistcoat had not barrelled up to them and suggested that they might wish to take their mooning elsewhere. He suggested it so roughly that Russell was moved to suggest in return that unless the gentleman in question wished to wear one of the great spars of wood that were piled on the dockside as a suppository, he might like to moderate his manners before ladies.

Russell had turned round by this point to stand in front of Thomazine lest matters come to that pass and so the large gentleman's comical change of expression when he recognised Russell went unnoticed by her. The large gentleman's profuse apologies did not, however. Things were all at sixes and sevens on the docks of late. Strangers coming and going at all hours — murders —

Russell had often known murders down here on the docks: sailors, drunk, knifing each other in brawls, or brawling whores drowning one another. It still offended him rather badly that some ne'er-do-well had come down to his docks, where his ship was moored and done this dreadful thing. The man told them there had been a murder and a fire, and Russell was not sure what was worse, for he had known Tom Jephcott. Not well, he had not been an intimate of the man, but he remembered passing the time of day with him before.

"Strangled," the large gentleman said, with grim relish. "Strangled him black, they did, with the eyes popping out of his head and —"

"That is sufficient, sir," Russell said sharply, more out of concern for his own sensibilities than hers, for she was all eyes and ears listening to this ghoulish talk.

"Talk of the town, it is, for by God's grace some of the lads off the Perse was in the Devil's — uh, the Pelican, and they put the fire out before too much damage was done, but..." His face clouded. "Done a mort o' damage to the warehouse, mind. God alone knows how much it'll cost Master Giddings to put right, for it were the better part of the Go And Ask Her's cargo, and her new-unladen. Year's earnings, poor old sod. And he wasn't the only one to be so afflicted, for 'twasn't only his cargo in there."

"And the Perse?" Russell said sharply.

The shipmaster shook his head. "Not a mark to her."

"Then I'm sorry for Master Giddings and will do aught I can to help him. Send word if I may be of any use, Master — um, I'm sorry, I know your face, but I —"

"Aye, and I know yours, Major. You're a hard man to mistake, no matter what they say. Keziah Dolling, as is ship's master to the Ariadne." He swept his greasy bonnet off his head to reveal a head of close-cropped badger-grey hair and made an unexpectedly genteel bow. "At your service, mistress — your daughter, Major?"

"My wife," Russell said with indignation, and then realised by Dolling's horrible grin that he was being made game of.

"They was celebrating a safe return," the man went on primly.

"In the Devil's Tavern? Hm. Very safe. So the Perse came in —?"

"Perse come in on the evening tide on the Wednesday, and she was all right and tight, empty as a whore's purse — sorry, miss — by Friday morning, not so much as an old stocking left aboard."

"Splendid," Russell said happily, and then remembered they were talking about a man's death.

"She done well, the old gal. Aye, some of them lads was paid off with full pockets, Major, they done well this time around, and there was some serious lifting the elbow going on in the Pelican that day." He closed one eye thoughtfully, "You ever considered a new master for the Perse?"

Russell said nothing, for he had a new ship in mind one day. Give the Perse her honourable retirement and send the Fair Thomazine out adventuring in her stead. But that was for a long time hence, God willing, and before then —

"So, what? A fight?"

"Seamen ain't much given to wearing ribbon," Dolling said grimly.

Russell frowned, not understanding.

"Thomas was choked with a ribbon, Major: pretty little trinket, like a gentleman wears, all 'broidered by a lady's clever fingers. Bloody funny choice o' murder weapon, you ask me. Almost as if someone were trying to make a point. Like it was a token or some such."

"Jephcott was a married man to my sure and certain knowledge," Russell said, and then — "Oh. Oh I see. You think —"

"We-ell," the ship's master drawled, "well, that's what some of the lads are saying. Choked with a lady's ribbon for putting his hands where they ought not to go. Some fellers is like that — possessive, you might say." He closed that bright eye again. "And then some of the lads is saying that maybe Thomas come across a thing he should not have come across, late one night in a warehouse where they was unloading ships all full of silks and spices. Maybe a ribbon was what some bright spark had to his hand, if a watchman doing his duty happened to find him in a warehouse full o' silks and spices."

"I think I am being stupid," Russell said.

"I don't think you are, Major. I think you are very far from stupid. I think you know very well what I mean and I reckon you would do well to be mindful of it. Folk talk. Stupid talk for the most part, but there it is. There was damage caused here the night Tom Jephcott was throttled. The Ariadne's going to be out of the water for the better part of a month —"

"Will you want for work, sir?" Thomazine said.

"Me? No, though I thank you for asking: no, she's a fixer-upper. There was a bit o' damage to a few of the ships that are laid up fitting for the long voyages, but nothing a good carpenter can't mend. A dozen bales o' silk — cargo, for the most part, stored by, and had it not been for them lads off the Perse, the whole boiling lot would've took fire, the whole far end of the dock gone up in smoke. Four ships just come in after the Perse, and they'd have lost the lot. All English trade, though, Major. East Indiamen, you get me? English East India Company. Four ships damaged, a warehouse full o' cargo burned up, and not a scratch on the Perse. And for meself, I happened to be playing both sides off against the middle, I might watch meself. Eh?"

"Master Dolling," Thomazine said sweetly, "would you let me go on board your ship?"

He did, of course, and she tucked her hand into the crook of his elbow and trotted about the deck with him while he pointed out the bits of the Ariadne that needed repair and told her enormous lies that Russell was too polite to call him on.

Russell skulked behind them, amusing himself by placing his feet precisely where hers had trod, half-listening to Dolling's phenomenal tale of a great whale he had seen off the coast of Norway once, and wondered what the bloody hell had been going on in that last week.

Murder. Arson. Profit. Greed?

War, for sure. Were the two connected? He didn't know — although in his experience it wasn't unlikely.

Bloody George Downing, the King's erstwhile ambassador to the Dutch — expelled from the Hague for his perfidious politicking, poking and poking until the King thought war was the best option. Russell wasn't so sure. He hadn't took to war when he'd been a seventeen-year old lieutenant in the New Model Army, had liked it even less when he was in Scotland under General Monck and half-dead of a fever, and thought any man who wanted it now had to be out of his mind, but it was different, in all probability, if you were the one giving the orders and not the one taking them.

George Downing was a bloody turncoat regicide — not that he had turned his coat by turning King's man after the wars: God knows there were enough of them who had had the sense to see which way the wind was blowing after the Commonwealth and swear a pragmatic allegiance to His Majesty, but Downing had betrayed his old comrades, sold them to a bloody traitor's death for a mess of pottage, and Russell trusted that man like he trusted the Devil. Not much moved George Downing but profit and the hope of more profit and if he wanted war it was because there was gold at the bottom of it.

Russell sighed and eyed the rats-nest of rigging consideringly. He hooked his elbows through it, put a foot in the bottom and leaned experimentally into the rope cobweb. Once you got used to the swaying, like a fly in a web, it was remarkably comfortable and he closed his eyes and turned his face into the fetid breeze with a contented sigh.

"What are you doing?"

Thomazine's voice broke into his drowsy awareness. He didn't open his eyes, but cocked an eyebrow at her.

"Sleeping, tibber. I'm a poor frail invalid, remember?"

"He has been abed with an old fever for the last week. This is his first day out of bed," she said to Dolling.

Russell opened one eye and tried to look reproving, which was difficult when you were hanging like a spider in a web four inches above the deck.

"Missed him, then, when the old gal came in. We said it wasn't like you to be absent when she was due, Major. Wondered where you was the other night. Some of the lads said they reckoned they'd seen you come down for a look at her the night Jephcott copped it — just like you done today, thought you might have seen something. Well. Can't have been you, then, if you was ill, can it? But they'd have swore to it it was you, for you're a hard man to mistake —"

Russell must have bridled for Dolling shook his head, realising he had given offence. "No, Major, not the look of him, no more than he was a size o'you, with pale hair and he took pains to be sure that his face was hard to mark. Which is, you'll own, a trick you have?"

"Had," Thomazine said firmly at his elbow. "I like to look on my husband's face. I happen to think him perfectly lovely. But it couldn't have been you, dear, for you were in bed all week and I was with you all the time. Wasn't I?"

Russell said nothing. But he could feel Thomazine's eyes on him.

"So, husband."

Thomazine was dismembering a pie in the shadows of a bakehouse.

"So?"

"Don't change the subject!" He had that lovely bright-eyed innocent look and it was very pretty, and she wasn't fooled for a minute. "Trade."

"Trade?"

"You are engaged in trade with the East India Company, sir. Aren't you?"

He lifted one shoulder. "Well. True."

"Which?"

He realised she wasn't in a teasing humour. "Both," he said, and her mouth fell open slightly, "— but, tibber —"

"Don't you 'but, tibber' me, you bloody — pirate!"

"I am engaged in perfectly legal trading, madam!"

"Oh, are you? Are you, indeed? Free trading with a nation with whom we are at war —"

"Mind your tongue," he said against her mouth. "That is not common knowledge." He sat down, taking a deep breath. "If you are asking did I send you out on an errand the other night so that I might spring from my sickbed, throttle poor Jephcott, and set fire to the English East Indiamen to promote my own enterprise — er, no, Thomazine, I did not."

She felt her cheeks flare and mutely cursed a fair-skinned redhead's complexion that gave away her every temper. "I didn't say —"

"No, tibber, I know, and nor did you believe it —"

"Really," she amended, honesty being one of her besetting sins as much as it was his. "I wondered if —"

"And now you know. I did not, Zee. Could not, and did not. Well. We are at war, so much you know: every man in London sees the Dutch under the beds and in the closets —" He shook his head, grimacing. "That wretch Downing. He would give us war and men in this country are hot for it. So, war we shall have."

"But —"

"But whose interests — other than my lord Downing's, of course — would be served by war? Not the King's. Not the nation's. And the King knows it, sweet. He is not his father. He is not bloody stupid. On the one hand Downing pushes for it and men of like temper whip the people up to want it — greedy for gold, as ever. The King is hot for the gold — and to make sure that none of my old comrades in Europe come home to start stirring up any further republican trouble. We ageing rebels being the very devil for insurrection. On the other hand, he can't afford a war. And he surely cannot afford to risk losing what trade routes he has, if the Dutch start to fire on our spice fleet." He thought about that. "Again. They've tried that already and we didn't like it, d'you remember? After Smyrna."

"But the Dutch do awful things to our men —"

"Oh, do they hell, Thomazine! I have been engaged in talks with Mijnheer di Cavalese these six weeks and more and not once as he tried to eat me, convert me to Papistry, or torture me. I have been trading with the Dutch in my small way for — what, three years? — I still have all my own fingers and toes and my head is still on my shoulders. You read too many pamphlets, gal!"

"But —"

"Tibber, in Amsterdam I used to lodge with a very nice family called Brouwer. They live up by the Kalverstraat, the flesh-market. You'd like Mevrouw Brouwer. She feeds me. Very respectable people, very devout. They sent one of those horrible blue and white jars that's neither use nor ornament for our wedding. But it was more expensive than they could rightly afford and they bought it for me — for us — because they were happy that I was to marry a woman I loved. Does that sound like the sort of person who eats babies, Zee? Really? Any more than I was when they said it of me? Or your father?"

The thoughts flitted across her mind, like the wind over the river, all the awful things they'd said about profane, drunken Dutchmen, torturing Englishmen wherever they could capture them. All the awful things they'd said about crop-headed Roundheads, twenty years ago, in the wars then: all the atrocities her father's men had apparently committed, everything just shy of the sack of Magdeburg.

There was some truth in them. There was always a grain of truth in such. But not enough for blank hatred. Injustice had always roused her worse than anything else, even as a little girl and if he had not been passionately fair, always, she should not have loved him. Her eyes dropped and then she leaned across the table and took his hand.

"Sorry," she said, and he gave her a wry smile.

"So the respective governments of England and the United Provinces get their war and all the people cry huzzah and all the naval officers rub their hands in glee at the prospect of making their names in glorious battle again. And all the merchants who think they can take over the Dutch trading routes at nothing a pound clap their hands for joy and all the more practical merchants who would rather not have a very disruptive and very expensive war get on with the business of talking to each other to ensure that we — um, they — can protect their interests and any warfare that takes place is going to take place somewhere else. We enjoyed a period of co-operation between England and the Low Countries in Indonesia until Amboyna, so it is possible."

"And the King knows you are doing this?"

He dropped his eyes, startled, and then looked up with the most delighted smile. "Oh, yes, best-beloved. He knows. He pays me to do it."

9

It was a faint, hazy morning and Thomazine squirmed blissfully against the bolster and stretched her toes out to brush against her husband's foot. The sheets were cold and she sat upright with a muttered word she should not have known.

Russell's clothes were not folded neatly on the press at the foot of the bed. He had not been here for some while, by the coldness of the sheets. She tightened her lips and dressed and went downstairs to the widow Bartholomew, who was just as tight-lipped, but not for the reasons that Thomazine had suspected. It seemed the day was far advanced. Ten of the clock, by the chime of St Gabriel's, and the Major gone since before daylight, when a messenger had come for him — had the bloody man not slept at all, she thought irritably, picking at the plain brown bread and bacon the widow had set before her. He was supposed to be recovering, damn him.

So ill, then, that he did not reappear at noon. Nor by the time the bells at St Gabriel's rang for evensong and nor was he at home when they returned from evening prayers. The Bartholomew-baby was fretful, wanting to be attended to, and the widow was anxious, flitting like a bat between cooking-fire and table, trying to oversee a supper for the wrong number of people. Her food was good, Thomazine must acknowledge that.

Thomazine hefted the whimpering child into her lap — a solid little boy, who wriggled, but whose warm weight was oddly homelike and reassuring. It was raining again as the sun set, one of those bitter spring squalls that seemed to blow up out of nowhere.

The shutters were shut, the bed was warmed, grace was said and supper was eaten, and still he did not come.

She wondered how she would know if some harm had befallen him. If they would bring him here, or carry him to some other place — to Four Ashes, to be buried.

How she would manage and how she would go on when she was a widow at twenty-one? She went to bed. He did not come. She undressed and slipped between the warm sheets, and still he did not come. She had just decided on finding his brace of travelling-pistols somewhere in the bottom of the clothes press and going in search of his poor broken body when she heard a noise.

So, clearly, did the widow, who came scampering out of her room with a glint of martial zeal in her eye and the poker in her hand.

But it was only, finally, Russell, tripped over his own feet at the worn bend in the stairs and sprawling headlong and foolish over the attic threshold. He propped himself on his elbows and peered up at her where she stood in the doorway and by the light of the banked kitchen fire downstairs it was possible to observe that the errant husband had one eye swollen almost shut and the evidence of a badly stifled bloody nose. "Have you been set upon?" Thomazine said warily. He panted at her with his mouth open, blowing bloody bubbles. "Thankful —"

She was concerned, she was afraid, she was — suddenly sniffing his breath, she was furious. "Get in here, sir! All is well, Mistress Bartholomew, no cause for alarm, my husband —" and her fingers bit into the flesh just above the bones if his elbow as she hoisted him to his feet, "is as drunk as fiddler's bitch, sir, what d'you mean by it?"

That last was not intended for the widow's ears and so once the door was closed she gave him every single choice epithet a decent upbringing amongst soldiers had taught her, and a few more she had acquired more recently. "I have been worried sick!" she finished, "while you — look at the state of you, Russell, I don't imagine we will ever get the stains out of that waistcoat — drinking and brawling, sir, I thought you had grown past that foolishness twenty years ago!"

He sat on the bed and blinked at her earnestly, which would have been a considerably more appealing sight without the bloodstains. "Tibber," he said. "You really cross with me, darling girl?"

"I am bloody pig-livid, Thankful! I think you need to tell me all," she said firmly, and he raised his head and gave her a shaky smile.

"You still love me? You will still love me?"

"Because you have been out on the spree with —" she sniffed again, delicately, "Master Pepys, I surmise, for he has less expensive tastes in liquor than some? Always, Thankful."

He closed his eyes, and his hand closed on the soft flesh of her hip, hard enough to hurt. "Not. Sam," he said. "Not my friend. He — sorry. But he cannot remain my friend. When. I am so —" A deep shaky breath, but he straightened up. "Thomazine, I am removed from my duties with the Dutch negotiations. The letter that you took to Mijnheer di Cavalese?"

"It arrived?" She had almost forgotten that letter, after so much had happened.

"It was received. Dear God, tibber, I must have been sicker than ever I imagine to write such — He did not take it kindly."

"But why —?"

"He did not take kindly to my apparent suggestion that we arrange reciprocal trade in butter, cheese and whores."

She could not help it. She laughed. "You said such a thing? Oh, hardly! Any man who knew you —"

"Would know that I am the kind of duplicitous filth who could murder his own sister, debauch an innocent young woman, and spend what time he has left over from murder and rapine in drinking with Rochester and his cronies. Which, in addition to making me deeply morally suspect, implies that I am of His Majesty's inner circle. Which means, my tibber, that any right-thinking Dutch trader would — not unreasonably — not consider me a fit and proper person to enter into any negotiation with, while our two countries are at war."

"But Thankful that's silly, you're talking about — about a few nutmegs, the world won't end if — no one would believe that you would insult him, deliberately. You are not made so."

He put his hands on her shoulders and looked into her face with eyes that were bloodshot, but steady. "Sweeting. I was sick of that infernal fever. I could have said anything for aught I know."

"But you wouldn't have —"

"Thomazine — my dear, my very dear love — I am known to speak more freely than perhaps I might otherwise in fever."

"He's being silly. Look, if I —" She took his cold hands in hers and squeezed them, "I will go round and say to this man, I wrote the letter, I have these antic fits, I thought it would be funny?"

"I am not sure that would help. But thank you for thinking of it."

"You are sure it was your letter? I mean, it was the proper one, it hadn't been mixed up with, I don't know, a poem or a pamphlet or something?"

"He threw it across the desk at me, love. I barely knew my own writing, such a scrawl, I should have believed another had simply made a crude attempt at copying my hand — he believed I'd been so drunk when I wrote it that I might barely form my letters — but I do know my own seal, God help me, for it's our rosemary branch. I wrote that letter, Zee. I must have, for it had our seal on it. I don't know why I would do such a thing but I did it." He put his head against her shoulder and sighed. "That, and there appears to be some ludicrous fiction that I rose from my sickbed like Lazarus and spent the evening of Wednesday last haunting Wapping docks strangling the watchmen. As if I have nothing better to do with my time."

"You did what?"

"Zee, I am missing a ribbon. I imagine half of London is aware that I am missing the ribbon you gave me at our wedding, for I have made some endeavours to locate it, and I know you have —" He gave a woeful sniff. "It was a gift and you took care to make it and I am sorry I was so useless as to lose it. They are saying that Jephcott was strangled with my ribbon, darling, and what with bloody superstitious sailors putting it around that there was a man in a cloak on the quay, as if most of London does not wear a cloak in bloody spring — Oh, damn it, Thomazine! Why must I be thought responsible for every flood, fire and famine that occurs in this bloody city? Bloody gossip: rumour and vicious tattle — I'm tired of it, Zee, I am tired of it!"

"But you were here, dear," she said patiently. "I can vouch for that. You never left the house. So I can just say so, can't I?"

He sighed and rubbed his cheek against her shoulder and then pushed himself off. He paced about the attic, narrowly avoided cracking his head on the pitch of the roof, and glowered at her. "If any man came out and made an allegation, tibber, then possibly, you could. But they haven't. They whisper, and Mijnheer di Cavalese and his associates prefer not to be associated with a man that is the subject of such low common gossip." He gave her a shaky grin that did not reassure her in the least. "Flung mud sticks, darling. It seems my name is the subject of every vile rumour this morning — every word I have ever spoken, taken out and turned over to see if I may have meant some evil by it —"

"But it is just words, Thankful! They cannot blame you for a thing you did not do! No one can!"

"Yes they can, Thomazine." He ran both hands through his hair, his loose, ribbonless hair, the irony of which was not lost on her. "I make a lovely scapegoat, darling. I am not popular, because I am too bloody honest."

"Then be honest!" she said ardently, "Tell them!"

"Tell them what? That I am answering a case that has never been put to me — oh, aye, and then they will say there's no smoke without fire, and what is my guilt that I must protest my innocence so much — Thomazine, love, I cannot defend myself against an enemy I cannot see!"

"I am not just going to let you be accused of — it's ridiculous, Thankful, you wouldn't murder anyone, never mind go about London knocking people on the head left and right, it's comical, you can't just —"

"But they want to blame someone, dear. Dolling said as much, did he not? I should have known. I should have known he was trying to warn me — what they were already saying —" He closed his eyes again and his mouth set in a straight line. "Well. We do not, God be thanked, want for money. We can go back to Four Ashes and —"

"And what, Thankful? Run away?"

"No!"

"What else would you call it? You know you did nothing, but you would rather hide away than —"

"Than be stared at? And whispered about? Yes! Yes, tibber, I would! I loathe it! You have no idea how I loathe it — and I pray God you never will, wife, for it is a horrible, horrible feeling, that you walk into a room and everyone go silent, or look at you out of the tail of their eye — that you are the subject of every idle conjecture, every —"

"So bad?"

He tossed his hair out of his eyes and he was panting with the force of his emotion, vibrating with it. "Thomazine, when I — when it became common knowledge that I was to marry — people asked, you know, they wondered in my hearing, what manner of girl might — choose to bed a man such as I. What might be — made amiss — in you, that you would love me: if you pitied me, or if you were one of those perverse women who came into heat at the thought of being bedded by a monster —"

"Oh Russell, you are not a monster!"

"I am, Thomazine! Marred and bloody mad and I do not know what you love in me and it frightens me — it scares me out of what bloody scattered wits I have left, that one day you will wake up and wonder why you have shackled yourself to this, this thing, this ageing, ruined, thing—"

She wondered if he knew that he had backed himself, almost imperceptibly, against the wall and that he had turned his face aside so that the scars on his cheek stood out in stark relief in the unkind candlelight. Wondered if he forgot, too, that she had known him all her life and that it did not matter how plain he made his scars, for she had never known him any other way.

"That does not make you a murderer, Thankful," she said calmly.

He closed his eyes. "It does not, love. But it makes me afraid. I care nothing for other people's opinion of me — save yours, my tibber, and if you decided I was not worth the trouble, I — I don't know what I should do."

"Are you not angry? That someone can say such things and go unpunished?"

He shook his head. "No. Not angry. Frightened. Please, Thomazine. In most things I count myself to have sufficient courage, but not — I am not brave enough for this. I am sorry. I cannot."

He was one of the bravest men she knew, he had suffered hurt and privation and fear and misery and he had done most of it as lonely as a man could ever fear to be in this life. He did not fear pain. But he feared other people and what they might make of him. And that was a terrible thing.

She held her hands out to him, palm up, and he looked at her warily and then took a step away from the wall. And another, until he stood in front of her and then knelt on the bare boards to take her hands.

"Do we need money?" she said again.

He shook his head and would not meet her eye. "The Perse—"

"I will not go back and hide at Four Ashes, Thankful. I won't run away. I'm not made like that. But nor, if you wish it, will I make you a public spectacle." He put his head in her lap with a sigh. Her fingers found the stiff knots of muscle across his shoulders and worked at them. "But I cannot promise you that I will not speak if I hear someone repeat that lie in my hearing."

"What do you mean that we should do?" he said and he sounded like a little boy, frightened and hopeful and shy all at once, that he could put a problem that he could not bear into her lap so that she might take it up and share it with him.

"Carry on living," she said gently. "That is our best revenge, I think. To live — and be happy — and not to be frightened. We can do that." Her hand slipped over his shoulder, her fingers tracing the ridges and rags of his ruined cheek. "Will you trust me that far?"

"To the ends of the earth," he said, and she felt his shaky indrawn breath. "When — when do we start, tibber?"

"When are we next engaged to dine?"

"Tomorrow? With the Talbots — provided they do not choose to cut our acquaintance."

She ignored that. "Would you like to attend the theatre tonight, husband?"

The look on his face was a joy. "Thomazine, I am supposed to be disgraced, I —"

"Am no such thing. Master Dryden has written a new play, I believe. The Indian Empereur — Master Fairmantle saw it on its opening night, he says it is very edifying and most educational."

"Does he, indeed. And how many ladies in dubious states of undress does it contain, dear? Master Fairmantle not being known as a patron of the arts?"

"He said it was very suitable for me," she said primly.

He raised his eyebrows. "Did he now? Do you think people would be very shocked, were I to attend?"

"Horrified, darling. Especially if you were to enjoy it. Perhaps we ought to see if we can find a rather more spectacular waistcoat for you, too?"

"I think that might be going a little bit too far, my tibber."

But he was smiling as he said it, no matter how faint and tremulous that smile and she thought that possibly — just possibly — whoever it was that had thought they could make malicious sport of her man might have underestimated him.

PART III: FIRE

10

"I have been thinking," Thomazine said firmly, the next morning. "*You* know you didn't murder Thomas Jephcott —"

"Stop saying that!"

"*I* know you didn't, because I was here with you all along. So really, since we both know you are nothing of the kind, the easy part is telling people the truth, isn't it?"

"But no one has said anything, wife." Russell gave her a horrible bleak smile. "To me, at any rate. We had this discussion yesterday. We can do nothing, my tibber, and that's the worst of it — we can only stand by and lead as blameless a life as possible —"

"What did my father always used to say, when you served with him?"

"A number of very unhelpful things. Which, particularly?"

"Regroup and come about and re-engage the enemy in a rearguard action," she said primly.

He gave a bark of startled laughter. "Doubtless useful, but — "

"Carry the war into the enemy's camp, o my beloved. And take them up the arse."

That did make him laugh, properly, and then he gently disengaged himself from her and lay back in the rumpled blankets with his arm over his eyes and said he didn't even know who the bloody enemy was. But that didn't matter, not really, because they had the wonderful, gossipy, unstoppable force of scandal-broth that was Charles Fairmantle in their armoury on his perpetual busy quest to find a lovely scurrilous new bone to take to his master Wilmot.

"Thomazine, what have you got in mind?" Russell said suspiciously.

She laughed and smoothed his hair into a tail between his shoulders. "If the world wants scandal, Apple, scandal we shall give them."

"But —"

"But, my sweet, nothing. It is a scandal. You are innocent and let us prove it. We'll get the King himself to own it, if we have to. Let us make your poor injured innocence the talk of the town."

Russell swung his head and looked at her, saying nothing. There was a very little colour back in his lips and his cheeks and his eyes were not so blank.

"You don't mind," he said, sounding as if he did not quite believe it. "This is an adventure to you, isn't it? If I was spat on by every man at court, it would trouble you not at all."

"If every man at court is stupid enough to believe you capable of a thing you plainly did not do, love, then the opinion of stupid people is of no importance to me."

"But it's twice now," he said. "They said — at Four Ashes — there was the same rumour there, too, and it has followed me here. Perhaps it's me, tibber. Perhaps I am cursed. Perhaps —"

"And perhaps, Russell, the same person — people — is behind both rumours here, have you thought of that? I mean, you did say you made a lovely scapegoat, for you would never dignify gossip with a reply. How many people here knew of your sister's death? How did you hear of it, if you had not seen her in years?"

"Chas Fairmantle told me in the middle of a crowded room," he said gloomily. "I was so surprised I crushed my wine glass, bled all over His Majesty's carpet, and bloody Fairmantle must have apologised to every footman in Whitehall for being the cause of it. That man is a bloody fool, he really is. He has no more wit than one of the King's spaniels. He just opens his mouth and out it comes — Thomazine, what have you got in mind?"

"So pretty much everyone at court knew — but how many of them knew her?"

"None, I thank God! She was not a woman who would stoop to mixing with degenerates like the present crop —"

"So people could say anything they liked about her, lamb, and no one would have known any different? There would be none to say — this could not have happened, or, she would not have done such a thing. Well. That would make someone's job much the easier, then, wouldn't it — for people always talk, don't they?"

"They have no right to!"

"No. But they do. And people make up what they don't know. And you — being gorgeous and mysterious and, oh, all those things — you're interesting."

"I am no such thing, tibber! I am a plain man who likes his supper and his bed and his wife. I am not interesting! In any capacity!"

"Poor Apple," she said and kissed the top of his head again. "You're interesting to me, sweet."

"You're enjoying this," he muttered darkly and she squeezed him gently about the middle.

"I have a brain in my head, husband, which I have not been permitted to use this three months and more, in case it scares the horses. Well. It seems to me, o best beloved of men, that you make a lovely subject for gossip because unlike some people, it is impossible to get you to confirm or deny a rumour. And if one was in the market for scandal, what better as the subject for tattle than a few juicy unsolved murders?"

"Couldn't I just be a plain regicide and be done with it?" he said in a rather forlorn little voice.

"Someone evidently thinks not, sweet. Oh well. A friend loveth at all times —"

"And a wife is born for adversity," he said wryly. "So you keep telling me."

The play was doubtless as edifying as Fairmantle had promised. Thomazine wouldn't know: she watched it through a haze of tears and Thankful at her side never took his eyes from Lord Egmont up in his box.

They were not intimates of Lord and Lady Egmont, but on nodding terms, almost beginning to edge away from the tarnish of an acquaintance with the Merry Gang. It wouldn't have been long before they'd have been asked to some large, impersonal social occasion, some courtly supper or masque, something where they would be on trial to be found fit, or not, to be allowed more confidence in polite society.

Well. That wasn't going to happen now.

Thomazine had inclined her head respectfully to the older woman, smiling, and her husband had bowed. They had done nothing to provoke Lady Egmont's outraged stare, pulling away her sweeping swagged skirts as though Thomazine had spat on her. They had certainly done nothing to provoke His Lordship's stiff, glowering fury, sweeping past them on the steps of the theatre so close that they had to step aside in haste or be knocked down.

It might not have been so bad if someone had not laughed. If Lady Egmont's little black page had not turned back to pick up Thomazine's spilled gloves with a look on his face that was both sympathetic and sad at once. If the lady had not said, loudly, "Nero, sir! Put those down!" — and then, when he would have handed them back to her, "Where you found them, boy!"

People had began to stare, the orange-sellers falling quiet to gawk around them. Lady Egmont twitched her head aside, so even her eyes were not sullied by their appearance. His Lordship turned his head very slowly, changing his course so that he brushed by them so close that she could see a louse crawling in the curls of his wig. He meant that they should step aside from his path. He did not know Russell very well, then, for her husband straightened his back and stopped dead on the steps, so that Lord Egmont must himself turn aside first.

Egmont stopped and he said nothing, though he was white to the lips and two furious spots of colour glared on his cheekbones. "Out of my way," he said icily. "And take your accomplice with you."

Thomazine heard her husband's sharp indrawn breath. Under her hand his arm was vibrating like a plucked lute-string.

"Russell," she murmured, "be —"

"You will apologise for that," Russell said, and it was so silent in that little space around them that she heard the grit of his back teeth.

"I don't think so," Egmont said pleasantly.

Russell's hand dropped onto the hilt of his sword, quite reflexively. He did not wear an elegantly-chased French rapier at his hip like a fashionable gentleman, but instead wore his old plain, worn, munitions-quality backsword. Not a weapon for grace, but a declaration that he had been a soldier once and he was yet a man who knew the business of steel. It had not glinted in the torchlight outside the theatre, but had seemed to suck in the light instead.

"Intending to murder me, too, Major? I don't think so. Even your little accessory couldn't deny it before so many witnesses." Egmont smiled, showing all his teeth and made to pass them.

That was when someone laughed: a nasty laugh, the sound of someone enjoying watching a good man's overdue come-uppance, and Thomazine's husband, who was a good man, stiffened and tossed his head as if he did not care that he was being laughed at. He and his wife had been insulted by a man who was even now looking about him to see what acclaim he might gain from a fashionable audience — look at me, gentlemen, baiting this most vicious criminal.

"Sir," Thomazine said plaintively and her voice trembled with a thing that if you did not know her well you might take for a most becoming timidity and not a roaring fury — "will you not listen to me? A moment only, sir, I beg you?"

Egmont stopped again and his eyes raked her with utter contempt. "Say on, then, if you must."

She blinked, clutching her gloves to her bosom. "Sir — my lord —" Might as well be hung as a sheep, as a lamb — "Your wife, sir, is a poxed whore and sleeping with my lord Dorset — check your privy member for sores, sir, were I you, for 'tis common knowledge Dorset won her from Wilmot in a card game and everyone knows he has it."

She left him gaping and Her Ladyship — who was sleeping with both Dorset and Wilmot, on Chas Fairmantle's word of honour — scarlet-faced with mortification. Thomazine made her obeisances, took her husband's arm and went to see the play.

Thomazine felt hot and miserable for the rest of the night and was sorry she had said it.

"I'm not," Russell said grimly, without taking his eyes from Egmont laughing in his box.

"I'm not sorry I said it. I'm sorry that I made you conspicuous. And now everyone is looking at us."

She squeezed his hand, and for the first time he stopped looking at that shadowy box up above the stage,and looked at his wife. "Are you? Sorry?"

"If it makes you unhappy, love. Yes."

The princess onstage had flung herself to her knees, clutching the villain's thighs and orating for all she was worth. The theatre was hushed as she approached her doom.

Russell dug his thumbnail into a somewhat disreputable orange and tore a great strip of peel loose. He cocked his head and looked at her thoughtfully and then dissected the wet flesh neatly, licked his fingers clean of the bitter pith and held a segment to her lips. "Well, they will continue to look," he said with resignation. "So —" He bent his head and kissed her, orange segment and all. "Let us give them something to watch."

And that was how it began.

It frightened her, a little, how easily it happened; that one day they had been a decent, new-married couple and looked on with indulgence, if not precisely warmth. And the next, they were existing in an odd, shadowy half-world, where he was not quite a murderer and not quite a traitor, but definitely a villain, and where she was an accessory to the fact and neither of them were welcome and doors that had been open to them yesterday were barred and bolted in their faces today.

Money bought you nothing. Money bought you food to go on the table and put a roof over your head and clothes on your back, but it did not open doors that had been slammed shut, or compensate for friendships — acquaintances — lost. You could not buy back honour. You could only try and make up for the things that had been lost with the loss of it.

She had not known that the loss of an intangible thing could be as physical as the loss of a limb. And all the silk gowns and all the jewels — which she did not have, but could have had for the asking — in the world, did not make up for the fact that she was lonely. She had Thankful and he was all the world to her, but increasingly he was bright and black by turns and she never knew which he would be.

She had the uncomplicated company of Chas Fairmantle and she thought without his good-humoured interventions she would have run stark mad, for at least he did not take things to heart so. You could have a civil conversation about a play, or talk of the illness that was beginning to afflict the poor: they had buried the first poor lady who had died of the new disease not a week ago in Covent Garden and there were rumours that the contagion and the new comet that was seen very bright in the sky was a sign of God's having turned his face against them in this war against the Dutch.

Fairmantle very carefully did not mention the murders, although there was a multiplicity in the City now, where life was cheap and death was cheaper. Or rather, he mentioned them once, with a horrible cautious avidity to see what she would say: where Russell had been that night, or that afternoon, when another life was snuffed out somewhere in their little circle of streets. She did not say he was in bed, or he was at the docks, working, setting all to rights for the Perse, or finding work for some of the men who had crewed the burned ships that they and their families might not want for bread. Increasingly she grew to appreciate her husband's stubborn view that the more credence you gave to such contemptible stories by treating them seriously, the more you appeared guilty. If someone wished you to be so.

And so they drifted, purposeless, rootless, only existing when they were in the hard, glittering company of the outcasts of Court. It was not, she thought, a life she could maintain indefinitely. And nor could he.

But tonight, Thomazine smiled at her raven-elegant, dangerous, gorgeous husband and patted his hand with her ivory fan. "You look lovely, Apple."

He still sulked, so she leaned sideways, spread the fan over her lips and whispered, "May I invite you to my bed, sir?"

He gave her a wry look. "You're the third one tonight to make that offer, my tibber."

She swapped the fan for an equally elegant fork. "Oh, am I, now. Who was she?"

"Lady Talbot," he said and laughed, rather wildly. "Asked if I'd wear a highwayman's mask and put my hands about her neck whilst — this is not a nice conversation to have with my wife, Zee. The answer was no. To either."

"Oh, dear, Russell!"

"As in — oh dear, Russell, or oh, dear Russell? The pause is significant — to me, at any rate."

"Very dear, and very silly, Russell." Behind the fan again she blew him a kiss and his dark eyes lit with warmth.

The world said she was leading Russell a merry dance of her own. He a murderer and she a whore: another thing they whispered, behind fans, on the edge of his hearing, it seemed. That the Puritan's bride was too young and too gay to be happy with her dour Caliban. That the Puritan's bride might, perhaps, seek amusement elsewhere. She had not known they thought he was fair game, though, and had not known how he must feel, until she had just now learned of Lady Talbot's unusual offer and felt as if she had swallowed a fish-bone.

Lady Talbot had rather remarkable grey-green eyes, wide and long-lashed and slightly bulbous. Thomazine laid the fan on the table, took the heavy chased silver fork in her right hand and stabbed the pale green, slightly bulbous grape on her plate with venom. Then she met Lady Talbot's gaze, smiled sweetly and bit the grape in two.

"At least your teeth are your own, tibber," her husband breathed in her ear and she nearly inhaled the damned thing.

"Russell," she said, without taking her eyes from the notorious whore who had importuned her man, "who was the second?"

"Her husband," he whispered back and then she did, in truth, choke. "Asked if he might be allowed to watch."

"Oh, dear God."

Because these were the invitations they received now. The rakes, the whores, the hangers-on. The daring, who wanted to see if he was in truth a murderer, would spring snarling across the table with a knife between his teeth and commit horrible acts on the assembled party. They wanted him to. That was the worst of it, that the same ladies and gentlemen who had mocked him as prim and ordinary previous were so quick to believe his guilt. *Not quite one of us, you see. Always knew there was something.*

The green-eyed trollop who was whore to the Duke of Buckingham was eyeing her husband again like a dog eyeing a meaty bone and Thomazine twirled the fork thoughtfully in her fingers. If the bitch thought she'd get him in her bed drunk, she had another think coming. She slipped her hand under Russell's elbow and switched her meagre glass for his full one.

He was drinking more than he should lately, but why should he not? Sometimes it lightened his mood sufficient to forget the whispers. Sometimes it made him irritable. Tonight was one of his black nights. Lady Talbot had not improved his mood.

Buckingham — what fool had invited both of them to the same supper anyway, save possibly a fool who craved attention? — was playing silly buggers, idly baiting Lord Talbot about his horns. Lady Talbot was in her twittering element, thinking she might play one off against the other and display her overripe charms to the company as she did it.

Thomazine was tired and bored and had heard nothing tonight more than the same lacklustre rumour than she had heard from a hundred lips for the last fortnight and the long-boned waist of her bodice was tight around her overstuffed middle. Getting poddy, my tibber, Russell had said drowsily to her in bed last night, folding his hands over the little pot she was acquiring from all this rich living.

Her husband looked stone-cold furious and that made Thomazine sad, as she took her own place at the outcast end of the table. They had seated Russell near to Lord Talbot — between Francis Talbot and Lord Kettering and opposite the Duke of Buckingham — the better to observe him, she thought, like a wild animal at a menagerie. And they'd set her with the undesirables, where a girl of no account from a quiet Essex bywater might be conveniently ogled and propositioned, but not expected to participate.

There was a woman she did not know to her right, a chubby, happy, slatternly wench with a laugh that jiggled her fat white breasts like a half-set blancmange — "Mistress Behn," she said, beaming at Thomazine. "And you're my Crophead's squeeze, then?"

"His wife," Thomazine corrected coldly.

"How very unfashionable, to bring a wife to such a gathering! All the rest of us are whores, darling," Mistress Behn said languidly and there was a little round of applause from the rather gaunt, poetic-looking gentleman at her elbow, who did, in fact, turn out to be a poet and who was quietly tucking fruit up the voluminous sleeve of his shirt as fast as he could without attracting attention. She must have been staring, because Mistress Behn nudged her hard under the table. "Nat and I are whores of fortune," she said and looked at Thomazine through brown eyes as soft and protuberant as a spaniel's. "Fortune's not paying well this week."

"No doubt, but in any decent household we do not talk of whores at table!" Thomazine snapped, all too aware of Lady Talbot's white hand on her husband's midnight sleeve and his fair head bent towards hers.

"Surely," Mistress Behn agreed, following her gaze. "We sit with them in this company. And in this household, madam, the honest ones steal and the arrant ones pander. But we never talk of it, of course."

"What are you saying?"

"I'm wondering what manner of whore you are, my lady. At this end of the table we gamble our wits for preferment. And at that end..." Mistress Behn trailed off, still looking at Lady Talbot and the Duke of Buckingham and said nothing — very pointedly. "Your good man was honest when I knew him —" her eyes rested on Thomazine, thoughtfully — "in Den Haag. Though he did not know you then, for he is much changed, I think?"

"Married," Thomazine said through shut teeth, as if that might account for it.

"Sad. No man of sense should marry."

"Or woman," Nat the poet said softly and looked at Mistress Behn with liquid sympathy until she stroked his dark curls like a lapdog.

"Marriage is a noble institution, sir. But who wants to exist in an institution?"

"You knew my husband in the Low Countries?" Not that Thomazine did not understand this flighting wit, but she did not consider herself a whore, Fortune's or otherwise.

"He was very kind to me," Mistress Behn said and dipped her lustrous eyes with a sigh. "Had he not worn his hair cropped like a yard-brush at the time, I might have let him be kinder. So unflattering."

"You had an affair with my husband?" Thomazine flattened her hand on the tablecloth, where the starched linen had crumpled in her grip and patted it smooth.

"No, mistress, I owe him — something in the region of two hundred pounds, I imagine, for six months' rent and keeping. Living is dearer at Court, you know. One is obliged to keep up a pretence —" Mistress Behn grimaced. "As you see. Smoke and glittering mirrors. I imagine I should have been cheaper to keep as his mistress. And I imagine the world would have understood it the better if he had."

"Why should he feel any obligation to you then?"

"My husband died and left me drowning in duns, madam. This is common knowledge. Ask —" her spaniel's eyes flicked to Fairmantle, braying on the opposite side of the table. "He hears all, doesn't he? Hears all, tells all and knows nothing. I am much attached to His Majesty. He never has any money either, the poor darling, or he would have helped, I'm sure. No, behold poor Astraea, running distracted from the debt-collectors with little to commend her but one set of glass pearls, one silk gown, much turned, and her wits. Enter one slightly sardonic Caliban, a little ragged at the edges."

"Oh, please don't call him Caliban!" Thomasine begged impulsively. "My lord Wilmot began it. He hates it. He is not a monster, he —"

"Began it himself, mistress," Mistress Behn said gently. "Not honour'd with a human shape, the man-beast in The Tempest, d'you see? He signed himself so when he made his reports. 'Tis a humour, no more. He had always a perverse humour, my poor Crophead, and much misunderstood."

Thomazine blinked at her, struck briefly dumb. "You and he were spies together?"

"Did I say so?"

"I did," Thomazine said. "He has told me as much."

"Well, love makes fools of us all, doesn't it?"

To which Thomazine, sitting in an overstuffed room in a gown that was too tight in the breast, with tortuous loops of her hair pinned to her skull with great jewelled pins and full to miserable overflowing with fancy cream sauce, could only agree.

Mistress Behn smiled at her and took the poet Nat's inky white fingers in her own. "I believe my lord Talbot needs to piss," she said sweetly. "We are, remember, Fortune's whores. Observe the trollops of Cheapside. The tuppenny strumpets display their wares like a market stall." She gave her hostess a charming smile up the table, "Those who would rise are more audacious. Ask Nelly Gwyn. She's made her way in the world with little more than wit."

"You are suggesting that I become an actress?"

"She's suggesting that you move up the table and sit in Talbot's chair while he's not in it," Nat said mildly. "Though, you know, if you've a mind to go on stage, Aphra is the lady to write it —"

"Hush, Nathaniel. Women playwrights? Shocking!"

Leaving them giggling at some shared private joke, Thomazine made her way up the table and then the rich sauce made its way up her throat and with one piteous look at the back of her husband's head, she fled.

11

Thomazine did not feel so ill, lying down.

Lady Talbot's maid was very kind: a plump, motherly woman who reminded Thomazine of her own mother and who did not show any revulsion at all at her heaving up most of her supper into one of Her Ladyship's bowls, though she was a little bit cross at Thomazine's tight-laced stays.

"Well, young lady?" she said. "How long d'you mean to go on with this?"

"Until I get the names I need," Thomazine said wanly.

The maid — whose name was allegedly Hortense and who had dropped her genteel French accent almost as soon as Thomazine had collapsed in a sad puddle of emerald silk on the banquette — looked at her blankly.

"D'you not know, then, girl? How many might it have been?"

"How on earth would I know?"

"Well, I assume you were there at the time, mistress! Unless —" her eyes flickered — "you weren't — I mean — has he promised you marriage, dear? Because most of them are already married and not like to put her aside for such as you."

"I'm already married myself. The tall gentleman with the fair hair in black is my husband."

Hortense patted her hand. "Well, I'm sure it will all work out then. Not John Wilmot's, I hope, young lady — not that it's any of my business, but he's not known for his kindness to his girls when he tires of them and I'd not look to him for help—"

"Why on earth would the Earl of Rochester help me? Unless he happens to know something useful —" Thomazine struggled upright and gave a sigh of relief as the stiff bones of her unlaced stays parted over her tender belly. "And I imagine it would be the first time in his life if he did!"

Hortense was staring at her. It seemed she grew stupid, as well as queasy.

"I think we may be at a misunderstanding," Thomazine said with dignity. "This is my husband's child. Not the Earl of Rochester's. You didn't really think I would — oh, please!"

"You wouldn't be the first, madam."

"I'm sure. London draws fools faster than a turd draws flies."

The Frenchwoman's lips twitched. "Surely. Well, that is some relief, mistress, for if your husband is the fair gentleman he'd not own a son that favoured my lord Wilmot, who's as black as a raven. D'you mean to do that child a mischief, coming out so tight-laced? That babe needs room to grow! For you're no tiny thing, if you'll pardon my free speaking and your man's a fair height — does he know?"

"Don't you dare tell him."

"Is he daft altogether that he hasn't noticed?"

"He hasn't said," Thomazine corrected gently. "I think he — he hopes. But I would rather he did not know until he — until we — until I know. For sure."

"Don't tell my lady," Hortense said and her eyes darted suddenly sideways, as if the willow-light, romantic figure of Lady Talbot might suddenly drift through the wall. "She's slipped two before now."

"Oh, I am sorry —"

"One was her husband's and she didn't want to lose her place with Buckingham. And t'other was Buckingham's and she didn't want His Lordship to know. She doesn't care for children, her ladyship. Not if they might disadvantage her."

"What has that to do with me and my husband?"

"She won't like it," Hortense said firmly and Thomazine still did not understand, "not one bit she won't like it. You do not want to put yourself out of favour with Her Ladyship, madam. If you draw the attention she's marked for herself she will not care for it. She is a jealous lady and hot-tempered."

"Is she known then, for such malice?"

Hortense's face stilled and she shook her head. "I could not comment, mam'selle," she said, in her best careful Parisian accents. "I will leave you to rest, if you please. To be careful of the child, you see?"

She bustled out with the bowl and its horrid contents, leaving Thomazine in peace.

The room smelt of rosewater and a little of spice and here, in the little-used apartments at the back of the house, Thomazine could not hear the laughter and the voices from downstairs. She felt very lonely and she wanted, very badly, to be in her mother's house, being petted and made a fuss of. One hot tear slipped from the corner of her eye and burned its way down onto Lady Talbot's damask upholstery.

She heard the door open. "Tibber?" Russell whispered, "Are you all right?"

She sat up and put her arms out to him like a child wanting to be picked up and he came and held her with a great sigh.

"That lady gave me a — garment — for you to borrow," he said and rocked her gently against his shoulder. "She said she forbade you to lace your stays so tightly as previously as you had, for the sake of what reason you knew. Are you feeling better?"

"The better for your being with me."

He smelt of smoke, sweat and stale food-smells, but under that he smelt of Russell and home, and she buried her face in the ribbed silk over his warm shoulder and felt the solid curve of muscle and the bone beneath it. "Shall we return to supper, then?" she said against his arm.

"Unless you would rather we made an early night of it, tibber? We don't have to — we are not obliged to be polite — we could go home, we could — you could read to me and I could comb your hair out, like we were used to?"

Oh, but she wanted to. Wanted to go to their plain, warm lodgings where she could take her shoes off and sit with her feet in his lap and he could rub her aching feet and they could talk of what had been and what might yet be, God willing. But then there was Lady Talbot, whose malevolence might not extend to ruining a man's reputation for the joy of it, but who might take pleasure in a woman's sickness and exult in having seen a rival off. "I would rather go back in," she said. "I was enjoying the company, you see." He looked so forlorn and at the same time so indignant. "Oh, lamb, it's not that, it's just — Lady Talbot —"

"You would rather spend time with Lady Talbot than with me?"

There were times when it was tempting to slap him for his stupidity. "No! But I'll not have her think —"

Russell stood up and his mouth had taken on that prim, twisted look, as if he had bitten into something not ripe. "I see. I see. Well. I shall keep you no further, Thomazine, if you prefer to keep the company of that — that —"

She stood up as well. Her bodice was not closed and her stays were loose. Once he would have looked down at her undress and kissed her, or at the very least he would have put his arms round her. Tonight he held up Lady Talbot's elegant fur-lined velvet jacket and thrust her arms into it as if she were still a child. He hooked it closed and tugged it straight with the cool efficiency of a man who has had a lot of practice. Thomazine had never seen one of these jackets before.

"Most women wear them in the Low Countries," he said absently, and she looked up into his face, startled — when had he grown so experienced in the matter of Dutchwomen's dress? — but he didn't look back. Not once. His eyes were fixed on the closing of her jacket. "As undress," he added, sounding quite critical about it. "Not in a public place."

"Well, if I had not your —" She stopped herself, because it was not a thing to share like this, in anger, and she would not use their child as a weapon. "Temper," she finished, which did not make sense, but was a little needle. "May we return to supper?" she said stiffly and held out her arm. He nodded equally stiffly and took it.

No one laughed and no one was surprised to see them return, only perhaps there was a little ripple of what you might call astonishment, if you were sensitive to such things. Thomazine returned to her place at the foot of the table, with the groundlings and Russell resumed his, where he could be baited like a bear and he knew it. But he could see her from here and that steadied him a little, though if he kept his head down she would not know he was looking. Even in that dreadful ill-fitted jacket Thomazine was radiant, though the pale amber colour did not flatter her much, which, he suspected, Lady Talbot knew. It had not been a charitable attempt to make Thomazine comfortable, it had been meant to make her look pallid and dowdy.

He heard Thomazine's giggle again. He hoped Aphra was not filling her head with total fabrication. Mistress Behn meant well and there was a head on those plump white shoulders that many of the men around this table would have wondered at, but she had a history of — well, romanticising her friends. But

160

she had had a time of it, with the late Master Behn. He had not been kind, always: certainly not kind enough to leave her in a position of independence and she had been in a sorry way when Russell had first known her. He had not rescued her, he had not been her protector, he had certainly never done any more than lend her money for rent and food in Antwerp. She liked to imply that he had, though. She reckoned people understood her relationship with the world if they thought she was a whore.

"We're all whores, chick."

It was her catchphrase. They laughed at her for it. She was a funny lass, Mistress never-quite-legally-Behn. She was possibly the most loving, generous spirit he had ever met, with the two possible exceptions of his wife and his mother-in-law. One day it was always going to be wine and roses with Aphra. But it was always going to be tomorrow and she lurched from crisis to crisis cheerfully living on her wits till then. Because like St Martin, what she had, she had a habit of giving away.

A lot of people called her a whore but she had never, ever, in the — what? ten years? — he had known her, sold her body. But she had sold her wits, a good deal. That was what she meant. They all did that to a greater or lesser degree: sold their gifts to people who did not deserve them in order to live.

She was, though, a bugger for trying to make things nicer for her friends and that was not always helpful. There were a number of people in Antwerp who were under the impression that plain Thankful-For-His-Deliverance Russell was a noble scion of the House of Stuart and that he had been of the King's household when he'd come by his scar at Edgehill. She had meant well, bless her. She had thought he wanted for society and she meant that he should have none but the best.

He had a dark suspicion that going by the laughter, she was telling Thomazine some similar faddle about exactly what he had been doing in the Low Countries: thinking, no doubt, that a pretty, gay young woman should rather believe in her husband as a tragic figure of romance than a rather plain information-gathering merchant. Which he had been. And that Thomazine, because she was her plain-dealing father's daughter, would not see it as a rosy-tinted fiction, but think that he had lied to her.

"How soon one whore knows another," he heard Talbot sneer, just on the edge of his hearing. "Birds of a feather, eh?"

Kettering, the nasty little bastard, passed some remark about plucking.

He saw Talbot look his way. He knew he was being baited. "The little red wench has been plucked by just about every man in the Gang, don't you know? Plays the whore for Fairmantle —"

"I grow tired of that word," Russell said, very clearly and all of a sudden it was very quiet about that table.

"I understand you are not comfortable with the truth in any of its guises ... Mijnheer Russell."

Someone giggled.

Russell held Talbot's eye until His Lordship flushed and looked away. He picked up his delicate wine glass, twirling the twisted stem between his fingers. Then he shrugged and threw the contents in Talbot's face. "You. Outside. Choose your seconds."

Hell broke loose.

Talbot reared up, dripping and stuttering, with his bitch-wife squawking in outrage at the side of him and Russell suggested that she might care to hold her scold's tongue also, lest she join her benighted husband on the point of his sword.

"Are you going to let a — a murderer talk to me like that, Francis?" she yelped and the murderer swung his head and grinned at her — not pretty, he could feel it, the muscle going taut on the scarred side so that all his teeth showed.

"Your husband is too much of a coward to allow else, my lady. And on the matter of whores, my lord, you are not sufficient of a man for Lady Talbot, either, I understand. Or else why should she choose to bed Buckingham — who's not much of a man, either?" He pushed his chair back and there was part of him that wished Thomazine did not see this and there was a part of him that thought it was about time she saw what they truly said about her — about both of them. "Anyone else wish to claim to have slept with my lady Talbot, or are we keeping tally at two, so far? I understood her to have been like Newmarket races — everyone's been there?"

"Oh, I have," Sedley said cheerfully. "There's an echo, you know. Or maybe that was her husband, got lost?"

"You dare!" Talbot screamed. "You dare to —"

"Of course he bloody dares, Talbot, you just called his wife a whore. Which is, if you ask me, the kettle calling the pot black, for I'm not sure your lady hasn't taken Strephon to her bed," Wilmot said from the head of the table. He threw a grape with deadly accuracy at Russell, who caught it, unsmiling. "Don't poke Caliban, Francis. He don't like it."

"I demand satisfaction!"

"Good for you. I suggest Mistress Abrams in Covent Garden. Very reasonable rates, clean girls, I'm sure they won't mind your little habits, Francis." The Earl smiled at Lady Talbot, ever so sweetly. "There you go, madam, no need to defend something that's as fictional as one of Master Dryden's plays."

Lady Talbot's face blanched, her slightly bulging grape-green eyes turning in the Earl's direction, shiny with loathing.

"Try it," Wilmot said pleasantly and the ape leapt into his lap and he fed it another grape. "Just try it, madam, and I will see your name ruined. Imagine. No parties. No games. No intrigue. You might be forced to rusticate, my lady, somewhere dull, where they would not tolerate your little games." He smoothed the rough little grey head and Strephon chittered, showing sharp yellow teeth.

A deceptively dangerous little beast, that one. Russell didn't trust the monkey much, either.

"Francis —" Lady Talbot said faintly.

"Is going to sit down and behave like a man of sense. And Caliban, you are going to do likewise. You will apologise to my lord Talbot and his good lady for that lamentable misunderstanding and you will put your sword away — right away, there's a good man — and go and sit elsewhere. Go on. Banished, Major."

And gladly so, for Russell was shaking so hard he must sit down or fall and his heart was choking him. He would have killed Talbot, here, in front of them all —

That poor frail wine glass wouldn't take such treatment and the stem broke in two as his fingers closed on it in astonishment. Wine and blood spattered the pristine linen tablecloth and the Earl of Rochester sighed and handed his napkin over with a flourish. "Dear me, you are determined to see blood shed this evening, aren't you? One might argue that under that rather unpromising exterior you are a seething hotbed of unresolved passions, sir. One *might*."

164

Russell sat with his mouth open and said nothing, which gave him the opportunity at least to suck his bleeding fingers and look at the Earl for some clue as to what the bloody hell—

"No, I didn't think so, either," Wilmot said blandly. "Because you didn't do it, of course. And I wonder why someone is at such pains to make it seem as if you did."

"I am a man of blood, sir, did you not know —"

"Oh, come off it! I am not so new-fledged as that, Major. You haven't been a man of blood for some time — if you ever were, and that not merely a tale put about to explain your somewhat individual charms. You intrigue me strangely, you know. You will persist in being stubbornly who you are, despite it making you the butt of every man's wit. Which is interesting, because you share that fair mantle. And we mock him, because he is precisely nobody. A desperate, scrabbling, encroaching person of no significance whatsoever. How very strange, wouldn't you say?"

"That your little coterie seek to destroy that which they do not understand?"

"No, Caliban, for so far as Chas is concerned there is precious little substance to understand. Were he forty years younger I should send him to bed with no supper and tell him to stop pestering the grown-ups. As he is, we can only ignore him and hopes that he goes away. Which he does not. You are always quick to see offence, sir, aren't you?"

The ape put its hairy little hand on Russell's knee and he looked down at it and smiled in spite of himself.

Wilmot leaned his elbow on the table and rested his chin in his hand. "Now I wonder, sir. I wonder if you were always so hot at hand, or if it is a thing that comes with being so — marked — that you think yourself the object of every eye, when you are not?"

"Perceptive."

"Oh, no, sir. I don't pay you the least mind, usually. But I do like to watch your wife — see, there you go again, Major, stiffening up — I like to watch people. To see how they work and —" he shrugged his elegant shoulders — "to meddle, perhaps, a little. She is hardly the serpent of the Nile, your Thomazine. She doesn't trouble to hide her feelings. See — she is worried for you, she's looking this way and trying to pretend she isn't, in case you don't look back. You may as well, Major. She has seen you. She's smiling. I don't think she means to, but — look."

She was. Very, very shyly, in case someone should see — should know. Russell smiled back at her and her whole face lit with a secret joy, as if there were not the best part of a quarter-mile of table between them and the better part of thirty inimical gossips.

"Mainly, Major Russell, I take an interest in you for her sake," Wilmot said wearily. "Because she is a nice little thing, and honest, which is about as rare as gryphon-shit in these parts, and because she was kind to me. She is a little less kind, now, since she knows my reputation. A nice child. Two nice children, Major."

That was supposed to be a surprise. "I know," Russell said, and Wilmot smirked.

"You are not entirely made of wood, sir."

Russell was not. He felt, actually, as if he were melting like butter, basking in her confidential smile. Thomazine had not tired of him. Other people marked it — it was not just the wishful thinking of a foolish, ageing man —

"Well, then. What do you propose to do about it?"

Russell turned his head, looked at Wilmot and said, dreamily, "Love her. And the child. Always."

He was rewarded by an expression of grave amusement on Wilmot's perfect features. "Of course. And presumably the whispers will go away by themselves? Dear me, you are a romantic. Who'd ever have thought it?"

"If I find the source of the rumours, my lord, I will kill him," Russell said.

"And you not a murderer," the Earl said mournfully.

Russell was beginning to rather like Wilmot, who was a reprobate and shockingly without either conscience or moral compass, but who was — amusing. Cheerful, funny and wholly untroubled by anything that resembled a scruple.

"D'you know then, I think you may be rather fun after all, Major. Do let me know when you plan to carry out the deed of darkness, won't you? I think I might like to hold your coat."

Russell stood up and all the tongues started wagging again: another table they would not be welcome at then, in the future. Thomazine put her hands on the table, as if she meant to come with him.

"You ready, then, my girl?" he said, and she linked her fingers in with his.

"Shameless," Lady Talbot said, very loudly. "The hot-tailed little strumpet."

Thomazine curtseyed. "My thanks for the loan of the jacket, madam. Mistress Behn, should you choose to call on us for supper —"

"The widow will have an apoplexy?" Russell suggested, and his wife snorted.

"You will be most welcome, Mistress Behn."

They did not call a carriage and no one asked them if they required it.

"Not a long walk and a fair night," Thomazine said comfortably.

"As long as you're comfortable with it." Russell stopped and turned her gently to face him. "Both of you."

She said nothing for a moment. "I wondered if you'd noticed."

"I had noticed," he said gravely. "A fair night, then. For the three of us to walk home."

12

Thomazine was drowsing, midway between sleep and wakefulness, when she heard the tinkle of breaking glass and a brief commotion of shouting and banging in the street. Then there was one high, piercing scream from downstairs and the sudden angry roar of the Bartholomew-baby woken untimely from his dreams.

Widow Bartholomew's voice raised in outrage, topping the shouts outside and then Thomazine felt the bed lurch as Thankful was out of it and across the room in one lithe movement, jerking open the stiff casement.

"You will disperse!" he roared out of the window, evidently forgetting in his agitation that he had been a civilian this twelve months and more and had no more authority over a mob than the kitchen cat. He leaned forth to brandish a thing menacingly from the window. It turned out to have been the chamber pot, the contents of which were a remarkably efficient means of breaking up a party.

The widow looked furious. This was a quiet, respectable working neighbourhood. People did not throw rocks through the windows of decent folks' houses without something being done about it.

Russell turned the rock over in his hand. Thomazine unscrewed the paper that the missile had been wrapped in. "Death to the duck lovers?" she said blankly, and her husband snorted with more honest amusement than she'd seen in him for the better part of a month.

"Something like, my tibber."

"You recognise the handwriting?" she said warily.

He stopped with one arm in the sleeve of his coat and gave her a grin of sheer, wild joy. "No, my tibber, don't be daft. What d'you think I'm like to do, go round to his house and run him through? This piece of villainy is going straight to the local Justice, Zee, and nothing will satisfy me but to have the bugger what set this in motion strung up by the cods from the nearest chimney —" He stopped, cocked his head, considered. "Transported as an indentured servant. That'll learn the sod."

It wasn't funny and she ought not to laugh, but it always tickled her a little when he got cross and his careful, precise voice went slightly country.

"Nobody is permitted to hurt and distress the people I have a care for, tibber. There will be no more. It stops here."

He still sounded like a backcountry boy from Hughenden and a sudden chill went down her back. For there was a certain turned-inward look he had — had always had when he was on his mettle, the look of a marksman sighting down a gun barrel and it boded ill for someone. He was not yet sighted on his enemy. But he would be, because he was not made for forgiving, and then it would go hard with someone.

"Thankful," she said, putting her hand on his arm, feeling the muscle of his sword arm tense under her fingers, long and lean as a hunting-dog. He was, still, dangerous. He looked down at her and the unmarred corner of his mouth twitched.

"Thomazine." Not a question, but an affirmation. She was here and she was with him. He tipped his head until his forehead rested against hers — this close, he had beautiful eyes: slate-grey and shot through with sparkles of silver and black, with gold tips to his dark lashes.

"Be careful," she said.

"Have you ever known me else?"

And there was no answer to that, because she had not known him else. But then — he was a man who helped desperate Scottish prisoners of war to escape and then employed them in a public capacity and counted them as friends. A man who engaged in peace negotiations with Dutch merchants, whilst his peers courted war with the Dutch government. A man counted by half the world as cold and unemotional, who had wept for joy on his wedding day and at the birth of his friend's first daughter.

No, there were any number of things she did not know he might be and after a bare six months of marriage she was learning that he was not, quite, the rebel angel she had thought he was.

"I have never known you careless," she said.

Russell was as good as his word. The note was presented to the local Justice, who promised to make an investigation.

Russell found a glazier and then lurked over the man's shoulder asking intelligent questions all morning until Thomazine imagined the poor soul was glad to finish his task and escape. He probably thought he was being quizzed by a suspicious householder, poor thing, and in fact Thomazine had a dark suspicion that her husband was filing away the information for a future point when they returned to Four Ashes, when she was going to find Thankful somewhere unlikely with an empty window frame, surrounded by splinters of glass and strips of lead, whistling sibilantly and having a marvellous time.

"I will be at my business again tomorrow," Russell said firmly and blew in Thomazine's ear so that she whooped in tickled surprise and earned a second reproving look from the widow.

"What business, husband, might that be?"

He gave her one of those long, slow blinks, like a happy cat that passed for an expression of joy with him. "I am still a man of business, darling, and I have yet an interest in a ship. I note that Mijnheer di Cavalese withdrew from negotiating with me but he has not withdrawn his interest in commerce. I have a share in the Perse and I am under an obligation to your Uncle Luce to maintain it —"

She made a noise of surprise, for the firmly inland Uncle Luce and ships was still an unlikely combination.

He laughed. "D'you think she was named the Persephone by chance, love? Luce has a part-share in her too. She was named after your cousin and, God willing, we shall have the Fair Thomazine in the water for next spring. No, my darling, I am not wholly a lily of the field for I do toil and I do spin. Doubtless my lord Rochester will have some comment to pass about soiling his hands with trade, but then, I thank God, one of us means to meet his obligations!"

He spun her about and kissed her soundly, and even the widow's lips twitched, so he kissed her too, on the cheek, very respectably.

"We shall stay?" Thomazine said.

Russell gave her a cockeyed grin. "Oh, yes. I have business to transact, Thomazine. I have a ship to outfit and a second to build and you have seen barely a fraction of what there is to see in London, and —"

"*And*, Thankful?" He had stopped rather too suddenly for her tastes.

He shrugged. "I have always had a mind to join the Royal Society, dear. Haven't you?"

It seemed he had been giving much thought to what she had said, so ardently, about having his vengeance against those malicious, anonymous gossips.

"Gracious, dear. If we cannot gain access to civilised society without the aid of a gang of horrible reprobates like the Earl of Rochester, what hope have we of gaining access to the Royal Society?"

"Oh — well, you know. Anyone might attend their lectures and learn fascinating things about the wonders of reason and science. They are the Royal Society of London for Improving Natural Knowledge, dear. Perfectly fascinating."

"Why, darling, since you are become a man of some leisure you are grown quite the man of letters, too. Science, Thankful?"

"Reason, then." He knew he was being made fun of and he still didn't know how to take it, quite, so he wriggled a little. "I know I don't make a habit of going about London throttling people, Zee, and so do you, but I wondered if there might be a way of saying for sure that I had not done such a thing? For in the wars your Uncle Luce said he could tell much from the wound a man took — whether his opponent was left-handed, or how tall he was —"

"Dear, the watchman was strangled. There would be no wound to show, would there?"

"Surely. But tibber — they are enlightened men, they must find something! I mean, it might be that the image of the murderer will be in the poor man's eyes and I am quite distinctive to look on —"

"Thankful, that's horrible!"

"Isn't it?" he said cheerfully. "There was a Frenchman — he was a Jesuit, I'm told — Shiner? Schoner? — he was doing dreadful things to frogs and he said that you would see a thing

173

on a frog's eye when you cut it open to — observe. Your Uncle Luce told me. You know he has an interest in such things."

"I will speak very sternly to my Uncle Luce when I next see him," Thomazine said with a strong desire not to continue this conversation.

"But if we were to gain access to the Society and to set our case before them as a matter of rational interest and not as a topic for lewd intrigue, well, just think! They might — I don't know, dear, they might perform any number of public marvels. They have a journal which is published every month —"

"You have been looking into this, haven't you?"

"You know what their motto is, Zee? *Nullius in verba.* Take nobody's word for it. It could be the King himself trying to say that I did these things and they would pay it no heed — oh, love, if they cannot prove my innocence beyond a shadow of any man's doubt, no one can! And they would prove it by reason and logic that cannot be disputed — not by one word against another, but by evidence, for they don't take any man's word for anything unless it can be proven!"

She had not the heart to look at his excited face and say that he was a disgraced intelligencer with a shadowy reputation and no matter how interesting his proposition might be, he was still not likely to get through the door. He could pay his subscription and stand at the back and gawk like all the other gentlemen who admired reason and discourse and paid their subscriptions, but get so far as to lay out his proposal? To one of his scientific gentlemen in person for long enough to explain himself, and he whispered as a murderer and a traitor to his country?

In his dreams, the poor sweet.

She could not bear to disappoint him, though. "How do we gain access to this society, then, husband?" she said.

He huffed into her loose hair. "Prince Rupert," he said smugly. "I had considered that."

She said nothing, for — well, nothing that was said about that old Cavalier could shock her, she had been brought up believing that Rupert of the Rhine was something next to Antichrist in his ability to perpetrate supernatural acts of daring villainy against his gallant Parliamentarian opponents. Her father had hated Rupert worse than he hated the Devil. He'd been one of those gallant Parliamentarian opponents. So had her husband.

"He is a scientist in his own right," Russell said, mistaking her silence for disapproval. "He is apparently a very educated man."

"And — um, what, love? You will go to the Royal Society of whatever-it-is and say that you and Prince Rupert have a prior acquaintance? But dear — the only acquaintance you have is —"

"I might have shot his dog at the battle of Marston Moor," her husband said and she felt his chest vibrate with amusement, "and I may have knocked his hat off at Edgehill."

"Dear God, Thankful, don't tell him who your father-in-law is! Daddy's done considerably more than knock his hat off, in his time!"

His arms tightened about her middle. "Oh, I do love you, tibber. You make me laugh. No, sweet. I have no intention of presuming on my acquaintance with Prince Rupert — which, as you say, has been somewhat, ah, cool in the past — unsolicited. I cannot say that were he and I to be at the same — say — supper party, I might not, perhaps, angle for an introduction to one of the members of the Society who may have a particular interest in matters of anatomy."

"Oh, be sensible, love! Who do we know who could get you an introduction to Prince Rupert?"

He kissed her shoulder. "The Earl of Rochester, my tibber. The Prince is a bachelor gentleman of, ah, well, bachelor personal habits. He takes as much pleasure in the arts —"

"You mean actresses," she said tartly, since he would not. "Thankful, if what you mean is that Prince Rupert has a habit of getting —"

"Indeed he does."

"— with the Earl of Rochester, then, sir, I am —"

"Not at all surprised," he said primly. "In my humble opinion, he would be better served finding himself an amenable lady and settling down to a blameless life —"

"Strangling watchmen and selling state secrets to the Dutch. That way, you wouldn't have to do it, darling."

13

Russell despised slinking around Whitehall, being fed chicken drowned in sickly cream by some fledgling rake right in the darkest, coldest corner of the great draughty dining room in the company of the least liked, least popular men at His Majesty's court.

Lord Crediton was helping Thomazine to a further slice of chicken breast, which she didn't want and her eyes met Russell's across the frigid expanse of glittering tablecloth. She looked as if she might cry and he wanted, very much, to be at home at Four Ashes with her, not here.

There was a sharp rap over his knuckles. "Your attention is wandering, Major Russell," a cracked old voice said at his elbow and he very deliberately tucked some loose hair behind his ear so that the scars on his cheek showed full in the unkind candlelight.

"On the contrary, Lady Endsleigh. My attention is fixed exactly where it should be." He glanced down at her. Not an edifying sight, the old harridan, three inches thick in powder and rouge and hung about with pearls the size of duck-eggs. "On my wife."

She chuckled. "So there is some blood in you, Major. Despite the rumours."

"Rumour is a lying jade. As ever."

"New-married, then, I take it? Since we've not had the pleasure of your marred face at court this six months and more."

"A little less than a month, madam. I prefer not to discuss my marital affairs with all and sundry."

"Heh, hoity-toity, sir! You were keen enough to discuss your marital affairs when you were tendering your resignation from the Army, young man. Very keen that all and sundry might know you were leaving the business of the defence of the realm to go scampering back to Buckinghamshire and get on with the serious business of begetting some heirs, now the place is your own —" She cackled again. "Well, God bless you both, Major Russell, for I declare you blush like a maiden, so she must be doing you some good." She had dreadful teeth and he wasn't actually sure they were her own for they seemed somewhat too large and numerous for her withered mouth. Of all women, he should have preferred to be trapped in a broom cupboard with Castlemaine, who had the advantage of being an honest whore, than with Kitty Endsleigh, who was solicitous and affectionate and had wandering chicken-claws for hands and a marked partiality for vulnerable young men.

She was kind, though, and he had been glad of her kindness, once, though perhaps not as glad as she might have liked him to be. His gratitude had never gone as far as sharing her bed — although there had been times when he'd been so miserable and so lonely in his first days on Monck's staff that he would have, if she'd asked him openly. "Looks like a nice girl," she said, following his gaze. "If you've got any sense, Major, you'll get her as far away from this sink as you can, get her bred, and keep her hands full with managing a household and her belly full with nice rosy fat fair-haired babies."

He dropped his eyes and said nothing, because he did like to maintain the illusion that he was a stern and upright gentleman in charge of his own destiny, rather than his wife's fond and rather foolish cavalier and no more in control of his own household than a mayfly. Lady Endsleigh chuckled again. "I take it we won't be seeing much of you, either, sir, when you go to become a turnip in the country." She sighed, which was unexpected and almost dislodged her pearls. "There's not many will say it, Major, but I'll miss you at Whitehall, your funny ways. You're honest, and that's rare."

"Too honest," he said.

She looked at him thoughtfully and for the first time did not rattle her society-laugh. "I note you don't ask if I believe the tales, then, sir. Which I don't. There's a lot of bloody fools that do, ain't there? Not the tales that you are a turncoat, which is ludicrous, and nor yet the tales put about by that equally rattle-pated ninny Fairmantle, that you are being groomed for execution by some anonymous black-cloaked ne'er-do-well who seeks your downfall." She snorted. "He over-eggs the pudding, that fool. If he would have the world believe your innocence, he'd do better to keep his blabbing mouth shut, for having him bleat your innocence does you no favours, young man. What a world, Major Russell, what a world we live in where a man is passed over for an excess of honesty and yet John Mennis, who is a delightful gentleman and an utterly inadequate administrator, remains Controller of the Navy."

"No one has ever suggested that Sir John is dishonest, madam," Russell said gently.

"No. Well. An old fool, perhaps, but not dishonest, except by omission. Nonetheless. You will be much missed, Major, by those who value intelligence and plain dealing. Which is to say, not many." She shot a glance of loathing across the table at Crediton, presently endeavouring to force another morsel of chicken between Thomazine's lips. "What in God's name possessed you to leave that poor little maid sitting next to that one-man boarding party?"

"A lack of alternative? What would you suggest, madam, that I challenge him to a duel? Nothing short of ravishment across

179

the table would shock this party — and that only if the wine were spilled."

She nodded. "I believe you're right, sir. Perhaps I should follow your example and likewise rusticate. This dreadful place! The end of days, I swear it! First the murders and then the sweating sickness and now the Dutch — I swear, sir, damme if those of us who don't die of a fretting leprosy won't be burned in our beds by those infernal Butterboxes, pox on 'em!"

"Ah?" he said, only half-attending, watching Thomazine stiffly take a morsel of chicken from Fairmantle's fork, followed by a grape from the man's greasy fingers. "That would be a great grief to your family."

She gave him a forlorn look across the table and he was already half out of his seat. "I must go to her. My poor girl, she is unwell."

Thomazine put her head against his shoulder and whimpered and it was all he could do not to pick her up in his arms and carry her from this hot, stifling, overstuffed room, stinking of sweat and perfume and over-rich food. "Oh, husband," she murmured piteously, "I beg — take me hence, lest I faint and disgrace myself in such exalted company —" She pressed a hand to her mouth delicately.

Crediton removed himself and his hovering fork with equal delicacy. "Well, well. How remarkably old-fashioned of you, sir," he sneered. "D'you think I'm not upright enough to take care of your wife?" He leaned back in his chair, thighs lolling suggestively apart just in case no one had got the joke and one of his cronies snickered at his elbow.

"Please, dear," Thomazine said against his chest, "I find the heat oppressive and my stomach is queasy —"

Which shifted Crediton, in his expensive embroidered silk, quicker than the rumours of plague. Poor little Thomazine lolled against him so piteously that he was forced to pick her up, long-legged as she was and she nestled against him with her head against his shoulder to murmurs of shock and disapproval from the party, and for once, he did not care, because she was ill and she was his dear love and he had promised to protect her and cherish her all the days of his life.

This wasn't his life, not any more, even if it ever had been. If Rupert planned to attend — if he had ever planned to attend — there would be other times, because as he ordered their carriage to be brought round, he made a decision. They would go home. What mattered was Thomazine —

"You can put me down now," she said, in a perfectly cheerful, happy, healthy voice, once they were outside.

"A remarkable recovery, madam," he said dryly.

She put her hand on his waist and grinned up at him. "I was very much afraid that our host might do himself an irreparable mischief if he persisted in trying to fondle my thigh under the table. I did not think that would bode well for your future prospects, Russell — your wife having emasculated one of Prince Rupert's drinking companions. And I believe the prince is presently abed with a recurrence of his old fever and is not likely to put in an appearance this night — or, indeed, for some days hence."

He stared at her.

"If Rupert's not coming," she said gently, "I have no intention of spending more time with that appalling pack of loiter-sacks than I have to, dear. I should rather be at home. With you. I believe we were discussing the matter of vineyards and little foxes, yester'e'en."

"Oh, you clever wench," he said. "But Zee. My employment prospects are husband and, God willing, father. And no more. Those days are done. I am no intriguer, remember? I am dismissed. What ambitions you may be cherishing in that deceptively tricksy head of yours, madam, forget it. I have no intention of taking up a post on His Majesty's staff again."

"Of course not, darling." She stood on tiptoe and kissed his cheek. He was not so daft that he was fooled, though he enjoyed the being kissed. "Crediton is a disgusting creature. I do hate a man in one of those absurd wigs. I should much rather have a good, plain, honest gentleman who wears his own hair —" She tucked a loose wisp behind his ear, allowing her fingers to drift over his cheek with a tenderness that still undid him. "Horrid man. He was trying to frighten me. Plague, indeed."

"M'lord, your carriage."

It was still cold and Russell was glad of the stout wool of Thomazine's plain, countrified cloak as he settled it about her shoulders. She settled his hat more firmly over his eyes. A fine pair they must have made, each dressing the other, like a pair of children. "Not a night to be keeping men or horses standing," he observed to the driver, who looked at him in some surprise.

"Sir?"

"Nothing. Aldgate, sir, if you please. Fenchurch Street, near to the church of St Gabriel."

He thought he might grow to like carriage travel, with his girl sitting opposite him with her feet in his lap and her slippers off, while he rubbed some warmth and some blood back into her poor pinched little toes. They both concluded they did not take to fashionable life. Russell would not, in this lifetime or any other, wear high-heeled shoes, no matter what the reigning fashion dictated. It seemed that my lord Crediton was a victim to that particular vanity. "Which must mean he barely comes to your shoulder, husband, in his stockinged feet," Thomazine mused.

"Indeed?"

"Thankful, you are looking thoughtful. Are you planning some kind of vengeance on my lord Crediton, in which case I —"

He set her feet back down and leaned forwards. "I am thinking, my tibber, that we could have walked from that house to Fenchurch Street by now. And I am thinking that perhaps I did not put up with your uncle's poeting all the way through the Wars of the Three Kingdoms to be murdered by some ungodly ne'er-do-well in a London slum."

He leaned forward and rapped on the roof of the carriage in an instruction to stop.

It did not stop. Instead, he heard the crack of a whip and suddenly the carriage lurched as the horses startled into a gallop, rocking and pitching from side to side at a speed that was almost unthought-of in these city streets, creaking like a ship in a gale. "He does not mean to stop," Thomazine said and she looked up at him as if he would know how to make it go away. "Thankful — what does he intend should happen to us?"

"I suspect we are being carried off," he said, but smiled at her reassuringly. "Ah well. Over my dead body, tibber." She stared at him for a second and then she shook herself, quite briskly, because she was the daughter of a fierce and inventive soldier and she was, he thanked God, the wife of another. She unhooked her skirt and kilted up her petticoats between her legs, which gave her the faintly comical appearance of a baby in clouts, but which freed her from six yards of clinging heavy silk. Her face was dead white, her eyes enormous.

He lifted the leather screen of the window and looked out at the rushing night. "I've not a clue where we are, tibber. Which means we're out of the City. Choose your weapons."

She looked down. Swallowed. Looked up. "Pistols. Russell. Must —"

"You can load and fire?"

"Whose daughter am I?" she said scornfully and put out her hand for his pistol. His own hand was shaking.

"Tibber. This —" Her eyes met his. "I love you. Give me your hand. We do this together."

"As ever," she said and smiled, shakily. She put her hand into his as the door cracked open, swinging wildly on its stiff leather hinges.

She thought that he meant that she should hit the cobbles on top of him and she hadn't. She had twisted like a cat in reflex and they had gone down in a sprawling tangle and for a minute when she heard something crack she thought she was dead, everything gone white in a blinding flash of pain. But then she could breathe again and she realised it was a snapped bone in her stays and it was jabbing into her flank like a dagger. She was not dead after all, though she feared from Russell's stillness that he might be. She dared not panic, but had started to rifle his clothes, trying to find a heartbeat, blood, a bruise —

"Jesus bloody Christ!" he gasped, sounding so utterly unlike his decent upright self and so much like her father in one of his more temperamental moods that she giggled. He rolled over onto his front and tried to get up. "Tibber, I reckon I've broke my ankle," he added, quite conversationally, and then she thought he might have fainted, because he dropped flat to the wet cobbles with a weird whooping yowl and did not move again.

She could hear the clattering of hooves crashing on into the night with a slapping that sounded horribly like flesh on flesh as the door swung to and fro on its hinges, fading into the dark. Between her white underlinen and Russell's pale hair they were sticking out like a pair of sore thumbs and all she could do as she heard the sound of hooves joined by the rumble of wheels was to drag herself and her limp husband into the shadows between the looming houses and crouch down and throw her cloak over the both of them. Disguised as a midden, she thought wildly, and pressed her face into his shoulder, with the broken bone of her stays tearing at her belly and a warm stickiness running down her flank, feeling as if all her bones had been smashed like eggshells.

She could hear a stick tapping on the cobbles. A stick, or the click of high heels. One of them was shivering and she wasn't sure which of them — she, with her legs and her feet indecently bare and her shift tucked up between her thighs like the worst slut in London and her bare skin pressed unpleasantly against the rough, gritty, slimy stones of the alley, or Russell, with pain.

"Major Russell — ah, Mistress Russell — I do apologise. Most profusely. All a terrible misunderstanding. I really ought to have made the effort to attend that soiree this evening. I had not realised you wished to discuss a matter with me of such urgency. Mistress Russell, I may offer you a token of my good faith, though I would beg of you, consider an old man's infirmity. I knew your father, madam. Knew him and respected him greatly, though I suspect he might not acknowledge the recognition." The speaker coughed and spat with an audible splat. "God damn, I hate these wet nights. The damp gets to my chest. I met your father at Bristol, Mistress Babbitt. He asked me if I thought it was worth it. I said no. Does that satisfy you as to my good intentions?" Prince Rupert of the Rhine blew his nose noisily. "And may we now repair to my carriage, before I catch my death of cold altogether?"

The rain had stopped, the moon was riding high above scudding silver clouds and Thomazine was long abed.

It had been an accident, Rupert said, and he had been so distressed about it that Russell had had to accede. Rupert had not meant to attend Crediton's supper, with the pain from old wounds that always flared up in the damp and gave him grief and a recurrence of his old fever. To which Russell, who had taken a pike in the cheek at Edgehill in a battle against this man, twenty-five years ago and who likewise found that all the bones in his head throbbed when the wind backed, could only agree with heartfelt sympathy. But later, Rupert had thought that actually, as the man was a friend and might have gone to some trouble for this, he would endeavour in courtesy to at least attend briefly, even walking with a stick and in considerable pain. As he was drawing up to the house in his carriage he had seen the Russells getting into a carriage of their own.

"I knew your wife, you see," Rupert said simply. "By the hair. There are so few ladies at court with such bright hair."

The driver of the hired carriage must have panicked at seeing Rupert's own vehicle clattering in pursuit. That was all Russell could think. A plain man, a common hired carriage, suddenly pursued with intent about his business by a very official, crested, gilded, expensive-looking vehicle — such a man would not be unreasonably afraid.

That was what Rupert thought, anyway and seeing the older man's embarrassment and distress at thinking himself the cause of such an incident, Russell was not of a mind to argue.

The whole thing was just odd — that Russell was standing in his old enemy's personal quarters, while a man he'd faced down across a battlefield and cordially loathed twenty years ago fussed and fretted like some greying old mastiff, muttering self-reproach. Rupert had summoned his own personal physician to examine Russell's ankle. Russell's ankle was not broken, though it was badly sprained and had it not been for the presence of his wife he would have sworn more considerably than he did, having a prissy gentlemen in a nightcap wrenching at it.

Russell was tired. He was getting old and he was not used to being thrown around the cobbles as much as he might have been twenty years ago. He wanted nothing more than to limp to his bed. Rupert had been very apologetic about Thomazine's state of undress and had been very courteous to her with his eyes averted, which was somehow rather touching. Still, he was a bachelor and not well-equipped with ladies' clothing and so he had lent her a vast silk brocade dressing-gown which had pooled about her feet, tall as she was, and she had sat with her dirty bare feet tucked up underneath her in the big carved chair by the fireside with her chin on her hand and her hair in a wild tangle about her face.

Thomazine was now long in bed and still Rupert would go on and on, talking of the good old days. There was a beautiful little French clock, all gilt and intricate traceries, chiming the quarter hour, the half hour, the hour... Russell could have willingly thrown it on the fire. It was relentless. Russell pitied Rupert that he had no one else who would talk to him of those days when he had been a man of fire and glory and not an ageing, ailing man of letters living on memory. Russell, who had been a man of fire and a little glory himself in those days and who was now a staid old married man with a throbbing ankle and not an inch of his person that was neither scraped nor bruised was just plain weary and he wanted to go to bed, and not re-live the great battle at Edgehill.

Struggling to keep his eyes open in the stuffy warmth, half-numb with too much good brandy, he sat upright quite suddenly and said, "Willis."

Rupert, stopped short in the middle of an anecdote of some petty skirmish at some bridge or another, blinked. "Was he there?"

"No. Willis. Royal Society Willis. You mentioned him."

"I had not realised you were interested in natural science, Major Russell? Perhaps you would like to join one of the society's lectures at another time? Master Willis is one of its founders, you know. He has done some fascinating work into the brain —"

Thankful Russell's brain had ceased to function with any clarity about an hour ago. "Tomorrow," he said firmly and stood up. Being on the outside of the better part of a pint of brandy and having forgotten all about his sprained ankle due to the numbing properties of same, he gave a yelp of anguish.

Rupert grinned. "Help yourself to a cane. I've a number. And — welcome to the society of the walking wounded, Major." He raised his glass mockingly. "It only gets better. Good night."

Russell got lost, of course, but there seemed to be silent and officious servants in every corridor and they were all very kind. Hobbling along, slowly and painfully, he tried not to crane his neck at the works of art so casually displayed on the clean sky-blue and gilt walls amongst the antiquated and downright bizarre weaponry — dear God, he'd never seen so many paintings of ladies with their shifts off.

"Here we are, sir. I'll have a man bring you hot water and fresh linen in the morning."

"And, ah, my wife?"

Which embarrassed the servant not at all.

"I'm sure something may be found, sir. Good night." He departed as noiselessly as he'd come, leaving Russell wishing, most fervently, for a length of twine with which he might later find his way back to Rupert's parlour, like Ariadne in the maze.

"Russell, 'sthat you?"

Thomazine sounded sleepy and cross, and did not sit up.

"You stink of brandy," she muttered and then rolled over and looked up at him through a red-amber curtain of loose hair. "Well? What did you discover?"

He yawned. "That I've no head for spirits?"

"Thankful!"

He thought she might have hit him, but since everything hurt anyway, one more jab in his much-abused ribs more or less was little hardship.

A while later, when she folded her arms over his about her middle, over the solid little prominence that was going to be his son one day — he lay there thinking that life was rather wonderful. It was not going to be wonderful in the morning, but right now, right this minute, he could have asked for nothing more.

14

More than suffering the after-effects of a night on the tiles with a prince of the blood, the next morning, Russell woke up frightened. That was a thing he had not been in twenty years and more. He could not see how the things were connected, but there was starting to be a pattern, of blood and fire, and of — of coincidence. What he could not conceive was why some vengeful eye might have chosen to light on him. He was in no way remarkable — he was known for not being remarkable. He was a plain administrator and a man of business with a wife and a house to run. There were no women in his wife other than Thomazine, no unnatural lusts, no gambling debts, no secrets. He was — he had always been — honest and plain in his transactions and decent. People had remarked on it. People had mocked him for it.

Twenty years ago he might have tossed his head and said that it was evidence of his having been marked especially for the Lord's trials to test his mettle. Now, with dependents, with roots and ties and obligations — he tossed his head and said, under his breath, that if he found the son-of-a-bitch who was behind this he was going to skin them and roll their bleeding carcass in salt.

Thomazine was wan and a little forlorn this morning and there was a bluish-yellow to her skin like spoiled milk that he did not like. Not sick, not feverish, but wanting sleep and wanting to be comforted and he could comfort her a little, but not in Prince Rupert's lodgings, which were not home. She had crumbled her bread on her plate at breakfast and smiled nicely at the Prince, but her eyes were heavy and her mouth had a sweet downward curve. He thought her cheeks were thinner, too, and he did not care for that. He might have words with this son of his if the child was going to wear his mother to a pack-thread before even his entry into the world.

When they arrived at Willis's address he appeared to be a sober, respectable gentleman of prosperous appearance and intelligent demeanour, the sort of kindly, trustworthy doctor that would see to a family of the better sort in a little country town — neither too high nor too low, not too plain and not too fashionable. He bowed politely over her hand and Thomazine caught a glimpse of something dreadful on the elbow of his good black coat and her eyes flew to Russell's face in absolute horror.

Not quite so much like a plain county-town doctor as Russell had thought, then. Thomazine's Uncle Luce was a sober and mostly-respectable medical man of prosperous appearance and Russell was fairly sure that he'd never been seen in public with the contents of a man's brain-pan on his sleeve.

"Charmed," Thomazine said faintly and looked at her husband instead, he being apparently easier on the eye than a thing that looked like grey porridge.

Rupert had not accompanied them. He had looked somewhat wan himself that morning, picking at his breakfast like an ageing raven, peevish and sore. He hadn't had his wig on, either, and Thomazine had been hard pressed not to stare at his close-cropped head. It was not a look she had ever taken to, she said afterwards, and she had not the faintest idea why a man should choose to crop himself like a convict in the name of vanity. He had written them a note of introduction to Dr Willis and then he seemed relieved to be free of them.

It was a relief to Russell too, to be fair, because he could not be comfortable in the apartments of a man who'd spent most of his gilded boyhood attacking not only Russell himself, but his father-in-law and most of his friends. He seemed very old — and he wasn't so much older than Thankful, but being dark and sallow, he seemed that much more — well. Aged. Thomazine put her hand his again and he squeezed her fingers comfortingly, and then glanced down at her, frowning slightly. "You all right, my tibber? Hands are cold?"

"It isn't the warmest," she agreed faintly.

"We had something of an accident yesterday evening," Russell said absently, watching the door swing ponderously closed behind her. "Unsettled in her stomach, poor maid. She didn't sleep well, either."

"I've a colleague who'll see to her," Willis said and left his cadaver with as much good cheer as if he'd been getting up from his armchair to greet a guest.

"Sorry," Russell said to the flabby, bluish-white body on the table. Seemed rude not to.

It did stink, mind, though it wasn't a smell Russell was likely to forget. He had spent rather a lot of time after the battle at Edgehill with the scent of his own decay in his nostrils. He had every sympathy for the ne'er-do-well on the table with his greasy, hairy scalp peeled back like the shell of a boiled egg.

Willis came back in, dusting his hands on his white linen apron like a grocer. "There we go, Major, your good lady all settled in the kitchen with my housekeeper. They can have a lovely little coze while we talk of — what was your interest, sir? Anatomy?"

"I imagine," Russell said warily, because he wasn't quite sure what his interest was.

Willis nodded. "Poor soul," he said and Russell had the disconcerting impression the doctor was talking of the body on the table and not Thomazine. He advanced on the cadaver with an air of purpose and a saw and Russell winced.

Willis glanced up, his eyes bright under fierce triangular brows. "It's all right, Major. He doesn't mind. He can't feel it, you know."

"I'm sure. I was shot in the head myself, after Naseby. I have a degree of fellow-feeling."

"Ah? You intrigue me, sir. Pray, be seated."

Russell had little choice, unless the man was likely to provide himself with a mounting-block to poke at the dents in Russell's skull, which ordinarily pained him not at all, until the man started jabbing his sharp fingers into the scar. "Any pain, sir? Tenderness?"

"Yes!"

"Ah, I see why you have consulted me, then!" The wretched leech was actually reaching across the table for a pair of scissors with every intent of cropping Russell's hair to the skin for a better poke.

"It hurts, sir, because you are pulling my hair! Kindly desist!" Russell yanked himself free and glowered, panting, with most of his hair worked free from its bindings and fallen in his eyes.

"Do you suffer from the headache at all? Any disturbances in your vision, or imbalance?"

Only, Russell thought, after an evening with the indestructible Rupert. "Not in these twenty years, doctor, and I am not here to discuss *my* anatomy."

"Such a shame," Willis said and his fingers lingered tenderly over the old scar on Russell's head. "Would you consider —"

"No."

"In the interests of science, you understand. It would be perfectly safe. Fascinating —"

"No!"

"Would it not be astonishing were we able to see a man's bones without harming him?" Willis said longingly, and Russell, who was presently in possession of those coveted bones, bridled.

"Indeed, sir, but I happen to be using them at the moment!"

"Ah, but Major." The doctor's eyes were bright with longing. "You would be amazed were I to reveal to you the secrets of the human frame."

"I should probably be as sick as Thomazine," Russell said dryly. "But it is, indeed, of bones — and, possibly, of brains — that I wish to speak to you."

"Then you're in the right place, sir. Shall I call for some refreshment, if you don't require a professional consultation?"

The man was stark mad. No, that was untrue, he was enthusiastic. Evangelical, even. Russell's experience of the human body was that it broke far too easily, but Thomas Willis was determined to demonstrate the beauty of a man's inner workings, thinking he had found a fellow enthusiast. He had not. He had found a man with a slightly stronger stomach than most who was capable of looking on flayed scalps and opened heads without puking up his breakfast (and that by the simple expedient of reciting the Acts of the Apostles from memory).

The circle of arteries at the base of the brain was the latest discovery. Russell was never going to eat blood pudding again. Or, possibly, drink red wine.

The clock was almost chiming the noonday hour when the man finally ran out of specimens. "My dear Major," he said happily, "I hope I have been of some help to you?"

"Surely, sir. This — that —" he pointed at the convict's peeled skull — "what might you tell, from a — a body? A corpus?"

The doctor blinked at him, frowning. "What do you mean?"

"Well, if someone were to be killed unlawfully and their body put into a fire, how should you know? That they hadn't just died, I mean? By accident?"

Willis gave him a reassuring smile and tapped Russell on the side of the head. "By the bone, sir. The secrets of the bones. A man whose neck is broken —" he prodded the cadaver and the flayed head wobbled rather horribly — "the bone would remain broken, did you bury him, burn him, or hew him in pieces. 'Tis a common misconception that a fire will hide all. The soft flesh may wither, Major, but not the bone. Oh no, sir. Only God's fire will consume whole. Why do you ask?"

For the first time Russell thought of Fly with sympathy. She'd always been keen on the flames of hellfire, especially where other people were concerned. It had a certain black irony that Fly Coventry might have burned. But not alive. She had not deserved that. No one deserved that.

He shook his head, trying to clear the shadows. "My sister," he said, "she — died. I was away." And thank God for that one bright mercy. "I was abroad." Suddenly his eyes blurred and he had to put his hand on the table to stay himself. "I was not there. There is talk, you see. That she, perhaps, was —"

He loathed Fly, he'd hated her when she was alive and he hated her just as much now she was dead, but he could not stop that picture in his head, of her, her hair as pale as his own flaring out in strands of bright fire across the bare boards, her cap spilled, her skirts starting to catch in traceries of flame — "Was murdered," he said in a strained voice that he did not recognise. "It makes." The muscle in his scarred cheek was starting to twitch again, a thing it had not done since he was married. "Makes my wife. Fearful."

Willis nodded, understandingly. "Of course."

Was it Russell's imagination, or was the doctor looking at him oddly for knowing that? "I wondered. You know."

It was not a question. Willis raised an eyebrow. "Do I know what they say of you, sir? I do. And yet you say you were overseas when your sister was burned."

"I was. I am — in addition to my duties as a soldier, which are light — I am engaged in trade. I was about that business. I did not know I was to be married, you see, I had no idea that she — that I —"

"You have no need to convince me," Willis said gruffly.

Russell nodded. "To convince myself, perhaps. But I had no reason to wish her harm — she and I had led wholly separate lives for twenty years and more — I had not spoken to her since the year of Naseby when she asked me — told me — to come back and play the man of the house in her widowhood."

"You would not, truly, have held the reins?"

Russell laughed, for it still made him bitter. "An excellent metaphor, sir, though I think an unwitting one. When a man mounts a horse, who holds charge — the beast, who may be the stronger, or the man with the bridle? No, sir, I would have been in charge of nothing. I should have been her puppet, her mouthpiece. I am not ashamed to own that, either. Death was the only thing that could have broken a habit of twenty years' standing, whether it be hers or mine. No — 'tis not her death I seek answers to."

Willis' eyebrows raised. "You make a habit of it?"

"Someone would have it so. A watchman at the docks — strangled, and someone tried to set the dock alight. A few ships were damaged, but the crew of my own — the ship in which I have an interest, then — were, uh, celebrating their safe return and saw the fire and raised the alarm."

"And you were?"

"In bed, quite blamelessly, sick of a recurrent fever."

"Alone, I assume."

"But for my wife and the widow who keeps our lodgings. I am not accustomed to make illness a social occasion. So, both times I have been elsewhere and both times the only people who can vouch for my innocence are people whose word is not — wholly — unbiased. How, then, would I prove for sure that I had not strangled Thomas Jephcott?"

It was not one of Russell's better mornings, watching Willis strangling the life out of a corpse that was already dead and leaking fluid to prove it. In Russell's feeble, squalmish opinion, Willis could simply have told him and not sought to demonstrate.

"*Nullius in verba*," Willis said happily and applied his own strong fingers to the livid bruises on the poor body's abused throat. "D'you see?"

"What am I looking for?"

"Put your hands next to mine."

"I thank you, no!"

"The pattern of bruising, sir. Your hands are bigger than mine and you have a greater reach — being, as you see, taller. On the other hand, I flatter myself that I am the stronger — experience of lifting dead weights, you might say — and so the marks my fingers leave are deeper."

"That's revolting," Russell said, quite involuntarily.

"And anyway, you didn't do it."

"Your confidence heartens me, sir. On what evidence? The honesty of my countenance?"

"Have you ever been strangled, or throttled, or hanged, Major?"

"I am pleased to say, not being a felon, I have not!"

Willis nodded and then, quite without warning, lunged with his hands outstretched and grabbed Russell about the throat — quite gently, as it happened, but sufficient to startle him. Russell broke a number of glasses and pieces of surgical paraphernalia, he almost overturned the table, corpus and all, and he came embarrassingly close to breaking Willis's nose. And when his heart had started beating again and when the good doctor had finished stanching his nose on a square of linen that had been used for God knows what fell purpose, Russell yelped, "What the hell d'you do that for?"

Willis looked smug. "What did you do?"

"I damn near pissed myself, sir!"

"You went for my hands, Major. As any man would." The doctor put his square, workworn surgeon's hands up against Russell's throat again. "You sought to break my hold. And that, sir, that will leave a mark. If you throttle a man, he will fight you. He will fight for his very life. It would have left marks on your fingers, Major Russell. Bruises, at the least — the desperate clawings of a man's fingers as he fights for breath. It is not a gentle death, sir, and I would judge that your preferred mode of execution would be a little kinder. But that I could not prove. No, Major, I can give you your evidence, for what good it will do you. Your hands are quite clean."

Thomazine looked up as Russell came out of the room with Dr Willis on a waft of cold and corruption. He looked as if he may have regretted his breakfast, but he was radiant, bloodstains and brain matter notwithstanding, and she found herself grinning at him quite helplessly. He wriggled back at her, almost imperceptibly, that lovely happy-puppy twist of the shoulders that was his expression of joy.

Willis was speaking to her and she was nodding intelligently and saying polite and meaningless things, and all the time she wanted to say — What is it? What do you know?

And then they were out in the street and she put her arm through his and said, at last, "Well?"

"I did not do it," he said smugly.

"I know that, Thankful!"

"So does the doctor."

"What?" She pulled her arm free and whirled to face him, much to the consternation of a portly gentleman with a beribboned cane who was edging his way past. "What do you — how did he — how can he tell?"

Russell held his hands up for her bemused inspection. "My hands are too big, tibber. Or too small, or something." He caught one of her hands and pressed his palm up against hers. "See? 'Tis a different shape to yours."

"Obviously, dear, but —"

"Then it would leave different marks on a man. Would it not?"

"But —"

"I know, my tibber, I know, the man was done to death with a ribbon. My bloody ribbon, damn it all, I was attached to that ribbon, but Thomazine, think on. Even those marks would be linked to a man's shape and size and as he assuredly was not me, they would equally assuredly not correspond to my form. And besides." He was looking smug again and she shook her head, feeling very stupid. "A man would not die so without a struggle. This is not a fitting conversation to have with my wife, dear."

"I don't understand?"

"Zee, if I were to show you in the manner requested by Lady Talbot, I imagine people would stare. If I were to put my hands about your throat — or a ribbon, or any other instrument — you would struggle and you would hurt me. Presumably, in poor Master Jephcott's case, not sufficient to make the culprit desist in his activity, but there it is. You would endeavour to break my hold in order to preserve your life."

"Yes?"

"And my hands — my shins, in all probability," he said dryly, "would bear the marks of it. A desperate man does not pull his blows, love. I have not seen that poor man's body and nor is it fitting that I should do so. But Doctor Willis can. And will. He believes me as innocent as you do, Thomazine. And I imagine that by the end of this week he will have absolute, irrefutable evidence that I did not harm a hair on that man's head and he will be more than willing to make free of it. And then let us see what the gossips make of that."

"You are exonerated?"

"I am absolutely exonerated, my tibber. And by the end of this week it will be public knowledge. As will be the information that some ne'er-do-well is slandering my — our — good name, for reasons of their own."

"What do you mean to do?"

"What I should have done a month ago. I am going to lay the whole matter in the hands of the authorities, love."

"But —"

"Thomazine. We have done enough. I will put you in no further harm's way. I will call at the Justice's house on my way about my business and I would like it above all things were you to go home. And bar the door, I think. I think I should prefer it if neither you nor the widow should be abroad without me, or without another."

"You are afraid?" And suddenly she was too, because he had that purposeful look about him and she did not know what he had sighted on, only that he feared a thing that she could not see.

"I am." That was an admission she had never heard before from her indefatigable darling. "For Zee — what if this is deliberate, my love? We have thought that this was no more than some clapper-tongued rogue seeking to attach my name to a murder for their own nefarious ends." He gave her a faint, unconvincing smile. "What if the rogue and the murderer are one and the same?"

And on that unreassuring note, he left her standing at their front door.

15

Russell was over-reacting. He was furious. He was terrified. He was as jumpy as a mouse in a room full of cats. He had made the local Justice aware and the local Justice had smiled at him and all but patted his head and sent him about his business for Russell had only told him the half of it. Had not mentioned that he was an intelligencer, he didn't think that would be helpful.

He thought, though, of all people Prince Rupert might be interested. He had detected a glimmer of sympathy in that ragged ageing raven that surprised him: like himself, Rupert was a man with a past of blood and fire, chained to a perch of respectability by circumstance.

Although he had something of a wait before Rupert was in any fit state to receive company.

"You have news?" Rupert said, squinting a little in the sunlight that gleamed on his fantastic brocade dressing-gown.

"I have," Russell said smugly. "Dr Willis is presently investigating the murder of a night-watchman at the Wapping docks."

Rupert scowled as if his head hurt — which, given the smell of stale brandy that hung about him, it probably did. "What does he want to do a daft thing like that for?"

"I posited it as a matter of some — interest."

"Oh? He has an interest in murders? Thought such matters were best left to the Justices, m'self." Rupert stifled a yawn. "Major Russell, is there a point to this? Given what they say of you, sir, I'd have thought you'd care to give the subject a wide berth."

"It does not trouble you?"

"If I were to bar access to my company for every man with blood on his hands, I'd be damnable lonely. The idea of a murder —" he shrugged — "aye, well. Add another notch to the tally, Major. How many men did you kill in the wars?"

"Too many for my tastes," Russell said. "Nor do I duel."

"Aye? Not what I hear. Heard you were very hot to engage at a recent supper, until Wilmot stopped you. Pity, for it would have been a pretty sight, you taking on my lord Talbot. You'd have whipped him, of course, and he'd have cried like a puppy for weeks over it. And then he'd have probably paid someone to cut your throat a month later. No, sir, 'tis not the deaths that intrigue me. Life's cheap, sir, you know that as well as I. You could have murdered half the whores in the City for aught I would care, so long as you left the clean ones —" He grinned ruefully. "Imagine the outcry an' you did not?" He took his wig off and dropped it on the little table beside him with a grimace. "Ah, damme but that thing makes my head ache. To the Devil with fashion, I say. You're too much the old Roundhead to turn up your nose at a man for his not keeping fashion in his own chambers."

"Indeed," Russell said dryly.

"No, Major, if you did put an end to that watchman, I'd be sure you'd a reason for it. Damme, sir, he was only a bloody watchman, what's the fuss? No. What interests me, sir, is why you set light to the dockside?"

"I didn't," Russell said. "But someone wants to make it look like I did."

He had Rupert's attention and he had it hard enough to make the Prince forget his hurts and sit forward in his chair, interrupting occasionally to ask questions, or merely to whistle long and low.

"D'ye say so?"

"I do. And so does Willis."

"For why, though?"

Russell set his shoulders. "Because I have been an intelligencer against the Dutch for the last — what — five years, my lord. It is not widely known."

"Be a damn poor intelligencer if every man knew you were at it, Major."

"Indeed. Well. It is now considerably more widely known than it was, sir, due to the public scrutiny of these incidents. Which was, I fear, the intent."

"And you reckon, what? Your man came across persons unknown up to no good in the warehouses and strangled him to stop him raising the alarm?"

Russell paused. "No, sir. I think that is how he wishes it to seem. The watchman was strangled with my hair ribbon — a distinctive thing, a wedding favour of my wife's that she had taken pains to embroider with sprigs of rosemary and I begin to wonder if someone chose the weapon because it was mine and known to be mine, rather than for expediency. And as an aside, my lord, I should like it back, if such a thing were possible?"

"Even though it were a murder weapon, Major? 'Odsblood, but you're a cold fish!"

"Love is stronger than death," Russell said fiercely. "I lost it, I can tell you the very night I lost it, it was at a supper party where half the Court was there and any one of them could have picked it up and marked it as mine, if they were so minded. So yes — I begin to believe that it is a man in your cousin's service who moves against me, which — it troubles me, sir for I can only think I am marked for a thing I am not. What I am, my lord, is a retired supply officer, a husband, and a, I pray God, a father, soon. I am not an intriguer. Not anymore."

Rupert blinked those crow-black eyes, slowly. "Major Russell," he said blandly, "are you suggesting that I might be in a position to direct my cousin's gaze elsewhere? Do you presume so much, sir?"

Russell blinked back at him, equally blandly, thanking God for that cicatrice in his cheek that made it perfectly possible to look inscrutable whilst his guts were in a quaking knot. "I, my lord? I suggest no such thing. I — muse. I wonder if someone attaches more importance to me than I merit. I was an intelligencer. I have been removed from that post due to that vicious gossip. I am, if you would have it so, harmless. Worthless, almost, save to my wife. I mean to do no more than to return to Buckinghamshire and live in quiet seclusion —" He was perhaps laying it on too heavily, so he stopped and cocked his head brightly, looking at the spot where Rupert's eyebrows met. "You might, perhaps, be in a position to pass on that information into a sympathetic ear?"

"My lord Downing?" Rupert suggested.

There was a long pause. That bloody French clock was still ticking brightly into the silence and Russell could willingly have thrown the damnable thing into the fire. "I think I am no friend to Sir George," Russell said eventually, because he must say something. "I —"

"Wonder if perhaps someone has been passing in information to Sir George already," the Prince said, reaching out and stroking the rim of his coffee-cup with a delicate forefinger. "I believe that my lord Downing is hot for the war, Major Russell. Now tell me. Are you?"

Russell did not know how to answer that. "I am not a traitor, sir."

"Which is not the question I asked. But is an answer. You think then that someone seeks to discredit you with George Downing, who may be my nephew's spymaster, but is not your master? Interesting."

"I — yes. Possibly. I don't — I don't know, in all truth. I do not think Master Jephcott was strangled because he saw too much. I think the intent was always to kill him." His cheek was locking up on him again, his voice starting to slur now, because this was not a thing he had said aloud, either. "It mirrors my sister's death, d'you see? She was done to death in a fire. At Four Ashes. And that bloody fool Charles Fairmantle had made this common currency when I first came back to Court after some time in — in service elsewhere."

"In Europe?" Rupert said.

Russell nodded abruptly. "Antwerp, to be specific. So I had not known of her death until — then. Charles is — he was — my neighbour, in Buckinghamshire. And an utter bloody fool. If brains were gunpowder that rattle-brain would not have sufficient to blow his hat off." He shuddered. "Which is unkind in me. He is a harmless ninny and he has been nothing but kindness itself to Thomazine and I throughout this time. I just wish he would mind his own business and not look on every man's misfortune as his own personal gossip-mill... Well. He did not mean harm, but he did harm. Every man and his dog knows my personal affairs. And someone has made use of that information to oust me as an —"

"Agent," Rupert finished.

"There was not a mark on my Persephone, who is known to deal with the Dutch East India Company. But the Ariadne will be out of the water for the better part of six months till they make her good again and that's before they can even start fitting her out for her next voyage. That's a lot of trade to lose for our East Indiamen, for she'll lose the fair weather and I doubt she'll leave Wapping until next spring, once the autumn gales set in. I am not always a soldier, sir. I find commerce endlessly fascinating: God willing, there will be peace in my lifetime and I would have a trade to follow when there is no more need for soldiers."

"Intelligencing is a trade, Major Russell," Rupert said.

"Surely. And no trade for a gentleman with a wife and a family."

"Ah? I was under the impression that your courtship was very much the blind for your intelligencing, sir. I liked to think that the lovely Thomazine had been much taken with — now, what was it, that Killigrew was squawking about so horribly — a lacquer box, was it? From China?"

Russell closed his mouth with a snap. "Japan. Bought her a little jade hare — now that's precious — too."

"Ah. Now this —" Rupert stroked the figured silk of his dressing-gown with a tender forefinger — "this is from China. Pretty trinket, no? Remind me, next time I get sight of any, I'll send her a length. D'you want to take it up again?"

For a minute Russell thought he meant the box, or the dressing-gown and said nothing.

"Do you want your post back, Major? Though possibly not working for Master Killigrew this time, but direct to the Admiralty. In an unofficial capacity, you understand. As an administrator or similar. You know the trick. You've fiddled enough books in your time to know the way of it."

"I have not!" Russell yelped, nettled, and Rupert's lean, dark face broke into a slow grin.

"I hoped you'd say that."

Thomazine had watched the straight tail of Russell's barley-pale hair, so distinctive against all those monstrous curled periwigs, until he was out of sight.

He could not mean it, of course. He could not mean that she must go straight home for she had to tell Chas Fairmantle or burst — well, apart from anything else, she had to let Chas know that he might start to noise it abroad that someone had made a fatal mistake and it would make him happy to know that his friend was exonerated. And so as soon as Russell was gone from her sight she caught Deb and they escaped to Birstall House — unannounced, unceremoniously, but with tidings of great joy.

But it didn't make Fairmantle happy. It made him very angry and that was a thing she had never seen before and it scared her a little, as she stood in his drawing room. She was not dressed for formal visiting and she was flushed and sweaty and her hair was coming a little unpinned, and she only had Deb for company, but that was how it was in Essex — and, she presumed, in Buckinghamshire: if you had an errand, or a matter of some import that you must tell a neighbour, you did not stand on ceremony for the doing of it, but went, like a person of sense. He was not dressed for formal visiting, either, but was in his undress, wearing an embroidered cap over his close-polled head and a long, padded chamber robe lined with pink and white striped satin.

"Well, that is not how it is in London, madam!" Fairmantle snapped at her, "and the sooner you realise that the better it will be, for you draw attention to yourself!"

"But this is important!" Thomazine snapped back at him.

"Indeed, and you not bringing the eye of half the world to my threshold is important, madam, I have business to transact!" Then his face softened and he looked down, looking almost ashamed of his outburst. "I'm sorry, Mistress Russell, but you have been much on my mind lately and I can help you no further, I think."

"But Chas —"

"No, dear, I mustn't. And I think I must be Master Fairmantle or Lord Birstall from now on."

"But I don't —"

"I know you don't, dear. And that's why it must be." He sighed and gave her a rueful smile. "Oh, there, now, you're looking at me like a kicked puppy and that breaks my heart. Come. Sit down, and — how does that old poem go, now? Since there's no help, come let us kiss and part. We are, I hope, still friends?"

"I do not understand," she said firmly. "Should we not be?"

He rang the little bell over the mantelpiece, his pink face reflected drooping in the big gilt mirror there.

"I imagine I should call for a dish of tea, shouldn't I? Or something fashionable? But you, my little country mouse, would like a mug of warmed ale or a similar rustic pleasure, I imagine. You never really have taken to the metropolis, have you?"

"I should like to try tea," she said. And then, "But not if it is any trouble to you, my lord."

He gave the order for it. He was right, of course, she would have preferred ale: her mother's, warm and a little spiced. Not that she was going to tell Lord Birstall why her stomach was in need of settling, not if he was minded to cast their friendship aside. The tea was not that marvellous, but she sipped it politely from its shallow dish, fragile as a thrush's eggshell. "We have dishes like this at home," she said coolly, in case he thought she was so much of a country mouse she did not even know real China porcelain when she saw it. "They were a wedding gift."

"Well, you have some very generous friends." Fairmantle smiled and sat down on one of the stiff, upholstered chairs opposite her. "Now, dear. I have cudgelled my poor brains to think of a way round this, but I am glad you have decided to make an informal call — a very informal call, dear," he said reprovingly, taking in her mud-splattered skirts and pattens, "it saves me the trouble of attending on you. A thing I should rather not do, I fear."

"What have I done?" Her voice sounded like a hurt child's and she tossed her head, wanting to look as if she did not care.

"You have done nothing, bless you. Oh, dear, what a tangle. And I had grown so fond of you, dear. Well. Mistress Russell, you should never have married that man," Fairmantle said and his lips pursed into a little pink drawstring of disapproval.

"I beg your pardon!"

"Well. You did, you have, and there it is, we have made our beds and we must lie on them. He is a sweetheart, madam, in his way. But you should never have married him."

Thomazine surged to her feet and did not care that the fragile dish slopped its fragrant contents over her skirts. "I will thank you not to speak of my husband in that way!"

"Oh, sit down, madam. I'm sorry, Mistress Russell, I am a member of Parliament and I am, I flatter myself, a man of some standing in society and I cannot continue to lend countenance to a murderer. No matter how fond I may be of his wife."

She wondered if this was how it felt to faint — not a thing she had ever done in her healthy life, but suddenly it felt as if her head were as empty as a bubble, all her skin shrinking cold on her bones —

And then she was sitting down again, with no idea how she got there and Fairmantle rubbing her hands anxiously between his own chubby, slightly sticky, fingers. "Oh my poor girl — my poor girl I did not mean — oh dear —"

"He is not a murderer," she said and all the stiffness came out of her suddenly, like a starched cap dropped in a puddle and her eyes and her nose began to run simultaneously. "He is not, Chas, he's not, and you know he's not! And that's what I came to tell you, he isn't, he isn't, he can't be —"

He did not touch her, other than to carry on holding her hands, gingerly. "Thomazine —"

"He did not hurt that poor man," she sobbed, "and we can prove that he did not, there is a doctor, a man in the Royal Society, he said he could prove it, he had evidence, real proof that could not be argued — Thankful is turning it over to the authorities even as we speak, to investigate properly, to clear his name once and for all —"

He hushed her, gently, as you might a fractious child. "I know he did not, dear. I know he did not and he could not. But Thomazine — oh, my poor girl — this is what I have agonised over, dear. He *did* kill his sister."

She said nothing, for she had no answer to that, she felt as if all the air and all the words had been punched out of her and her fingers crept all involuntary to her wedding ring. She saw his throat move as if he choked a little on something.

"I have known him — well, all our lives, you see, and he was always — I pitied him, poor boy that he was, I pity him still, do not think for one minute that this is easy. She — his sister — you know she was older than he? That she had the care of him since he was a small, a very small, boy. Barely lisping his first prayers, the poor mite. She was — she was zealous, I think you know. He has said. She was more zealous than perhaps is — natural, or normal, for a woman to be. And she hurt him."

Thomazine could not breathe. She could only stare.

"She hurt him very badly, dear. Some people might say she tortured him, poor little chap. And we all knew of it, everyone knew that she was cruel to him, that she — she made him a little mad, I think. More than a little. There is only so much torment a little boy might bear, you see, before he might — well. He thought, in the end, that he deserved it, what she did to him. That he was a bad, horrible, worthless little boy and that he did not deserve to be loved. I was at school with him, dear. I grew up with him. I wanted to be his friend —" Rather horribly, Fairmantle's eyes were filling with tears, too, and his hands were trembling. "You have no idea how much I wanted to befriend him, the poor lost soul, but he would never let me. Oh, Thomazine, he was so lonely, you have no idea, he would stand watching us at play, and he did not know — he would just stand, staring at us, with those dreadful greedy eyes and we would never let him in, and I am so, so sorry: I am sorrier than you could ever imagine that we did not let him be one of us, for he would have grown up with —"

He squeezed her hand very tight and gulped. "You know all this, dear, I think. He grew up a very sad and very lonely, little boy, with no more idea of loving than a beast of the field. I probably don't know most of what she did to him. He never told. He doesn't, does he? And — oh, Thomazine, I am so sorry. They hated each other at the end and he killed her, so that she could not carry on hurting him. He was frightened. I think he has always been frightened. That she would tell you what a bad, horrible, worthless child he had been and what a horrible, worthless man you were married to, and —" he seemed to shrink a little — "I cannot blame him, dear, for if she had been my sister I should have killed her years ago. She was a dreadful woman and I cannot blame him for it, but —"

He blinked at her, wet-eyed, and squeezed her hand again. "I think we need a drink, dear. Not tea. For myself, I think I stand in need of a restorative."

He stood up and took a turn about the room, stopping in front of her so that when she raised her head her eyes were on a level with the silver filigree buttons on his straining waistcoat. "You know he doesn't love you, don't you? He would, if he could — poor soul, he wants nothing more than to be — to be like other men, but she took all that away from him. He feigns it, because of all things he has learned how to dissemble — to appear like any other man, as if he thinks and feels just like any of us, but he doesn't, Thomazine, he can't. He doesn't know how to. And it doesn't matter how much you love him, because it can't be enough. It can never be enough. Like pouring water into a hole, dear — and I've tried, God knows I have tried, to stand his friend, but he will not let me."

Her face felt stiff and numb, as if it was made of marble. She had to remember how to move her lips, her tongue. "I." The oddest shrinking feeling about her bones, a cold, prickling sensation. "I know it. I know of her. She —"

Fly Coventry had not broken him. She had not. Thomazine would not have it so.

"How can it be enough, Thomazine?" he said sadly. "You deserve better than a man who will not love you. He will not ever love you. He has not the capacity."

It would be enough. Because she was a daughter of blood and fire and born when the world was turned upside down and she did not retreat. Not ever. It did not have to be a storybook love. She'd never took much to Sir Lancelot anyway. She lifted her head and looked squarely into Charles Fairmantle's moist, doggy eyes and she said, "He will. He does. That will be his revenge, sir. To be loved." And she almost believed it.

"You will stand by him?"

"Always," she said and it was starting to come easier. It was someone else's voice coming out of her mouth, but they were her thoughts at least.

He nodded. "I am fond of you, Thomazine. Were I not — did I not think we were truly friends — I would not tell you this. I feel sorry for Thankful, I feel dreadful that I knew what was done to him as a child and I did nothing, but it must stop. I cannot stand by and allow him to continue. I can't. I — well, if you had been unhappy, if he had treated you ill I should have helped, I would have given you money, found you a place, but —"

"I am well content, my lord. My husband —"

"Thomazine, I have spent the last quarter-hour very delicately trying not to tell you, and since you are determined to stay set on your misguided course: if you will have it in plain linen, mistress, if you persist in being obtuse, I will give it to you in plain words — your husband is a spy for the Dutch, my lady," he said stiffly.

She bridled. "He is not —"

"Will you listen to me! Do you understand nothing of what I've been telling you? That woman twisted him, she warped his loyalties, his honour, his —"

"That is not true!" she shouted back.

"Is it not, madam? Is it not? Then you will not mind, my lady, if I pass what I know to the authorities, either, will you? About how a retired Army officer on half pay might afford silks and porcelains and all manner of pretty things from his friends in Europe — he has never changed, Thomazine, can you not see that? He has never changed and he will never change, he is exactly the same damnable anarchist he was twenty years ago!" Fairmantle's face had grown red and he was leaning down into her face, but she wasn't afraid of him.

"Then I am glad you consider our friendship at an end, my lord, because I certainly do! How dare you — how dare you call him a traitor —"

"Because he isn't, mistress, not in his head, can you not see that? That is what I am saying to you! He is possibly the most fiercely loyal man I have ever known. He has never changed his loyalties, madam. Since — since Edgehill, I'll warrant! He is still loyal to his, his bloody puritanical, Dissenting, republican roots — well, I cannot stand by and let him do it, Mistress Russell, and I will not. I give you two days to make a decision: he either leaves this country and takes refuge with his dubious political friends on the Continent — and I will say no more of it — or he remains here and I hand over what I know to His Majesty. I know he killed his sister and I know he burned her body to hide his crime and God alone knows what else he might have done, Thomazine, for I fear there may be no end to his hunger for — for vengeance, mistress, I think he hates the world for what it has done to him, poor child that he was, but I must see justice done, can you understand that? I cannot keep this to myself any longer. For I fear — I very much fear, by the nature of the crime at Wapping, that someone else knows it, too. And for his own sake — and for your sake, dear, to save you from the shame of it — well, I must. And I hope you will forgive me for it."

She stood up. "You may do as you see fit, my lord. I will see myself out." And without looking back, twitching her skirts aside that she might not even have to touch the air around him, she stalked past the outraged butler and two scared footmen in the echoing marble hall and out into the street with her head up and Deb white and shaking behind her.

She held herself together for about a quarter of a mile and then she whirled and collapsed, sobbing, into Deb's arms and mistress and maid clung together weeping in the street while London whirled about them.

16

Thomazine sat in the kitchen, forlornly nibbling on a crust, with her mind in a miserable turmoil. Too fretful to think, even if she could have set her thoughts in order, she waited for Russell to come home because she knew it was not true, it was all a horrible lie.

It was a horrible lie that had been told to her by a man she had liked and trusted and who had been Thankful's friend all his life.

It was a lie that had its roots in what she knew to be truth and so she did not know what to think anymore, except that nothing was what she had thought it was and it made her head ache.

The Bartholomew-baby was on his feet and she watched him, idly, as he tottered under the legs of the table, purposefully pursuing a ball of rags across the kitchen. A nice little boy, sturdy, with fine dark hair that grew long enough to curl to ringlets on the back of his neck and little bracelets of fat at his wrists. He could not have been less like tall, slight, fair Thankful, whose pale hair was thick and as straight as a yard of pump water — whose features were delicately bony, not blunt and snub-nosed — who looked, at first glance, so frail and ascetic. An appealing child, the Bartholomew-baby. A happy, unquestioning child, content with his lot.

"Thomazine —" The street door flung open, quite unannounced, to admit her husband, windblown and mud-spattered and radiating excitement like a banked fire. He was aware of Jane Bartholomew's presence, he nodded politely to her and said something suitable, but had no more registered

217

her existence than he had registered the existence of the furniture. "Zee, you'll never guess —"

But the person who took most notice of him was, God have mercy, the Bartholomew-baby. He looked up, startled, his little round face crumpling in dismay, as the door opened; wobbling on his fat feet, rocking to and fro, his starfish-hands splayed in a desperate entreaty for balance, snatching at the air and finding no purchase, he had gone sprawling into the flames headlong.

His mother screamed, once. Thomazine was out of her seat so quickly the stool rocked and fell, but the child's skirts were already smouldering, the kitchen full of the sickening smell of burned hair, the little boy's screams of agony rising to a piercing pitch.

Even before Thomazine's seat had rocked back onto its three legs, Thankful had dived into the hearth and rolled the struggling little body in a fierce, stifling embrace. The note of the boy's screams had changed almost immediately, from agonised to afraid and hurting, beating with his fists against Thankful's rain-wet coat, where the pair of them lay half-sprawled in the hot ashes.

Jane Bartholomew was shaking. "Daniel," she said, in a small voice. "Daniel."

Russell was also shaking, holding the child far too tight.

"You're hurting him," the widow said wildly. "He is afraid, the lambkin, he wants his mammy —"

She plucked him from Russell's hands, the both of them sobbing now. The little boy was holding up his blistered fingers, not wanting them to be kissed better, still screaming. Hurt and frightened, inconsolably so, but — whole. "Thank you," Jane wept, "oh, you silly little boy — thank you so very much — you foolish infant, I have told you and told you, not so close!"

She whirled from the room in a flurry of skirts to fret over the most precious thing left in her world, leaving Thomazine with her husband: white-faced and stunned and shaking, blinking as if he did not believe himself what had just happened. He stared at her for a minute and then was suddenly and noisily sick into the embers of the fire.

She wanted to say any number of things. Instead, she took hold of his wrists, careful of his poor burned hands, and helped him out of the ashes. She brushed his hair back from his face and did not mind that the ends of it were singed off, or that his poor scarred cheek was pockmarked with burns. For he, too, was afraid and in sore need of comfort. She put her arms around him and held him against her breast and rocked him and said silly nothing-words until he stopped shaking.

He was afraid of fire.

He did not have an ordinary man's healthy respect for the flames, he was miserable, sick-afraid of it — of burning. He had nightmares of it. He had still thrown himself across the kitchen to pull that little boy clear. She had no words to ask why he might do that and yet he looked up at her through his ragged hair with eyes that were puffy and black-smeared and he said, "She burned me, Zee. Not much older than him." He gagged, retched, sat shaking again, panting with his mouth open. "Fly held my hands in the fire. To punish me. I was —" he had to stop, his teeth chattering — "was a little boy. Like that. And she hurt me."

Fly Coventry had taken her little brother's hands, when he was no more than a tiny toddling boy, and she had held them in the kitchen fire in punishment for some childish sin until his fingers had blistered and burned like a joint of meat. That thought made Thomazine's own mouth go dry and she could not speak for rage against a woman who had been dead and buried this twelve months, who had died in the most horrible way imaginable.

Russell buried his head in the curve of her shoulder and wept. "How could I let that happen to another child?" he said. "It hurt. It hurt so much. How could I?"

In the room next door, in that little, overstuffed room where Jane Bartholomew's married life was squeezed into half her house, her son was settling. Through the thin plaster his screams were dying to pitiful sobs, to hiccups.

"I love you," Thomazine said and the tears ran down her own cheeks unheeded, for that long-ago little boy, who had been hurt and who had not been loved. And she hoped it would be enough.

Thomazine would have told him what had happened, but she didn't want to distress him any further.

"Thomazine," he said, after a while. He still sounded shaky, but better. Steadier. Slightly muffled. "I'm sorry."

"Don't be sorry." He smelt of burnt hair and she bent and put her cheek against the top of his head. "It's not your fault."

"No. But I'm sorry you saw it."

He sat up and scrubbed his hands through his hair, wincing a little at the frayed ends. "Well. Now you know."

It would have been the perfect time, she thought afterwards. Now she knew why he had never spoken of his childhood. He had not shut her out. It was not a secret, or yet a conspiracy. He had not told her because he did not want to remember it and that made her sad. But it made her the more determined that their child should grow up happy and loved.

Then the widow came out of her own rooms with the Bartholomew-baby wobbling at her side, all fat and red and tearstained but beaming like a sunrise with that childish ability to forget hurt almost straightaway and Russell got to his feet and stood looking at the child with his hands behind his back.

"Well, sir, how do you fare?" he said and he sounded all awkward and shy and her heart quite turned over in her chest for loving him, for he had no idea how to be easy with children and he was trying so very hard. "Are you quite mended?"

The little boy looked at him suspiciously and Thomazine crossed to his side quickly before there were tears — from either party, for she suspected that her strained, over-weary husband might be minded to weep too, if the child was afraid of him. "Show me your hands, sweeting," she said, "show Zee?"

He put his little chubby fingers up and said, "Burn," solemnly.

Russell huffed and sat on his heels beside Thomazine and peered at the boy with more intensity than was possibly comforting to an infant, for the child shrank against his mother's skirts with his poor blistered fingers in his mouth.

"Daniel, do not trouble the Major —"

"I'd like to be troubled, mistress," Russell said. He glanced up at Thomazine, as though she might be angry with him for saying so. "I shall need the practice, you see."

And of course that suddenly diverted that sombre, fearful gathering into celebration, with Deb and the kitchen-girl pressed into service to run out and get feasts of fat things and the Bartholomew-baby bundled into Russell's lap whilst his mother and Thomazine whirled into impromptu gaiety and the evening ended with Thomazine's health drunk in good homely lambswool and wedges of bread and toasted cheese.

It was not, at all, what Thomazine had grown accustomed to these last months. It was not clever or witty or elaborate, but the company was sweet and the kitchen was warm and on a chilly evening in late spring it was the finest thing in the world to sit and talk and laugh with friends, to hold a wriggling baby or a cat in your lap, to hold your husband's hand between your own.

And not to be afraid. For once, not to mind what you said. To talk of things that mattered — real things, that were comfortable, that you could pick up and hold. The price of salt fish. Whether the baker in Pudding Lane gave better quality than the baker in the market at Leadenhall. How much rain they were having and how awkward it was to get clothes dry in such weather. How much notice the widow would require to pack her things and come to Buckinghamshire with them, when this was all done, to keep their house and run it with the same fearsome efficiency with which she ran this one. If there were any decent families of Russell's acquaintance of the captains and ships' masters at Wapping, who might wish to rent the house on Fenchurch Street. It was possibly not an elegant enough residence for any of his mercantile acquaintances, but it was a good, stout, well-appointed house, and did he wish that the furnishings should come to Four Ashes, or might they stay with the house?

Russell said he would ask questions in the morning and what did it mean when the child made such ferociously intent grunting noises, did the boy ail, what should Russell do to ease him. Thomazine sniffed, delicately, and suggested that the young gentleman had already eased himself and might benefit from a change of linen. To which Thomazine's beloved held the young man in question at arm's length with a look of some resignation and suggested that he might himself benefit from a change of linen, feeling somewhat damp about the breast.

It was a happy, ordinary, uncomplicated evening and as close as Thomazine had been to home since she had left Essex. And looking at Russell, with his fair head bent over the child's feathery dark one, she thought he began to feel the same way.

It was a promise of spring. And she forgot, in the warmth of that promise, what business she should have tended to, pushing it to the back of her mind.

Russell slept badly that night, whimpering and twitching in his sleep, coming awake blank with nightmares of burning.

That was when Thomazine remembered.

He could no more have burned that woman than he could have flown to the moon. Oh, she would have believed he could have killed her — and she imagined there were a number of people who might have held his coat while he did it, too. Thomazine's head was tight with rage at just the thought of what the godly bitch had put that poor long-ago little boy through. Fly-Fornication Coventry had stolen much from her little brother: his hope, his joy, his childhood, his faith. But more than that, she had stolen any ability he had ever had to deal with fire at close hand. He could not have burned her: he probably would have loved to, if he could, but he couldn't. Physically, he could not. He was too afraid of fire, she had seen it tonight, he would have been sick and shaking with it.

And if Master bloody Fairmantle wanted to try and blame him for that one, he could whistle. He was wrong. Utterly, utterly wrong, and she could prove it, and Charles Fairmantle could tattle to whoever he liked and she would tell him so, because fire was not her husband's weapon of choice. Cold steel was Russell's particular weapon; either in his hand, or in his backbone, and Master Fairmantle was going to find that one out if he persisted in his misguided beliefs.

She smiled into Russell's chest and wriggled a little for joy.

Thomazine was still smiling in the morning and promised Russell good things for supper and that she would come to his offices at the dock at noon to spend an hour in idle marketings like any country goodwife.

He went to his work with a rather dazed look of happiness, whistling a very reproachable little tune he'd picked up in the streets somewhere.

She sat down in the kitchen — if that overstuffed ninny wanted formality she would give him formality and be damned to him — and she wrote a very curt little note to Master Fairmantle requesting a few moments of his time at a convenient hour this morning on a matter of some import. Thomazine sent her note, asking a boy from two doors up whom the widow had taken to asking to run errands, since the murders. She asked him to wait for a reply — on promise of an extra penny for his time — and to run all the way home with it.

And then she waited.

"Well, madam?"

Fairmantle was beaming at Thomazine, as if yesterday afternoon had never happened and she longed to slap his beefy, stupid face for him. "May I offer you a dish of tea, Mistress Russell? See — we can retain the elegancies of friendship without laying ourselves quite so open to unwarranted intrusion as previous."

"Thank you, my lord, I would prefer not to trespass on your time. Or, indeed, to tarnish your reputation further," she added with a glower she couldn't quite help.

"Oh, don't take it to heart so, dear! Only think, madam. I am a respectable member of London society, an eminent public figure with a seat in Parliament. Do be sensible. How might it look if I am known to be intimate with a wife of an intelligencer for the enemy?"

"He isn't," she said flatly.

He nodded and smiled. "Well, you would say so, dear. Commendably loyal, I'm sure. But the problem is, *you* say so, but no one else of note will. He is disgraced — removed from his position: it's common knowledge that he is not wholly to be trusted, madam, and I am very much afraid that the authority of a young lady — a *very* young lady, if I might say so — of a somewhat dubiously republican family herself, will do very little to retrieve it."

"I am not here to have this conversation with you."

He inclined his head graciously. "You see sense then?"

"No, my lord. I am here to tell you that my husband is not, and cannot be, a murderer. And that I can prove it. So, if you choose to persist in what I can only call a blackmail attempt, my lord, you may take your allegation and stick it — as my dubiously republican father would say — where the Lord's grace does not shine. I'm calling you on it, my lord."

His face went as blank as a doll's for a second. "You cannot mean — Mistress Russell, you cannot intend —"

"On the contrary, sir. Be my guest. Go to the authorities with what evidence you have. My husband went yesterday and laid his case before the Justice — that his name is being unjustly maligned by someone for their own ends. I believe it is slander, my lord. I imagine that if he were to bring a suit against the person who is behind it, that person would be. Well. Very awkwardly placed, indeed, given my husband's friendship with Prince Rupert."

"Oh, madam, don't be ridiculous! I can prove that he —"

"And I can prove he is not, sir. And so can Doctor Willis."

"How?" Fairmantle demanded. She had the distinct impression he didn't like being challenged. "How might Doctor Willis, who has no intimate knowledge of your husband's family, prove anything?"

She sat back in her chair and folded her arms. "My lord, it is not necessary to have intimate knowledge of the living to defend a man."

"Meaning?"

"Meaning that my husband could not set a fire to save his life. He's terrified of it, sir. She made him so. And you could set him in front of any courtroom in the land and he would still shy off, were you to put a naked flame before him. He owns it himself. So he could not have killed his sister, my lord Birstall — or rather, he could have, but he would not have chosen fire to do it. And if he could not have burned her, under that provocation, no more could he have set the fire at Wapping docks where there was none. So that bird will not fly, sir. If he did not do those things, your evidence that he is a spy is no more than a cobweb."

"People will still talk, madam!"

She raised her head. "Then let them, sir. Let them prattle. If he had killed that man at the dockside he would have shown the marks of a struggle on his body. That poor man would also have marks and they would show the nature of his murderer — of what shape and size he was. There are no marks of a struggle on my husband's hands, sir, I may assure you. But there will be on someone's. No, we will not be flying to his friends — his decent, godly, respectable merchant friends, who are good people, who sent us wedding gifts and ask after our welfare — in Amsterdam for refuge, for we have no need. The truth will out, sir. So be my guest. Take your paltry evidence to the authorities and may the Devil fly away with it and you!"

Fairmantle stood up and took a deep breath and shook out the skirts of his coat. He was angry: his face had mottled an unhealthy rose and his lips had tightened out of that customary friendly smile, but he was trying to hide it and doing a good job of it, as he came and stood beside her, setting his hand on her shoulder in what she thought he imagined was a friendly, pacifying gesture.

She looked down at it in contempt. At the yellowing bruises on his white wrists and the half-healed, black gouges of a dying man's desperate scrabbles as those sturdy white fingers choked off his life.

She did not speak, she dared not lest her voice betray her, but she could not stop her eyes from widening in fear.

"Oh, Thomazine," Charles Fairmantle said gently and he stroked her throat with his knuckle and she felt the rough drag of torn skin where Thomas Jephcott's fingernails had torn his skin. "Why could you not have gone when I asked?"

The most frightening thing was he still sounded like himself, still sounded kind and cheerful, even as his hands closed around her neck.

17

Deb sat, and waited, and looked at her feet, and waited. She could hear voices — Thomazine's voice raised and she winced, because if Thomazine wanted to pass without comment in the city she must not act the country maid.

There was a long silence. The bell tinkled faintly in the echoing stillness of the house. An early fly bumped against the kitchen glass.

It was a quiet house, not full of noise and bustle like the house in Essex, or the sounds of the construction site at Four Ashes. It was a formal house, where everyone knew their place and pleasant country maid Deb was neither fish nor fowl, neither a proper ladies' maid nor a menial kitchen-hand but somewhere in between, a woman who was to be placed in the kitchen and left there until such time as she was needed.

She waited.

It seemed that Lord Birstall was dining out this evening. It was a source of great irritation to the cook, as they had just sent a maid out marketing for what had been meant as something of an elaborate little private feast, and now all would go to waste. This left Deb none the wiser, and so she waited some more, watching the sunlight creep across the kitchen floor.

The clock chimed, telling her she had been here almost two hours. It was not like Thomazine to be so forgetful of the maid who had served her since she was a little girl.

It had fairly spoiled Russell's temper, being kept waiting. He tried to think that Thomazine was just delayed, a press of traffic, an interesting thing in the market. He tried to think of petty, unkind things, because he wanted to believe that his wife preferred to buy ribbons than to meet him, or that she had a lover, or that he was of so little account to her that she had just forgotten. If he did not believe those things he might instead start to think of a racing carriage, rocking across the cobbles at a horrible breakneck speed, or of an embroidered ribbon wrapped choking around a man's throat, and the smell of burning silk —

Russell inhaled sharply through his nose, snuffing the bitterness of ink and tar instead and bent to his ledger again.

Thinking — absently — of the Kingdom of Cochin and Master Brouwer's consideration of the new Dutch regime there, twelve months in, and what that might mean for one small merchant in landlocked Buckinghamshire. He wondered if one day he might have a big enough ship to see Cochin for himself. The Perse was fit to make the crossing of the North Sea, wallowing like a laden cart between here and the Hook of Holland, she was solid and sure as a market-day mule, but —

One day. Maybe. To see the forests and the wonders — to walk in the Indies, or Cathay and see the things the sailors spoke of, the unicorns and the great whales and the strange and fantastic things from the bestiaries —

The Perse needed to be outfitted, he would have her go out again before the summer. The wool trade was picking up again in Europe and he thought maybe the Admiralty needed to know about that, because he wondered if it might make more sense if he were to be shipping fleece out soon. His own, likely, from Four Ashes, but he didn't think Master Pepys needed to know that. He was possibly the least inconspicuous smuggler in the south of England and it made him laugh that they let him do it. It would make Thomazine laugh, too, he suspected: she'd called him a pirate more than once and he thought she was quite coming round to the idea. But he needed to not think about Thomazine. About where she was. He would not give in to it, he would not go home, hours early, at two of the clock, because then she would know —

He had added up the same column three times and come to a different total each time.

Time to surrender, he thought.

Thomazine wasn't there. Deb said they had gone to Birstall House, but that Lord Fairmantle had taken her up in his carriage, to which Russell had replied, rather tartly, that he had not seen fit to put her down then, had he? — which had made the homely little Essex woman weep, because she was worried sick and the fact of placid and competent Deb in tears made Russell more frightened than possibly anything else had ever in his life.

He had smiled — which probably hadn't reassured anyone, he thought — and gone upstairs and changed from his plain working-clothes into something more sensible for visiting Master Fairmantle: a brace of pistols, a well-worn cavalry backsword and a palpable bad temper.

"If she comes home," he said sweetly, "Mistress Bartholomew, you are to lock her in her chamber and feed her nothing but bread and water."

Both Deb and the widow were sufficient worried that they were paying him no mind whatsoever. The widow nodded at him absently. She was bustling, purposelessly, like a bee in a bottle and that was going to drive him mad if he did not get out.

And then he thought of Thomazine, of her dear not-quite-pretty face, her level eyes all bright with love and humour and aliveness: he summoned her, in his head, the look and the feel and the smell of her.

"Hold fast, tibber," he said aloud. "Hold fast, dear love. I'm coming for you."

If she was not at Birstall House there was only one other place she was likely to be — with Fairmantle, while he was buzzing round the Earl of Rochester like a fly round a turd, craving Wilmot's notice.

To give Wilmot credit, he never turned a hair, disturbed at his breakfast — at three of the clock, the depraved young wastrel. He looked up with his glass in his hand and he said, quite sweetly, "I'm sure I don't know, Caliban. Where did you last have her?"

"She was with you!"

"No, she isn't. Why d'you think she's here?"

"She left to meet bloody Fairmantle! And he's not at home, so —"

"Language, dear, language," Wilmot said and twirled his wine glass by the stem. "You won't catch me using foul language in polite company."

"I am likely to become considerably less polite company, sir, if you do not stop fencing with me!"

Two pairs of dark, level eyes met and neither dropped.

"So you believe me to be abetting your wife in some sort of liaison with Charles Fairmantle, sir?" Wilmot sounded amused. "I quit your lady of so shameful a lack of personal taste, Caliban. A lack of discretion, perchance and surely a lack of common sense, or I'm sure she'd never have married you, but—"

231

Russell was proud of himself at that moment. Twenty years ago he'd probably have punched the Earl of Rochester in the head, repeatedly. He was an older and wiser man now and instead he drew his sword and rested the tip of it on the table, so that the shadow of it fell in a purposeful straight line across the frigid linen, pointing like an arrowhead at Wilmot's groin. "Don't piss me about," he said. "I'm not in the mood. Where's Thomazine?"

Wilmot glanced down and cocked an eyebrow. "I swear to you, Major. On whatever you choose, since I doubt you'd believe me if I swore in God's name — I swear to you, may my sceptre never serve me again if I lie. I have not seen the girl." He stood up and straightened his cuffs. "Despite what Master Fairmantle would like you to think, he is not a permanent resident in my establishment. For which I am more grateful than you will ever know, sir. So, assuming that he has not crawled into my privy and is even now locked in adoring contemplation of the contents, where is the creature?"

"Not at home."

"Master Fairmantle is very often not at home, Major — or claiming not to be, in the hope of feigning popularity. Are you sure he was not there?"

"Unless he was hiding under the bed, my lord, yes!"

"Now you're being silly," Wilmot said reprovingly. "Why on earth would a wench of some good sense choose to spend time with that dreadful, witless man? When she could be at home with another dreadful —"

Russell was not going to bite this time. "She thought he might be of service."

"Well, I imagine there's a first time for everything!"

"She thought he might be in a position to gossip —"

"Charles Fairmantle, gossip? Surely not, Major!"

Russell took a deep breath. "Gossip that we directed, sir, rather than whatever malevolent imp of mischief has been slinking around London telling the world that I have a habit of murdering my relatives!"

"My dear man," Wilmot said coolly, "that rumour *came* from Master Fairmantle. He is your next door neighbour, sir, he ought to know."

For a minute Russell could not speak. "He put it about that I had most foully murdered my own sister?"

"He has been saying it for months, sir. Not that anyone believed him, of course. I imagine I should get my coat, shouldn't I? You might want to leave yours here, Major. You'll only get blood on the cuffs and I believe it is the very devil to remove from brocade."

"Why would he? Why would he do that?"

"Well, I'm buggered if I know, Caliban. It makes a better story, possibly, and we might pay him some notice — is my guess. Why don't we go back round to his house and ask him? Bring your sword — I imagine you'll be wanting that. Paddle his flabby white arse, if nothing more gentlemanly."

But Russell had a horrible feeling he did know why. He wanted to weep and he wanted to run away, but most of all he wished to God he was the man that Charles Fairmantle had told people he was. Because when he got his hands on that slanderous gossip-monger — that duplicitous, sneaking, spineless lickspittle — he was going to commit murder.

18

"The Earl is not at home," the butler intoned and Russell did not trouble to reply, but walked in anyway, ignoring the man's protests, because he had his sword in his hand and he wasn't in the mood to listen to some squawking lackey. He had Wilmot cheerfully ambling behind him, who was armed to the teeth as well.

"What d'you think, then, Caliban? Shall we look under the beds?"

The Earl was quartering the parlour like a hunting-dog, busily moving the chairs and disarranging the drapery, lifting the lid of a great ornate tobacco-jar and peering inside, sniffing — "How very nasty," he said and dropped the lid onto the hearth, where it burst like an eggshell. He smiled his lovely, angelic smile. "Dear me, I am clumsy, aren't I?"

"Has there been a lady here?"

"No, sir, there has not, I beg you —" the butler stuttered.

Russell cocked his pistol and shot a hole in the rather horrible gilt mirror that reflected the street. He forgot, being slightly deaf in one ear at best, just how appalling the racket was in an enclosed space and how much sheer unbridled mess — of broken glass and silvering and plaster-dust — an intemperate pistol-shot was. In the tinkling silence that followed Fairmantle's butler was staring at them both as if they were dangerous lunatics and Wilmot very carefully picked a long, lethal shard of broken glass from his sleeve.

"Temper, temper," Wilmot said mildly. "Now, then, man. We mean you no harm. What is his name, Caliban?"

"How the bloody hell should I know?"

"Well, the Earl's your friend, dearie! According to him, you practically live here!"

"I can assure you he is not!"

"He puffed himself up that he was, I can promise you that." Wilmot's face went very carefully blank. "Ever since you grew dangerous. How very interesting."

"He made me dangerous that I might be a better subject for his intrigue?"

Wilmot shrugged. "As I said. No man of sense had any regard for it."

"But sufficient bloody fools did that I might be removed from my position!" Russell snapped. "Where is he?"

"He left on official business —" the butler started.

"Was he alone?" Wilmot said delicately. "Did he, in fact, have a fair companion — a —"

"Did he have my wife with him?" Russell said. The butler blanched a little and although his face remained perfectly innocent of any incriminating expression the answer was not one that he wanted to give.

One of the under-footmen wasn't so nice about it, though, and a couple of the likelier looking lads from below-stairs were lurking about the hall wanting to see what all the excitement was about and whether they might get a share of it. They were a bit surprised to see the Earl of Rochester in His Lordship's absence, but there was no accounting for the ways of the gentry — especially not when the gentry in question was the husband of the woman who'd apparently been hanging off the Earl's arm on his way out, earlier, and her with her dress all awry, drunk as a fiddler's bitch. She had been all over the Earl, she had. He'd had to practically carry her to his carriage, to get her out of the house.

Joseph had been given a shilling for his help in bundling her in. He had left her sprawling in sottish oblivion on the seat of the carriage with her skirts hiked around her waist. She had the look of a wench who had been well-pleasured and she cared not a blink when Joseph had had a feel of her pretty red garden, but had groaned aloud with the pleasure of it, lying there with her head lolling on her shoulders and her white throat all printed with kiss-marks.

"No," Wilmot shouted in warning and Russell had not realised he had done anything, that he should be near to choking the life out of one of Fairmantle's servants, let alone to knocking the man's brains out on the newel-post, that his shoulder was all but pulled out of joint by Wilmot trying to wrench him off the man, or that the servant's face should be the colour of raw liver, his eyes bugging from their sockets as he fought for breath.

"Russell, no!"

"You — they —" He was beyond speech, he wanted to growl like a dog. "If she is hurt," he said eventually and it wasn't what he meant, but it was all he could think of the words for, "if she is hurt, sir, if any of you have harmed a hair on her head, I —"

No. No, he would not come back here and burn this vile place to the ground, he would not sow the ashes with salt: he would not make it a haunt of owls and bats and every unclean thing, for God knows there were sufficient unclean things here already. But he would be the sword in her hand while she did it.

"Chatham," the frightened maid — the one who'd had hysterics, by the wan and red-eyed look of her — said, and the butler shot her a look of concentrated venom. "I heard him direct the coachman to Chatham, sir, he has business there."

"He often has business there!" the butler snapped.

"You mean he takes his mistresses there," Russell said and his hand tightened on his sword again. "Tell me, does he often take the unwilling ones, or is my wife just unfortunate?"

They were all staring at him. "Unwilling?" Wilmot said and his lip curled in unconscious contempt. "You mean he has kidnapped your wife? But they were friends, you are friends — This is not just some stupid game to draw my attention?"

That did not even merit an answer and Wilmot knew it.

Kiss marks and drunkenness, by Christ. This was his wife they spoke of, she would not —

"You will be requiring my lord's light carriage," the butler said.

"Oh no," Russell said, "no, I will be requiring his fastest horse. Much faster than a carriage, I find. Don't trouble with a harness, please. I think I shall manage swifter without."

He turned on his heel. He would have probably walked into the door frame for he was not quite sure where he was going, blind with rage and tears. The only thing that was real was the hilt of his sword under his hand, and the fury.

He heard a sigh at his shoulder. "Make that two horses," Wilmot said, with resignation. "And for myself, Caliban, I should prefer a saddle. If I must be cast as a gallant knight-errant for once, I should prefer to arrive without bruises on my arse."

It hurt to breathe and Thomazine's eyes felt dry and bruised, but dear God, not as much as her throat hurt. It felt like she was breathing through boiling sand. But she *was* breathing and that was a thing she was grateful for. The longer she breathed the more the stupid cleared from her swimming head and the more her boiling red-haired temper promised her that nobody throttled Thomazine Babbitt senseless and did not reap the whirlwind.

She ought to be afraid, but she had been brought up in blood and fire with the New Model Army and she was not. She was bloody livid.

"You." She gagged, choked, hawked a great clot of dried blood out of her raw throat and slumped back on the velvet cushions, panting. "You know he will kill you for this. Don't you?"

"I do hope so, dear."

"You. Hope?"

"Thomazine, dear, I have every intention of your husband meaning to kill me. I do not mean that he should succeed, of course. But I do mean that he should try. So, you know, do please feel free to scream and struggle a little when he arrives at our destination. It would add such a lovely touch, I think."

She lunged from her seat and snatched at the window-blind, but then fell back with a sob because the rushing dark outside was just that: dark. The carriage was rocking and swaying, pulled at a full gallop.

"I wouldn't jump, dear," Fairmantle said lazily. "You'd break your neck at this speed."

"What is it to you, you —"

"Well, I don't want you dead, Thomazine. I imagine that even your husband would balk at rescuing a dead woman." He pursed his lips and reached out to lift her chin with his horrible dry-scabbed knuckle, and she cringed back in her seat. "Although it is entirely the kind of foolishness he might countenance of late. I'd never have thought it of him, the silly boy. I should never have imagined him to be capable of such romantic foolery."

"Why?" she said.

"He never was before, dear. And I have known him for thirty years and more, and d'you know what? It seems I barely knew him at all."

It hurt her to speak and yet she had to ask, because it made no sense. "Why me? Are you carrying me off?"

He stared at her in comical shock for a second, as if she had made a lewd suggestion. "Mistress Russell!" he said, bridling. "I have a wife in Buckinghamshire, madam, what do you take me for?"

"Murder. Does not trouble you. But adultery. Does?" She wanted to laugh and instead she had to pant like a dog with her mouth open. This was a bad dream. She would wake up.

"Had you done as I asked, madam, we would not be in this position," he said primly. "I gave you the option of simply leaving the country. I was nothing but fair, Thomazine, you have brought this on yourself."

She shook her head — *Why should I have to fly the country of my birth at your whim?* — and he pursed his lips at her.

"I am very disappointed in you, dear. In both of you, actually. The boy I knew would have just gone away. Even when he was a little boy he would rather have hidden away than been exposed to every scrutiny, which would have been considerably easier on all of us, I may assure you. I do not like this course of action, madam, but you have made it quite unavoidable. Why do you think I looked to Thankful to oblige me in this enterprise? Because up until your arrival, he was the one man I knew who would rather perish than draw attention to himself! Always quite the little Spartan, even as a boy. And the man I knew would have taken his punishment — he would have taken anyone's punishment, dear, he deserves it, in his head, all of it. Well, you have changed him, madam, and I do not like this course of action, but you have made it quite

239

unavoidable. You have been a malign influence on Major Russell, Thomazine. He has grown perfectly reckless, since you married him."

She stared at him and he shook his head.

"Well, I'm sure we have no time for that, dear. I would estimate we will be arriving at Chatham, shortly, and I have much to prepare."

She would have said more, but the carriage was slowing a little and he reached across the carriage and grabbed her shoulders and yanked her roughly so that she fell sprawling across his thighs. While she was struggling with the jerking of the vehicle to get her feet underneath her, he caught her hand — one hand, then the other, in those strong white hands, gripping her wrists twisted behind her back so that the bones ground together. Off-balance, she could only heave and buck, she could not get her legs under her to fight. Her face was pressed into the meat of his thigh and she could not even bite, her teeth could not get a purchase in the rough, loose wool of his breeches. He tasted of sweat and layer on layer of stale scent. She ground her face against the flabby muscle, wanting to set her jaws in like a terrier. Caught. Held. His knee caught her a stunning smack in the face as his body convulsed with pain and she tasted blood, but she held on, meaning to tear, to rend — bite your bloody balls off, you murderous swine —

And then he was wrestling her arms up behind her back and he was brutal, he was cruel and he was meaning to hurt her, the muscles in her shoulders straining in screaming protest as he pinioned her wrists in the small of her back. Something soft was wrapping about them and the flow of blood to her fingers was cut short.

"Not one of your ribbons this time," he said, and she felt his belly heaving with breathlessness against her flank and she hoped the bastard would die of an apoplexy from it. "Pity, for I thought it was a nice touch."

She tried to scream when she was able to free her face from the cloying press of his thigh. She threw her head back and ignored the stab of pain in her bruised neck and she opened her mouth, but he stuffed a handkerchief in, a dry, stinking, dirty handkerchief that sucked all the spit from her mouth and left her choking and fighting to breathe through her bloody nose.

Then he threw her on the floor of the carriage and she saw his teeth flash in a cheerful smile above her before he flung a cloak over her body and set his boot heel on her belly.

"We approach the dockyard, Mistress Russell. Make a sound, dear, and I will crush the life out of that rebel's whelp you have in there."

19

"Sir." The watchman knew Fairmantle, then. Greeted him as if he were a regular visitor. Possibly, by the tone of his voice, not a popular one. "There a problem, my lord?"

"There might be, Bennett. There might be." There was an avidity in Fairmantle's voice that Thomazine had never heard, a horrible slavering greed that made her think of the people who gather around overturned carts and burning houses with their eyes on stalks, feeding on misfortune. "Who else is here?"

One of the horses snorted and she imagined them standing in the chill spring air — had the coachman got down? She didn't think so. She tried to ease her position, she was too tall for this, her legs too long to be bent under her –

His foot pressed down on the curve of her belly again, so that she felt the crescent of his heel bite into the unprotected swell of her flesh.

"What's amiss, my lord?"

"Expecting guests, Bennett. Unwanted guests. A gentleman of my acquaintance — a tall man, fair haired, with a great scar to his face, an ugly customer — I have received intelligence that he plans to set a fire here this night."

Thomazine could not help but squawk in protest and the boot heel came down with such a force that she thought she felt something break and all the breath came out of her.

"D'you hear a noise?" Fairmantle demanded. "Have they come already?"

"No one passed this gate but you, my lord, not since the ropers finished work and that'll be, what, a good three hours past?"

"He is a spy," Fairmantle breathed, "he is in the pay of the Dutch and he means to destroy the ships laid up here so that his masters may walk in uninterrupted. You have seen no one?"

"Not a soul, my lord, are you sure of this?"

"We have talked of nothing in the House for weeks but the imminent coming of the Dutch, Master Bennett. Believe me. War is coming. Traitors like him —"

"Won't get past this gate, my lord."

She felt the boot press down again as Fairmantle leaned forward in ponderous eagerness. "On the contrary, Master Bennett. Let him pass. Let him, and any that he might bring with him, pass. I will be waiting for them and believe me, they will feel England's wrath. But be vigilant. Alert your fellows. For if we fail, our country fails with us. But if we thwart them, Master Bennett, we are England's heroes. Mark them well, but do not raise the alarm, for he is a slippery fellow, this Russell. He will spin you tales. Don't believe a word of it. We'll catch the rogue red-handed, see if we don't."

Thomazine could not move, even if she had not been frozen with witless horror. Fairmantle continued to gossip and the man Bennett's cool disinterest thawed by the heartbeat with tales of rewards, of recognition, of what horrible fates awaited a traitor.

And that was what it was, wasn't it? That was all it was, to Fairmantle. A way to be noticed: a childish, pettish desire to be the centre of attention. To be finally acknowledged as a man of wit and daring by the men whose approval he craved and could never have. Thomazine gagged, choking on her handkerchief, and was determined not to be sick for she knew she would die if she choked and he would not lift a finger to help her, not if she lay strangling on her own vomit under his feet.

All those things he had said of Russell — that he had learned to dissemble, but that he could not love: that he was cold and had no thought of any other but himself, that he craved approval and belonging, but that they would not let him in — he had not been speaking of her husband at all. He had spoken of himself.

She was afraid, in the dark, under that cloak. She wept, silently, with tears running out of her eyes and soaking into her hair on the dusty floor of the carriage.

"It's not the most romantic place I'd choose," Wilmot said, sounding quite reasonable for a change. "For an assignation, I mean."

Black hulks of dismasted ships loomed up out of the darkness like great monsters of the deep, surrounded by the creak and splash of the ships in the water and the smell of the river, of tar, hemp and cut wood. It was a place that was like, and yet unlike, Wapping dock. For the docks thrummed with life always, with noise and with laughter from the disreputable taverns, with sailors coming and going, with all sorts of maritime hangers-on and minor celebrity and cheerful chaos. Here, all was eerily still, for work on the great ships ceased at dusk, when the light went. And these were engines of war. Not cheerful fat matrons like Russell's Perse, or sleek and beautiful like the Go And Ask Her, but huge, purposeful weapons of destruction, that were not meant to be beautiful, but were made for the purpose of crushing out life.

"What the hell has he brought her here for?"

"Perhaps he was hoping she will be so impressed by the size of the weapons that she'll overlook the paucity of his," Wilmot said cheerfully.

Russell shot him a look of loathing. It was too quiet. And no one had stopped them, either. If they thought he was so entirely shattered by the disappearance of his wife that he did not think the dockyard where the pride of the English navy was being constructed would be crawling with watchmen, someone thought he was dafter than he was.

Or someone was waiting for them.

Russell suspected he might have underestimated Charles Fairmantle. He cocked his pistol and Wilmot glanced over his shoulder.

"You mean business, then, Major?"

"If he's touched Thomazine I'll cut his balls off," Russell said curtly.

"Temper, temper. Leave some for me, sir. I am very displeased with Master Fairmantle, I can assure you. We have been quite deceived in that gentleman, I think. Not at all a fit and proper person to know. Now, where shall we start to look, do you suppose?"

There were too many hiding places here. Too many hulks he could have stowed her in — If he had to look under every coil of rope, on every deck of every ship, in every barrel, he would do it.

Wilmot had wandered off, whistling.

Russell stopped, flinging his head up, snuffing the air like a dog. Ridiculous. He could not scent her out, that would be absurd — he could smell tar. Tar and new-cut wood and the bitter green smell of new hemp from the ropery —

There were footsteps and he whirled, pistol ready — he could smell smoke, faint, thready, distant. Not woodsmoke. Bitter smoke, bitter like new wood.

Thomazine was sitting in the middle of the long, straight lane where they made the ropes, and she was alive.

In the warm amber glow of a lantern set on the walkway, there were great black bruises about her throat and on her face, and the gleam of tears on her white face, but she was alive, and Russell had never seen anything lovelier. Her hair was hanging from its pins, her skirts and her bodice were crumpled and splotched with dark stains. Her hands were tied behind her back and her cheeks bulged over a dirty rag that had been thrust into her mouth.

But she was whole and alive. Her eyes widened when she saw him and then another great fat tear glinted down her cheek and she blinked at him, slowly. Which was an expression he knew and he blinked back at her — *love you, tibber* — and stepped out onto the ropewalk.

"Let her go, Fairmantle," he said.

The man he had always considered — not a friend, but someone he thought he knew: an annoyance, a vexation, a witless lackey, a hanger-on — gave him a polite smile. "See, dear? I told you he'd come, didn't I?" Fairmantle twisted his hand into Thomazine's hair so that she reared back, choking, and with his free hand he pressed a duelling-pistol against her temple. "I don't think so, Thankful."

"What do you want from me?"

"You? Nothing. Nothing at all. What on earth do you think I might want from you?"

"Then why —"

"Because you're a spy, Major, a nasty little traitorous spy, and I'm going to catch you in the act of burning the King's ships laid up here. All the watchmen know you're here. They're just waiting for me to give the signal and then we will catch you red-handed."

Thomazine was shaking her head, no, and he wondered if Fairmantle actually believed what he was saying.

"I am a — what?" Russell said warily.

"Oh, come now! A spy! You know it, I know it, all the world knows it. You are a spy and a filthy deceiver and I am the man to give you your just deserts."

"Since when have you been a patriot, Chas?" Russell said without thinking, and Fairmantle's face twitched.

"Since I — since —"

"Since I ceased to be quite so obliging a target for your gossip?" Russell guessed and knew by the way the man's head jerked that he had touched him on the quick. "Why? Why do you hate me so much? How have I harmed you, that —"

But Russell had struck wide that time, for Fairmantle was laughing now, sure of himself. "Don't be absurd, Major. I don't hate you. You flatter yourself. But you must admit, sir, you make a most convenient man to accuse. Always a little bit too good to be true, as I recall. Always too pretty, in the old days, weren't you? — just a little bit too upright, too honourable, for my way of thinking. I just knew you had to have feet of clay. I knew it, for you could not be so — so bloody assured, all the time, as you seemed."

Russell wondered if he should shoot the man, like a mad dog. His aim was true enough, surely, for Thomazine was on her knees and he raised his own pistol without speaking a word, sighting down the barrel to the spot where Fairmantle's eyebrows met.

"Not quite so self-possessed now, Major, are you? 'Twas a marvel how many other men wanted you to be not quite so perfect as you seemed, too," Fairmantle added mockingly. "The world was very keen to take you from your pedestal. And your accomplice, of course," he said conversationally. "But then, I imagine she will have burned to death by then." He gave a slow, mocking blink of his own and kicked over the lantern, very deliberately.

For a second Russell thought the hemp waste had extinguished the flame and that it would not catch. But then it leapt to a small flame, and a greater, and then it started to run like water along the length of the ropewalk. "Now, you could shoot me," Fairmantle said, and his face was beginning to take on a cheerful, ruddy glow. "But then I might shoot her first, mightn't I? So what do you think, Major?"

Russell did not know what to think. "Let her go," he said again. "I will do whatever you ask of me. Just let her go."

"Well, that's very kind of you."

Thomazine was sobbing now, silently, and her eyes never left his. There was a quarter-mile of ropewalk between them. The fire was starting to crackle and spread, moving faster than a horse could run: cold sweat started to run down his back in spite of the heat, the hair was standing up on his arms and he was starting to shake.

"Frightened, Major?" Fairmantle said mockingly. "Thomazine tells me you're not an admirer of fires, sir. There's a pity. Though I believe your sister was already dead when I lit a fire beneath her skirts."

Russell knew what it would feel like, and the boards beneath his feet were beginning to grow warm, wisps of acrid smoke rising through the gaps in the planking. He knew how it would feel when he burned. He could do nothing, he could say nothing, his hands had grown numb and useless with fear, he could not fire a pistol with any accuracy.

He did not care for himself, much. But he knew how it would feel for Thomazine. And that he would not bear.

"Let her go, Sir Charles," he said, and his voice was his own again, above the rising roar of the flames.

As Fairmantle's head turned, Russell shot him.

Fairmantle went down, face first, into the flames, in a great shower of sparks. And then he rose screaming, flaming, and threw his dreadful fiery wig into the flames, where it burst like a comet with a smell of burning hair. He was swearing and crying, horribly, and yet he was still on his feet though his face was burned like meat and his clothes were burning, and he still held Thomazine's hair, in a long silken rope wrapped about his wrist, and she was trying to pull away from him, though it meant she hung over the flames, jerking most piteously.

There was a smell of meat, scorching.

The smoke thickened, choking him, his eyes stinging and watering, and he would go to her, though every breath was burning in his lungs, as if he were breathing in embers. He had a second pistol. It was an act of humanity to exterminate that horrible, burned thing that roared and stamped on the burning boards.

He could hear voices shouting somewhere. Not far away.

Thomazine was on her feet, God be thanked, and she was fighting like an Amazon. Fairmantle smacked her across the face with one of those horrible black-pocked joints of meat that had been his hands and she went sprawling across the boards with a scream. Sweet Christ, would the man never go down?

There was another shot. It surprised him for he had not fired and the voices were yet too far away, but suddenly there was an agony in his shoulder, just below his collar-bone and he tasted blood in his mouth. His left arm would not serve. "Thomazine," he said.

She could not hear him over the roaring flames, but her head turned. She was on her feet again. The burned thing almost had her, reeling like a drunken man to wrap his horrible arms about her waist.

"Thomazine!"

Russell was on his knees. His blood was on the boards, a spray of it, and with the last strength that was in him he fired into the churning clouds of acrid smoke and sparks.

He would have liked to see her one last time. But he lay with his cheek against the splintered wood and felt it shake with footsteps, and thought that it was enough.

20

Thomazine saw the shoulder of Russell's coat burst inwards in a great shower of black blood, but there was nothing she could do, for she was teetering against the rails herself now with Fairmantle's dreadful raw fingers scrabbling for her again. His face was a pocked mask of leaking meat — a horrible, homely smell of roasting, and then she was falling forward with a jerk as he grabbed her again, her loose hair swinging in her face and blinding her.

"Die, you little bitch," he slurred in her ear, and his forearm was tight about her throat, cutting off the last of the air.

There was a smell of burning silk as the last rags binding her wrists parted in the flame, and a brief screaming pain in her wrists as her skin scorched under it. The ends of her hair crisped and lifted in the hot air.

There was a blood-heat of metal between her scrabbling fingers as she caught one of her loosened hairpins. A pretty little enamelled flower at one end, set with a pearl. And three inches of sharp metal.

Her eyes felt like sand. She gripped the hot metal between her fingers and drove it back, up over her shoulder, into what part of Fairmantle's face chance willed. She did not think she would ever forget how it felt, the shock down her shoulder as the tip penetrated his eyeball, or the amount of sheer strength it took to ram a hairpin into a man's skull. Or the way he screamed when she did it.

And then she was free.

Russell's eyes were open. Thomazine could see the flames reflected in their darkness and gleaming on the silver filigree of his waistcoat buttons. His silver brocade had turned black with blood, which was pooling underneath him, spreading across the splintered boards towards her. There was blood spilling from his mouth and on his shirt — oh, Apple, so much blood — in his hair and darkening the plain respectable grey of the breast of his good wool suit — but he was alive.

She did not care about Fairmantle. He had ceased to exist and the world had narrowed to six feet of swaying boards inside Hell for she would not let Russell die alone, he was her dear love and she crawled, sobbing, across the boards, away from the heart of the fire, feeling her loose hair lift and banner in the hot air.

Sparks stung her face and her bare, scraped hands.

She was close enough to see the ragged black hole just above his collarbone where the life was pumping sluggishly out of him and she kicked like a swimmer across those last feet of wood, tearing at her skirts, at her petticoats, wadding great handfuls of cloth into the hollow of neck and shoulder — she had kissed him there, a hundred times, a thousand times — begging and praying and crying that he might live —

One handful of silk soaked through. It was growing hotter, harder to breathe. She did not mind dying with him in her arms, truly she did not, but she gave a little sob and changed hands, pressing down harder with her handful of sodden linen till she felt the faint, thready skitter of life under her fingers.

Was it slowing, or was there simply no more blood in him? His lips looked white.

"Thom'sin," he said and his voice was faint and slurred, but steady.

She almost took her hand from his wound.

"Call," he said. "Wilmot. Outside."

"What?"

He closed his eyes, but it wasn't in weakness. It was the old slow happy-cat blink of a man who would smile and cannot. "Looking for you," he said and his eyes filled with tears. "Wouldn't leave you. Came with. Wilmot. Call. Them."

"I won't —" Hers overflowed, too, and that was not helpful. "You will come too."

He closed his eyes again. No.

"Thankful you have a son, damn you, you can't die yet, you bloody fool!"

And then she did take her hand from the hole above his collarbone and she grabbed him by both shoulders and lifted his body from the boards, but she could not drag him and so she shook him instead, and sat defeated with his head against her thigh and wept awful tears of rage and shame and loss while Chatham docks burned around her.

And that was when the Earl of Rochester came bounding up the stairs and stopped, looking like one of the minor demons, all backlit rose and gold.

"Dear me, it's like the end of Hamlet up here — bodies everywhere," he said tartly. "That's not how this performance ends, Penthesilea."

PART IV: ASH

21

Russell had almost died and they had, in the end, not averted any battle at all. Six weeks later, on the thirteenth of June, war with the Dutch began in earnest, in the great sea battle at Lowestoft off the coast of Suffolk.

And Russell was very thoroughly out of the way and Thomazine was glad of it.

He had spent the next month flat on his back with his eyes closed, for the first thing he did when he stopped bleeding was to develop a recurrence of his old fever and almost die on her again.

Publicly, the Earl of Rochester said he refused, absolutely refused, to set foot in that house in Fenchurch Street, that his reputation would never stand it. The widow Bartholomew, blooming into her position as their housekeeper, said that was fine by her because her reputation would not stand having him in the house either. So Wilmot and the rest of his Merry Gang were banned from visiting, even had they wanted to: they sent carefully-scurrilous poetry to entertain and the occasional basket of oranges with instructions that the invalid was not to consume them peel and all and give himself the gripes in addition to a low fever.

Privately, though, John Wilmot was a fairly regular visitor, sans wig and sans silks. In a plain working man's suit of clothes he passed without comment amongst the working men of Aldgate, and he was in and out, running errands for the widow, fetching and carrying without regard for his position in the world. It was a game to him, though, and he was tiring of it even as they were packing up the house around Russell's sickbed, and Thomazine suspected that after they left for Buckinghamshire they would not see him again. That made her a little bit sad, because when he was not trying to be wild and shocking on purpose he was quite a decent, amusing, sensible young man, and he would make someone a good husband when he grew up. (Would be a pretty rotten husband presently, but that was by the by.)

No one mentioned Charles Fairmantle, and that was good, for she did not think she could think of him without flinching yet. She had dreams, still, where he rose burning out of the darkness, his face as raw as a haunch of beef, his fingers still clawing blindly for her throat. Dreams where she did not reach Russell in time and he had died, there on the boards, with his life seeping out from between her fingers. Where she could hear Wilmot shouting, but he could not find them, and they burned together with the English fleet. She thought Russell had those dreams, too, for he clung to her in his sleep some nights, shaking and twitching.

But by May he was sitting up in bed and having conversations that were intelligent, if brief, due to a lamentable habit of falling asleep mid-sentence. And by Whitsun they were making their slow, feeble way home, because he said he was hanged if he was going home on a bloody hurdle and he would ride home like a Christian or they could bury him with the rest of the plague-ridden of the City. And by June the first battle of the war had been fought and won.

It had been a near-run victory for the Duke of York as admiral of the fleet, with Prince Rupert commanding the centre, and she was glad for that ragged old raven of a hero for now he would have new battles to replay and new tactics to talk over, and new admirers, and he might be happy.

But he wouldn't be talking them over with Thomazine's husband, she was adamant on that head. Because for the foreseeable future, Thankful was going to be on a diet of gruel and barley-water, and when he was able to go two hours together without falling asleep in his supper, she might consider going so far as Dr Willis's strengthening diet of beefsteak and claret, but up until then, he was going to behave himself like a very proper model invalid.

He said he hadn't bled that much and that she was making over-much of what was no more than a scratch. He had only been stunned, he said, and he'd had worse, and what did he think she was, a child, to be babied? Thomazine, who had ruined a handkerchief and a good collar and a petticoat stanching the blood from the hole in her husband's shoulder, and whose skirts would never be fit for wear again, had smiled politely at him and nodded and returned to her mending the great hole in his good coat.

He had been holding her hand so tight at the end that her wedding ring had bruised her fingers. Wilmot had come racketing down the ropewalk with a half-dozen watchmen and warehousemen dragged untimely from their beds and they had carried him clear, and she had gone with them, weak with the weeping and the relief of a woman who was not dead after all.

They had put the fire out by dawn, with bucket-chains from the mast-ponds and the river. It had not spread so far, had not had the chance. Wilmot had heard the shots and raised the alarm and by the time he had found them the ropewalk was half-burned, but it was preserved, and had been repaired. And the Dutch — if they had ever had such a plan — did not come, not for another six weeks, and by then it was so patently nothing to do with Thankful Russell and his wife that the gossip had faded to a hush, in the new excitement of war.

Thomazine would have stayed with him, though, if help had not come. It was a sobering thought, that she would have sat amidst the inferno and held Russell's hand and burned with him if he could not have been brought to safety. She did not think she would ever forget his dark eyes holding hers at the last, as if she were the pole star by which he held his course. Not with softness, or with love, but with an absolute fixed intensity, as if she might pull him free of the jaws of the death by the strength of her will.

He had been in a deal of pain and not always lucid, and he had been very, very afraid and so she had held his hand and was afraid herself that even as the flames leaped below them his fingers grew cool in hers. She would have let go to wad up more of her petticoats against that great pulsing hole above his collarbone, but he would not have it.

It wasn't until Wilmot tried to have him taken up and he swore that he wasn't dead yet and he would walk free of this place on his own feet, that she wept. Then Russell had put his good arm round her and bled all down her decent grey bodice so that it had to be cut up for cleaning rags, before fainting. Wilmot had looked as if he'd like to bang the pair of their silly heads together for sheer wilful stubbornness and then he'd gone and put Fairmantle's horses to his carriage with his own hands, rather than wait for the Commissioner to be roused from his bed and give his authority.

Thomazine had only been able to think of Willis to turn to and he had been somewhat less than delighted at being called from his bed in the early hours of a spring dawn to deal with such a medical emergency. He was not that kind of a surgeon, he'd said grumpily. He had looked at Russell, though, limp and bloodied and lolling against Wilmot's fine linen despite the Earl's attempts to gingerly hold him away from the costly fabric and Thomazine swore that the doctor's eyes had lit up with anticipation.

They'd had to move the previous incumbent from the table in his surgery, although, being dead, the gentleman did not mind. Something had leaked from the flabby carcass and Russell's bright, blood-drabbled hair had stuck to it on the stained marble. That had made Thomazine retch and the good doctor had rather peevishly told her that if the sight of blood made her squalmish perhaps this was no place for her after all.

He had cut Russell's coat from him, and the blood-dark shirt underneath it, and Thomazine had made a little promise to God that if He brought her husband safely through this, she would see to it with her own hands that he had a good shirt to replace it. She would be a good wife to him: no more adventuring, she would be a proper, womanly wife, she would—

Russell's eyes were open, if not precisely brilliant with intelligence. His lips were parted, and very pale, and a little runnel of blood ran out of the corner of his mouth. He said something, too faint to catch, and Willis bent low to hear him, and her husband raised his head. "This is the only chance you get, sawbones," Russell said, panting slightly. "Make the most of it."

And then he'd fainted again, and Willis, whose fingers had been fluttering longingly over a bottle of the new tincture of opium that a gentleman called Sydenham had recently claimed such efficacy for, sniffed, thwarted. "Mistress, are you still squalmish?"

She was not — or rather, she was, but she dared not be, as she held Russell's head and Willis had probed and snipped and parted rags of flesh. He had left her darling delivered, God willing, from the mouth of the dog, crumpled and bloody and

259

with a neat seam throughout the fist-sized hole that was torn clear through his shoulder, but breathing. And there was, then, only one question she might ask.

"Will he recover?" She caught sight of herself in the polished glass of one of Willis's specimen jars — her hair disordered, her eyes huge and ashy-black in a dirty, pointed face — and then she had wept for shame. The doctor pinched his nose, looking embarrassed.

"I imagine on my previous acquaintance with the Major, madam, nothing short of chain-shot would finish him off." There was a solid, metallic chink as Willis dropped the misshapen ball of lead, wrapped about with shreds of flesh and torn linen, into a dish. "Which is no guarantee of anything, mind, except to say that he is a gentleman of a remarkably resilient constitution. I may give a cautious indication of his return to health, in time."

Mistress Bartholomew had wept horribly when they had rousted her out of bed, and that had set the Bartholomew-baby off, and that had set Thomazine to weeping again, and eventually poor Wilmot had had to find a pair of stout and sensible link-boys to carry Russell to bed, for there was not another living soul in their lodgings not nigh-insensible with grief and weariness. Her husband had, however, opened his eyes as she settled the pillow under his poor head. She had caught her breath, expecting tender words of gratitude.

He told her to bloody well stop fussing, which had made her laugh, and then made her cry again, and he had made a noise like a pot of water boiling over and flung his good arm out for her to weep on his chest.

It had been almost a month until he was fit to travel and then he managed to acquire himself an inflammation of the lungs on the way home and they had arrived back at Four

Ashes unannounced on a wet, chilly May afternoon. Russell was in a foul temper, coughing up blood and phlegm and muttering feverishly into a sodden handkerchief, and Thomazine was tired and stiff and hungry, limping on ahead into the parlour to find no fire lit and the celebratory supper she'd temped him into travel with yet unprepared.

"No supper?" he said irritably. "You've been strict on that head for nigh on a month, wench, and I'm perished for want of solid food!"

She ignored him, of course. He was at his testiest when he felt poorly, and she grew accustomed to it, after a month of him at his invalid worst. And, truly, better Thankful irascible and panting for a mutton pie, than Thankful wan and limp and quiescent.

"Do you have a fever?" she said sweetly, and he glowered at her. "Would you like one, dear? Because if you do not mend your tone, husband, you will be eating that supper in the sheep-pasture. In the rain."

His lips twitched unwillingly. "Tibber, I am tired, and wretched, and all my bones hurt. I am not feeling playful."

The widow was up to the elbows in the week's baking, not having expected them until the morrow, and Thomazine was half-minded to take her husband into the kitchens and wrap him in travelling cloaks and tuck him into the corner of the chimney-breast till he stopped shivering, but instead she ignored the widow's squeaks of protest and made him a mug of mulled ale with her own hands and raided the buttery for cheese and cold pigeon pie.

She was, yet, her mother's daughter. She had seen the King and she was married to an intelligencer and she had killed a man, and yet she was at heart a stout Essex goodwife who valued her hearth and home above all else, and who believed in the twin panaceas of good feeding and loving.

Once fed, Russell stretched his legs out to the parlour fire, which was beginning to crackle. Thomazine suspected much more feeding, and any more ale, and her husband would be asleep where he sat, and she looked around at her lovely magpie-room: at the firelight glistening on delicate porcelain and well-polished wood, the deep jewel colours of the Turkey-work carpet, the blue and white Delftware bowl on the coffer.

"Oh, Thankful," she said softly, and her eyes prickled again, "we are so lucky."

He had his hand to his shoulder, massaging the scar, at that moment, and he looked at her with that wry smile in his eyes. "Oh? I'll let you know when the wind is out of the east quarter, tibber. Hurts like hell at the minute." And then he'd closed his eyes with a sigh of contentment. "Aye, we are lucky, though I should consider myself a fortunate man to live in a cottage, so long as you were with me. Though I hope the next set of neighbours are not so prone to arson as the last."

Lady Birstall, five miles hence, had retired to live with her married daughter after the tragic death of her husband and the house was put up to let. It was understood that he had been carried off by the plague, poor man, like so many of the other citizens of the capital — like poor Major Russell almost had been, poor dear, and he coming home so wan and thin and weak — quite unexpected, and they had buried him in London. Very sad. They did not talk of it here — by mutual agreement, that was how it was. Poor, dear Chas Fairmantle was an innocent victim of the sweating-sickness, and not a murderer with the morals of a hunting stoat who would have killed them — all three of them — with less thought than he would have given to crushing a flea, with no better reason than that he craved John Wilmot's undivided attention.

It seemed such a paltry reason to murder. But then, Wilmot himself had been sent to the Tower of London in disgrace for the boisterous abduction of a young woman at the end of May. A young woman he had intended to marry, by all accounts, but the King did not approve of his methods of proposal. Yes, Thomazine thought murder was a little extreme, but on their current showing it seemed the only vice the Merry Gang had not seized on with both hands, and so — well, it was a thing that perhaps a logical mind might look to, as the only thing they had not yet tried, to fix their wandering notice.

Russell had given her one of his wry looks at that. "Logical," he said. "You suggested that the late Master Fairmantle was possessed of a *logical* mind?"

"If disordered," she said firmly.

"Indeed. A charitable perspective, my tibber."

The which she had to be, for if she was not — if she allowed herself to think that a man might murder another out of a childish desire for attention, because he could not bear that a fellow creature might be decent in truth, and would have him smeared with the same libertine slime as Fairmantle and his friends were themselves, well, then, she would be no better in her heart than the late and unlamented Master Fairmantle, and that she could not bear. "I think we might be a little more popular than your sister," she said gently, "and someone might miss us." For it seemed that in the end Fly-Fornication's only claim to significance to anyone in this world was for Fairmantle to try out his new-found capacity for murder. And that was a little tragedy all by itself.

"So if Prince Rupert his own self were to write to us, to both of us, and ask if we might consider a post — in an informal capacity, you understand — to carry on with our valuable intelligence work —"

"I should tell Prince Rupert his very own self to go to hell," she said, and settled her hands over her belly. She felt an elbow, or a knee, shift under her ribs.

"I imagine you could buy a deal of baby clothes with the consideration he is offering," Russell said, and set on the inlaid table at his side with a soft chink, a fine soft leather purse.

She opened her eyes again. "Thankful —"

"Both of us. He asks that *both* of us consider it. Together."

"Together? Well. That might be different." She put his hand over the violent activity of his offspring. "Do you think we might put off making any decision for a while, though?"

"What shall I tell him, then?"

"Tell him he can wait the same nine months as anybody else, dear," she said.

HISTORICAL NOTES

1665. Twenty years after the beginning of the wars that had divided the United Kingdom, England has lived through civil war, a Commonwealth under Oliver Cromwell, and now the Restoration of the monarchy in 1660.

During the Civil Wars, the Levellers were a political movement that emphasised popular sovereignty, extended suffrage, equality before the law, and religious tolerance, all of which were expressed in the manifesto "Agreement of the People". They weren't a political party as we now understand it; the "Agreement of the People" was not a formal political agreement to which members signed up. They were organised at the national level, with offices in a number of London inns and taverns such as The Rosemary Branch in Islington, which got its name from the sprigs of rosemary that Levellers wore in their hats as a sign of identification.

Their agenda developed in tandem with growing dissent within the Parliamentarian New Model Army in the wake of the first Civil War. Early drafts of the Agreement of the People emanated from the Army, and called for an extension of suffrage to include almost all the adult male population, electoral reform, biennial elections, religious freedom, and an end to imprisonment for debt. They were committed broadly to the abolition of corruption within the parliamentary and judicial process, toleration of religious differences, the translation of law into the common tongue and, arguably, something that could be considered democracy in its modern form —the first time contemporary democratic ideas had been formally framed and adopted by a political movement.

The soldiers in the New Model Army elected "Agitators", representatives from each regiment to represent them. (Amongst whom, in early 1647, are the young lieutenant Thankful-For-His-Deliverance Russell, and his colonel, one Holofernes Babbitt.) These Agitators were recognised by the Army's commanders and had a seat on the General Council. However, by September 1647, at least five regiments of cavalry had elected new unofficial agitators and produced a pamphlet called "The Case of the Army Truly Stated". This was presented to the commander-in-chief, Sir Thomas Fairfax, in October 1647, and demanded a dissolution of Parliament within a year and substantial changes to the constitution of future Parliaments, to be regulated by an unalterable "law paramount".

Thomas Fairfax and Oliver Cromwell, as the Army's commanders, were worried by the strength of support for Levellers in the Army, so they decided to impose a more conservative manifesto for the Army instead of the "Agreement of the People". When some refused to accept this, they were arrested and one of the ringleaders was executed.

The Levellers' largest petition was presented to Parliament on September 11, 1648 after amassing signatories including about a third of all Londoners. On October 30, 1648, the highest ranking Leveller sympathiser, Colonel Thomas Rainsborough, was killed. (Possibly murdered by Cromwell. Possibly murdered by the King. Possibly murdered by parties unknown who thought the act would impress either the King, or Cromwell.) His funeral was the occasion for a large, peaceful Leveller-led demonstration in London, with thousands of mourners wearing the Levellers' ribbons of sea-green and bunches of rosemary for remembrance in their hats.

On January 20, 1649, a version of the "Agreement of the People" that had been drawn up in October 1647 for the Army Council and subsequently modified was presented to the House of Commons — just over a week before His Majesty Charles I of England was tried and executed for treason against the people. In February, the Grandees banned petitions to Parliament by soldiers. In March, eight Leveller troopers went to Fairfax and demanded the restoration of the right to petition. Five of them were cashiered out of the army.

In April, three hundred soldiers declared that they would not give further service until the Levellers' programme had been realised, and were cashiered without arrears of pay. Later that month, in the Bishopsgate mutiny, soldiers stationed in Bishopsgate, London, made similar demands; they were ordered out of London. When they refused to go, fifteen of their number were arrested and court martialled, and six were sentenced to death. Of these, five were later pardoned, but the sixth was hanged on April 27, 1649. Later in 1649, Lieutenant-Colonel Lilburne, William Walwyn, Thomas Prince, and Richard Overton were imprisoned in the Tower of London by the Council of State. It was while the leaders of the Levellers were being held in the Tower that they wrote an outline of the reforms the Levellers wanted, in a pamphlet entitled "An Agreement Of The Free People Of England" (written on May 1, 1649) including reforms that have since been made law in England, such as the right to silence, and others that have not been, such as an elected judiciary.

Shortly afterwards, Cromwell attacked the "Banbury mutineers", forty troopers who supported the Leveller cause. Several mutineers were killed in the skirmish. Captain Thompson escaped only to be killed a few days later in another skirmish at Wellingborough. The three other leaders were shot on May 17, 1649, at Burford Church. This destroyed the Levellers' support base in the New Model Army, which by then was the major power in the land. Although Walwyn and Overton were released from the Tower, and Lilburne tried and acquitted, the Leveller cause had effectively been crushed.

So the old Levellers, then — those rebels and republicans who hadn't decided to come back to heel under Cromwell, seeing the error of their ways — what became of them? Some of them just put their heads down and got on with it, and — if all was not precisely forgiven and forgotten — were allowed to live in peace, provided they kept out of trouble and showed no further signs of dangerous insurrection. Some fled to Europe, specifically to the egalitarian Low Countries, where exiled rebels and republicans were ten a penny — as, indeed, were old Royalists. The English feared Dutch intervention in the Anglo-Spanish wars of 1655-1660 on the side of the Spanish: in part, because the Republic contained a strong Orangist party hostile to Cromwell. The leading personage of the Royal House of Orange was young Prince William, grandson of Charles I — later to become King William III — and not unreasonably, there were concerns that the Orange party was under the influence of exiled English royalists.

Following the devastation of the first Anglo-Dutch Wars, however, the Dutch were busy building up their shipping and trading fleet again, rather than poking in international politics. While the English had won a great many naval battles and destroyed a great many Dutch ships, they failed to win the war. The Republic was in a better financial position than the Commonwealth of England; as a result, the Dutch could keep on fitting out their naval fleet to make up for the losses they sustained at a pace the English were unable to match. So long as the war continued, the Dutch had also been free to expand their trade networks along the main sea routes outside English home waters without fear of English retaliation, due to the lack of available ships. English commerce was grinding to a halt as they lost access to the Baltic and the Mediterranean Seas, and when the two sides signed the peace treaty in 1654, the English were in essentially the same position that they had begun: watching the Dutch Republic outstrip their economy to become the premier European trade power.

Which matter brings us nicely to Russell's erstwhile paymaster, George Downing. Downing's family emigrated to America in 1638, settling in Salem, Massachusetts. He attended Harvard College — he was one of nine students in the first graduating class of 1642, and was subsequently hired as the college's first tutor. In 1645 he sailed for the West Indies with slaves in tow, as a preacher and instructor of the seamen, and arrived in England some time afterwards, becoming chaplain to Colonel John Okey's regiment (who had originally sponsored Downing's education in America).

It seems that the gentleman of the cloth preferred swords to ploughshares, though, and by 1650 he was scoutmaster-general of Cromwell's forces in Scotland. In 1657 he was on the public payroll, receiving a salary of £365 and £500 as a Teller of the Exchequer. His marriage in 1654 with Frances, daughter of Sir William Howard of Naworth, and sister of Charles Howard, 1st Earl of Carlisle, aided his advancement. In Cromwell's parliament of 1654 he represented Edinburgh, and Carlisle in those of 1656 and 1659. He was one of the first to urge Cromwell to take the royal title and restore the old constitution, but quickly became a prominent figure in Cromwell's dealings with Europe. In 1655 he was sent to France to remonstrate on the massacre of the Protestant Vaudois, and two years later was appointed resident at The

Hague, to effect a union of the Protestant European powers, to mediate between Portugal and the Dutch Republic and between Sweden and Denmark, to defend the interests of the English traders against the Dutch, and to inform the government concerning the movements of the exiled royalists.

He showed himself in these negotiations an able diplomat. He was maintained in his post during the interregnum subsequent to the fall of Richard Cromwell, and was thus enabled in April 1660 to make his peace with Charles II, to whom he communicated Cromwell's old spymaster John Thurloe's despatches, and declared his abandonment of "principles sucked in" in New England of which he now "saw the error". At the Restoration, therefore, Downing was knighted, was continued in his embassy in Holland, was confirmed in his tellership of the exchequer, and was further rewarded with a valuable piece of land adjoining St. James's Park for building purposes, now known as Downing Street. During the Restoration period, he was instrumental organising the spy-rings which hunted down many of his former comrades. He engineered the arrest in Holland of the regicides John Barkstead, Miles Corbet and John Okey, his former commander and sponsor, apparently after reassuring Okey that he held no warrant for their arrest. Downing's personal intervention violated normal diplomatic procedure and was widely condemned as a betrayal, particularly as he had once been chaplain to Okey's regiment — not to mention Okey's early sponsorship of his education. However, the King was pleased and rewarded Downing with a baronetcy in 1663. Samuel Pepys, who characterised his conduct as odious though useful to the king, calls him a "perfidious rogue" and remarks that "all the world took notice of him for a most ungrateful villain for his pains."

Downing had from the first been hostile to the Dutch, as the commercial rivals of England. In the first year of the Second Anglo-Dutch War, 1665, he was expelled by the Dutch because of his perpetual intriguing and spying activities and sent home. On his return, as a Member of Parliament, he attached a clause to a bill to fund the war's continuation which specified that the money raised could only be used for the war effort. This previously move was opposed strongly by Lord Clarendon as an encroachment on the royal prerogative, as it effectively made permanent the parliamentary appropriation of supplies — meaning that Parliament could then specify that tax revenues should be used only for a particular purpose, rather than spent as the King's government saw fit.

The real problem with the English trading system was that it was based on tariffs and customs while the Dutch system was based on free trade. Dutch goods were much more attractive around the world because they lacked the additional taxing on imports and exports that came with English goods. The end of the First Anglo-Dutch War had not changed this — in fact, it left the Dutch free to expand their trade while the English were still hindered by the same tariff system. Thus, another war seemed inevitable to many Englishmen at the time, lest the Commonwealth lose their naval and economical superiority for good.

The Restoration produced a further surge of optimism in England, as many hoped to reverse the Dutch dominance in world trade. At first, however, Charles sought to remain on friendly terms with the Republic, as he was personally greatly indebted to the House of Orange, which had lent enormous sums to Charles I during the English Civil War. Nevertheless, conflict soon developed with the States of Holland over the education and future prospects of his nephew William, over whom Charles had been made a guardian by his late sister Mary. In 1663, Louis XIV of France stated his claim to portions of the Southern Netherlands, leading to a short rapprochement between England and the Republic — during this time, Lord Clarendon, serving as chief minister, felt that France had become the greatest danger to England.

In May 1667, in the war's final year, he was made secretary to the commissioners of the treasury. His appointment was much welcomed by Samuel Pepys — which is interesting, as Pepys couldn't stand the man personally — and he then went on to take part in the management and reform of the Treasury, based on financial practises he'd observed in Holland.

An able — if unprincipled — diplomat, he was appointed a commissioner of the customs in 1671 and died in 1684 having accumulated a substantial fortune, though he was almost universally reviled for his reputed meanness and unscrupulous self-interest.

A word on John Thurloe, if you were wondering how Oliver Cromwell's spymaster who had previously spent his days overlooking the activities of unscrupulous Royalists in the Low Countries ended up working for the King. After Cromwell's death, Thurloe became the recognised speaker for the Cromwellian "court" party and for the established government, against the Army rebels and republicans. With the end of the Cromwellian Protectorate, after Oliver's death and his son's resignation, Thurloe was dismissed by the new Council of State in 1659, and refused to divulge his codes and ciphers when Thomas Scot resumed direction of the intelligence service.

He was restored to his offices by General Monck in February 1660. He tried to persuade Monck to reinstate the Protectorate and resisted the Restoration for as long as he could. Despite Monck's recommendation, he was not elected to the

Convention Parliament in April 1660. After the King's return, Thurloe was accused of treason and arrested in May 1660. He was released in June on condition that his knowledge be made available to the new government when required. He subsequently wrote several memoranda on state and foreign affairs for the information of Sir Edward Hyde, Earl of Clarendon. Thereafter, Thurloe lived quietly, dividing his time between Great Milton in Oxfordshire and his legal chambers at Lincoln's Inn, where he died in February 1668.

In 1664, however, the situation quickly changed. Clarendon's enemy, Lord Arlington, became the favourite of the king and began to cooperate with James, Duke of York, the Lord High Admiral. Both James and Lord Arlington agreed that war with the Dutch was more in English interest than war with France, and co-ordinated their efforts to instate it. This was not wholly without a degree of self-interest. James headed the Royal African Company, and hoped to seize the possessions of his trade competitors in the Dutch West India Company.

Charles was also easily influenced by James — who was, after all, his little brother — and Arlington, as he sought a popular and lucrative foreign war at sea to bolster his authority as king. Many underemployed naval officers expected a re-run of the first Anglo-Dutch Wars, in which reputations and fortunes were made.

As enthusiasm for war rose among the English populace, privateers began to attack Dutch ships, capturing them and taking them to English harbours. By the time war was declared, about two hundred Dutch ships had been brought in the English ports. In late 1663 James had sent Robert Holmes, in the service of the Royal African Company, to capture Dutch trading posts and colonies in West Africa. At the same time, the English invaded the Dutch colony of New Netherland in

North America on 24 June 1664, and by October had taken control of it.

Dutch ships were obligated by the new treaty to salute the English flag first, but in 1664, English ships started to try and provoke the Dutch by not saluting in return. Though ordered by the Dutch government to continue saluting first, many Dutch commanders could not bear the insult. The Dutch responded to English aggression by sending a fleet under Michiel de Ruyter that recaptured their African trade posts, captured most of the English trade stations there and then crossed the Atlantic for a revenge expedition against the English in America. In December 1664, the English attacked the Dutch fleet at Smyrna. Though the attack failed, in January 1665 the Dutch began to allow their ships to open fire on English warships in the colonies when threatened. Charles then used this as a pretext to declare war on the Netherlands on 4 March 1665.

The war was supported in England by much propaganda, particularly the alleged atrocities of the previous Amboyna Massacre of 1623. That year, ten English factors, resident in the Dutch fortress of Victoria on Ambon were executed by beheading on accusations of treason. During the trial, the English prisoners were allegedly hung up with cloth placed over their faces, upon which water dripped until the victims inhaled water. After some time, they were taken down to vomit up the water, only to repeat the experience. The Dutch also allegedly placed candles on the victims' bodies to demonstrate the translucence of the flesh. The English East India Company published a pamphlet in 1631, setting out its case against the Dutch VOC, which was used extensively for anti-Dutch propaganda during the First Anglo-Dutch War. Though the matter was supposed to be settled with the Treaty of

Westminster in 1654, pamphleteers reminded the public of it as the war neared. Additionally, broadsheets demonized the Dutch as drunken and profane, with Andrew Marvell's 1653 insult of Holland, "The Character of Holland," reprinted ("This indigested vomit of the Sea,/ Fell to the Dutch by Just Propriety"). When De Ruyter recaptured the West African trading posts, many pamphlets were written about presumed new Dutch atrocities, although these were mostly gross exaggerations and rumour.

After their defeat in the First Anglo-Dutch War, the Dutch began to construct a "New Navy", a core of sixty new, much heavier ships with professional captains. However, these ships were still much lighter than the ten "big ships" of the English navy. In 1664, when war threatened, it was decided to completely replace the core Dutch fleet with still heavier ships. Upon the outbreak of war in 1665, these new vessels were mostly still under construction, and the Dutch only possessed four heavier ships of the line. During the second war, the new ships were quickly completed, with another twenty ordered and built. England, meanwhile, could only build a dozen ships, due to financial pressures. The navy did not pay its sailors with money, but with "tickets", or debt certificates. Charles lacked an effective means of enforcing taxation. The only way to finance the war, in effect, was to capture Dutch trade fleets. The cash-poor English made the war's outcome dependent on the fortunes of its privateers; for every warship the English built during the conflict, the Dutch shipyards turned out seven.

Fighting began in earnest with the Battle of Lowestoft on 13 June, where the English gained a great victory; it was the worst defeat of the Dutch Republic's navy in history. The English, though, were unable to capitalise on the victory, because the leading Dutch politician, the Grand Pensionary of Holland,

Johan de Witt, quickly restored confidence by joining the fleet personally. Under De Witt's personal , ineffective captains were removed and new tactics formalised. In August Michiel de Ruyter returned from America to a hero's welcome and was given supreme command of the confederate fleet. The Spice Fleet from the Dutch East Indies managed to return home safely after the Battle of Vågen, though at first blockaded at Bergen, causing the financial position of England to deteriorate further.

In the summer of 1665 the bishop of Münster, Bernhard von Galen, an old enemy of the Dutch, was induced by promises of English subsidies to invade the Republic. At the same time, the English made overtures to Spain. Louis XIV, though obliged by a 1662 treaty to assist the Republic in a war with England, had put this off under pretext of wanting to negotiate a peace, but was concerned by the attack by Münster and the prospect of an English–Spanish coalition. Intent on conquering the Spanish Netherlands, he feared that a collapse of the Republic could create a powerful Habsburg presence on his northern border, as the Habsburgs were traditionally allies of the German bishops. He immediately promised to send a French army corps, and French envoys arrived in London to begin negotiations in earnest, threatening the wrath of the French monarch if the English failed to comply.

These events caused consternation at the English court. It now seemed that the Dutch Republic would end up as either a Habsburg possession or a French protectorate, either of which would be disastrous for England's strategic position. Clarendon, who'd always warned about "this foolish war", was ordered to quickly make peace with the Dutch without French mediation. Downing used his Orangist contacts to induce the province of Overijssel, which had been ravaged by Galen's troops, to ask the States General for a peace with England conceding — so the Orangists hoped — to the main English demand that the young William III would be made Captain-General and Admiral-General of the Republic and ensured of the stadtholderate. The sudden return of De Witt from the fleet prevented the Orangists from seizing power, but the Dutch were still unwilling to concede. Working through the winter of 1666, the Dutch formed an alliance against England with France and Denmark. In April, with his own lands threatened, Bernhard von Galen made peace with the Dutch, leaving England standing alone.

In June, the fleets met again at the Four Days Battle. Fighting to a draw, the new Dutch ships inflicted heavier losses on the English, signalling a shift in power.

English military fortunes improved in August when a fleet led by Prince Rupert of the Rhine defeated de Ruyter at the Battle of St. James' Day. This victory did little for the overall English war effort as Charles' treasury was almost exhausted, and the country demoralised by first the Great Plague and the Great Fire of London, hitting the only major urban settlement in the country. These events one after another virtually brought England to its knees. The English fleet had suffered cash shortages even before this, despite having been voted a budget of £2,500,000 by the English parliament. With his coffers almost empty, Charles again approached the Dutch seeking peace. Unwilling to negotiate, the Dutch declined. In early 1667, Charles' plight became desperate. With no money to refit the fleet, its largest ships were laid up at Chatham.

Realizing that he would either be forced to make concessions to Parliament or deal with the Dutch on their terms, he elected for the latter and talks began at Breda. With the English fleet removed from the North Sea, de Ruyter and Cornelis de Witt planned a daring raid on the English base at Chatham in Kent for June. Sailing up the Thames and the Medway, they stormed the fortress at Sheerness, destroyed fifteen ships, and captured the English flagship, Royal Charles, which was taken back to Holland as a trophy. The Medway raid was the most humiliating defeat ever inflicted in on the Royal Navy.

And that, right there, is the idea on which this novel is based. The impact of the Medway raid shook England and Charles urged his emissaries at Breda to make peace quickly. On July 31, 1667, both sides signed the Treaty of Breda which ended the Second Anglo-Dutch War. The treaty was a simple uti possidetis document, permitting both parties to retain those lands they had taken during the fighting. Among the territory to change hands were the English acquisition of New Amsterdam and the Dutch seizure of Surinam. The peace between the two nations was short-lived as the humiliated Charles joined with France to renew hostilities in 1672.

And did I invent the Merry Gang? I did not. That particular howling rabble — something like the Rat Pack of 1950s Hollywood — were a very real construct: a pack of over-privileged, over-indulged young gentlemen who lionised society for about twenty years during the Restoration period with Charles himself at their head, and then quietly faded into the Establishment. The irritating thing about the Merry Gang — a name coined by the poet Andrew Marvell, who flirted on their peripheries — was that they were pointlessly destructive, lewd, offensive, not infrequently murderous, arrogant, and often childish. If you were one of them — if you were privileged, if your face fitted — nothing was too low for them, so long as it got a laugh. Careers and reputations were ruined, marriages destroyed, murders committed — and because they were who they were, they got away with it. And if that was all they were, the Bullingdon Club writ historical, they would have very little significance. But, sadly, they were (on the whole) talented, as well as sexually rapacious — capable, competent politicians, when they put their minds to it, wits, poets and playwrights. They set the tone for the archetypal rake figure, who passed into theatrical myth as a stock figure in the Restoration comedies. They were often the patrons of artists and scientists — the Duke of Buckingham was the patron of Abraham Cowley, Thomas Sprat, Matthew Clifford and William Wycherley. He dabbled in chemistry, and was apparently "very near the finding of the philosopher's stone." He set up the Vauxhall glassworks at Lambeth the productions of which were praised by John Evelyn. John Dryden described Buckingham, the archetypical rake, under the character of Zimri in celebrated lines in the poem Absalom and Achitophel (to which Buckingham replied in Poetical Reflections on a late Poem ... by a Person of Honour, 1682):

A man so various that he seemed to be
Not one, but all mankind's epitome;
Stiff in opinions, always in the wrong,
Was everything by starts and nothing long;
But, in the course of one revolving moon
Was chymist, fiddler, statesman and buffoon.
Beggar'd by fools, whom still he found too late,
He had his jest, but they had his estate.

However, unlike the theatrical rake, who is traditionally redeemed by marriage when he meets a female counterpart as witty and unconventional as he is himself, most of the Merry Gang lived fairly unsettled personal lives: Buckingham was married to Thomas Fairfax's daughter Mary but scandalised Court — which must have taken some doing — by a series of affaires and duels, culminating in an illicit connection with the

Countess of Shrewsbury which led to a duel with her husband, in which the Earl of Shrewsbury was fatally wounded. The tale that the countess witnessed the encounter disguised as a page appears to have no foundation; but Buckingham provoked an outrage when he installed the "widow of his own creation" in his own and his wife's house. Sir Charles Sedley's first wife was incarcerated in a convent in Ghent with a serious incurable mental illness (possibly not unconnected to being married to Sir Charles Sedley) and he found a degree of stability, and two illegitimate sons, outside of marriage.

The most famous of the Merry Gang is, of course, John Wilmot, the Earl of Rochester. Bright, brilliant, and dead at thirty-three of syphilitic complications, after a wild rollercoaster of a life. Came into his title at the age of eleven, and abducting heiresses at seventeen — even more in and out of grace with the King than the Duke of Buckingham, due to his habit of combining wit and pornography to lampoon His Majesty. (Who sometimes took it in good part. And sometimes, very definitely, did not.) Wilmot was a mentor to some of the greatest actresses of his generation, when not removing them from active stage participation by keeping their bellies full or their reputations ruined, and wrote some of the filthiest, cruellest poetry of the period against the ones who earned his disfavour. A good friend to have, and a worse enemy — not like Buckingham, who might be inclined to assault you physically, and possibly terminally, but a man who could ruin you with words.

Wilmot's dark star had imploded by 1680, and the Merry Gang faded into middle-aged conventionality. The figure of the rake has passed into romantic myth — even now, we're still seeing him in popular culture, either as the wild man of rock who's redeemed by the love of a good woman (which, to be fair, none of the Merry Gang actually were!) or the sinister, debauched figure of the old roué who likes nothing better than destroying innocence.

And as for Aphra, the Divine Astraea herself — well, the Russells haven't seen the last of her...

A NOTE TO THE READER

Thank you for taking the time to read this adventure of Thomazine and Major Russell. If you've read any of my other books, you will already be aware of the various misadventures of Colonel Hollie Babbitt and his assorted rebel rabble — including one young lieutenant with an unbreakable habit of idealism — during the British Civil Wars. And if you haven't, of course, there's a pretty good chance that you might want to, after reading this one. There will, of course, be further adventures of the Russells — including smuggling off the coast of Essex and an unfortunate foray into Restoration theatre with Aphra Behn.

But more than that, I hope what you take from this book is that the seventeenth century is *not what you thought it was*. It isn't a period of drab religious and political reformation, all dotted about with worthy grey people. The world was turned upside down with the civil wars: women found a voice, briefly, petitioning Parliament in their own right, and "*the poorest he that is in England has a life to live as the greatest he; and therefore truly, sir, I think it's clear that every man that is to live under a government ought first by his own consent to put himself under that government; and I do think that the poorest man in England is not at all bound in a strict sense to that government that he has not had a voice to put himself under.*" (Thomas Rainsborough, Putney Debates, 1647.)

And then it was all taken away, and the people who had fought so hard for those outrageous unthought-of liberties were executed, or suppressed, or exiled, and the government under the Commonwealth as cruel and tyrannical as any the Parliament had protested under the monarchy.

And then it's all about-face again, and the King is back on the throne in 1660, and the pendulum swings the other way into a gaiety that's almost feverish. Something like the Roaring Twenties, with that same sense of grabbing life with both hands because it might all end tomorrow, but with added bosom and silk and old-school adventure, of Wicked Ladies and pirates and mistresses and theatres.

The world in the 1660s was a much more exciting place, I think, if you were of a moderate intellect and moderately well-placed in the world. Suddenly all the old myths were popping like balloons, and everything you thought you knew about anything was open to debate — the shape of the world, the way human beings were made, the role of women — painting, poetry, politics, religion, literature, sex, science, geography, it was all suddenly out there. Everything was to play for, and you could go anywhere, do anything, *be* anything. Like the days of the Tudor merchant-venturers, but without the obligation of Royal patronage, because in the 1660s the middle classes (many of whom had supported Parliament during the Civil Wars) had also developed their own identity, and although they were very fond of Old Rowley and his profligate personal habits, they weren't in the business of meekly submitting to any regal whims. They'd got rid of one King and they could do it again — and His Majesty was quite well aware of that, thank you. There were riots about one of his mistresses, whose religion did not meet with popular approval. Fortunately he was also knocking off Nell Gwyn at the time, and *she* knew how to work an audience.

And some of the politicians — dear God! George Downing: turncoat, regicide, notorious skinflint. Samuel Pepys, diarist and serial chest pest. Wilmot and the Merry Gang, who were all incredibly able, educated, sophisticated young men — well,

Johnny Depp's film "The Libertine" says it all. Witty and wasted. And it was also the age of Aphra Behn, of course, the first professional female author, without whom I would not be writing this. For more details of the actual persons mentioned in the book, see my Historical Notes below.

Reviews are so important to authors, and if you enjoyed the novel I would be grateful if you could spare a few minutes to post a review on **Amazon** and **Goodreads**. I love hearing from readers, and you can connect with me online, on **Facebook/MJLogue**, **Twitter (@Hollie_Babbitt)**, and **Instagram (asweetdisorder)**.

You can also stay up to date with all my news via **my website**.

M.J. Logue

asweetdisorder.com

Sapere Books is an exciting new publisher of brilliant fiction and popular history.

To find out more about our latest releases and our monthly bargain books visit our website: **saperebooks.com**

Printed in Great
Britain
by Amazon